```
D0016885
```

All the Stars Denied

GUADALUPE GARCÍA McCALL

A Companion Novel to *Shame the Stars*

Tu Books

an imprint of Lee & Low Books Inc.

New York

TU BOOKS, an imprint of LEE & LOW BOOKS Inc.,
95 Madison Avenue, New York, NY 10016
leeandlow.com

Manufactured in the United States of America by Worzalla Publishing Company

Edited by Stacy Whitman
Interior design by Neil Swaab
Jacket design by Christine Kettner
Book production by The Kids at Our House
The text is set in Espinosa Nova
10 9 8 7 6 5 4 3 2 1
First Edition

Names: McCall, Guadalupe García, author.
Title: All the stars denied / by Guadalupe García McCall.
Description: First edition. | New York : Tu Books, an imprint of Lee & Low
Books Inc., [2018]. | "A Companion Novel to SHAME THE STARS." | Summary:
When resentment surges during the Great Depression in a Texas border town, Estrella, fifteen,
organizes a protest against the treatment of tejanos
and soon finds herself with her mother and baby brother in Mexico.
Identifiers: LCCN 2017058034| ISBN 9781620142813 (hardback) | ISBN
9781620142837 (mobi) | ISBN 9781620142820 (epub)
Subjects: | CYAC: Race relations—Fiction. | Mexican Americans—Fiction. |
Deportation—Fiction. | Depressions—1929—Fiction. | Family
life—Texas—Fiction. | Texas—History—20th century—Fiction.
Classification: LCC PZ7.M47833752 All 2018 | DDC [Fic]—dc23

LC record available at https://lccn.loc.gov/2017058034

For my beloved granddaughter, Juliana Harley McCall.
Your sonrisa makes everything better.
Thank you for helping me with my revisions!

♥♥♥

And to my husband, Jim, el gran amor de mi vida.
To another thirty years together—and many,
many more fun-filled days with our grandchildren.

Other books by Guadalupe García McCall

Under the Mesquite

Summer of the Mariposas
(also available in Spanish as
El verano de las mariposas)

Shame the Stars
(a companion novel to *All the Stars Denied*)

Eco-poetry is a form derived from what used to be known as pastoral or nature poems. Eco-poetics is the study or creation of poems that explore the natural world, including the nature of humans. At its best, this seemingly simple form urges the reader to think critically about the layered meaning within the context of the poem. Eco-poetry has been around for many years and has been used by renowned poets from all over the world, including Walt Whitman, Emily Dickinson, Pablo Neruda, Langston Hughes, Ernesto Cardenal, and many others. Many modern eco-poets use the form to bring attention to environmental and ecological issues. In this book, the main character, Estrella, experiments with the form used by her favorite poets.

BEYOND THE CREEK

Joyful crabgrass sings; the simple beauty of its long
Thin fingers ascends to the sky on angled wings of tall
rachis.
Smiling florets on slim spikelets; arms that bend
Back and forth, and side to side; hands that swing,

And twirl, and glide. Its lovely dance seduces spring,
And summer's besot by the charm it brings. But
When the earth lies down to nest, the crabgrass dies
And leaves behind a void too great to sow with time.

CHAPTER ONE

I'VE BEEN THINKING A LOT ABOUT the desaparecidos in Monteseco. This morning in church my uncle Tomás asked what's left of our congregation to pray for our repatriated brothers and sisters. When the prayer was done, I looked around at the empty spaces, the missing smiles, mothers, fathers, brothers, sisters, entire families just gone—vanished. My best friend, Sonia, used to sit behind us. Nobody sits there now. She left with her family in May. Her family had a restaurant in town, but they lost their business with the market crash. Everything went downhill after that for them. He couldn't get government help, and nobody else would hire him. Her family took advantage of the free train fare program in Laredo, and they headed out to Michoacán, where she said they had an uncle they could stay with until things got better in the United States. Then, maybe, they could come back.

The market crash affected everyone, mexicanos and Anglos alike. According to national news, we are in a depression. My parents tried helping as many people as they could, but there was only so much they could do. Our property, Rancho Las Moras, is one of the last few places still owned by mexicanos in Texas. Most of the ranches and businesses in and around Monteseco have been bought out by Anglo immigrants. They've divided the town into two sections, our side and their side. They don't bother us if we don't bother with them. Not that there are many people to bother on our side. So many mexicanos have either left or been sent back to Mexico, our side looks dead—a patch of parched dirt, hollow and barren, compared to their side. That's what the poem I was working on was about, the sadness I felt when I thought about the missing mexicanos in South Texas.

"Estrella!" my mother, Doña Dulceña del Toro, called out from the porch of our ranch house. "Are you out there?"

I stopped writing, laid my pencil along the seam of my journal, and pressed my forehead against the page. *No. No. No.* My mind whirled with all kinds of excuses, all the reasons I could give for being out here, lying down in the middle of a field in our back yard, instead of helping our upstairs maid, Sofía, pull the sheets off the beds and take them out to the wash house like I'd promised.

"Estrella!"

I could tell by the way Mamá called my name, accentuating the last vowel with an assertive note, that this was absolutely the last time she was going to yell before she left the porch and came out to get me herself. *And God help you if I have to do that*, the tone of her voice said.

I lifted my head and looked back at the house. Yup. She had her hands on her hips and, more importantly, she was wearing an apron. She meant business.

"Housework," I groaned to myself. The worst business of all. Because no matter what anybody ever told me, as far as I was concerned, housework was the worst kind of evil ever imposed on women. I never got tired of saying it. And I suspected I would always feel the same way.

"Housework is punishment. Housework eats away at your soul! I don't care what anybody says, years from now kids my age will still be finding other, more interesting, more important things to do than housework," I'd told my father, Don Joaquín del Toro, that very morning at breakfast.

"That might be true. But things need to be done in and out of the house, young lady." My father had put his coffee cup down on in its small, delicate saucer, wiped his mustache and lips clean, and placed his napkin beside his empty plate before pushing his chair back to stand up. "Now, if you'd rather help Manuel shovel manure out in the stables, I have no problem with that. But we cannot sit idly by and expect others to do for us when we won't do for ourselves. Understand?"

"Yes, sir," I'd said, but I didn't quite buy the lot he was selling. I knew from firsthand experience that I wasn't responsible for everything my mother asked me to do, especially when it came to taking care of my little brother.

Wicho, christened Luis Aarón del Toro Villa at birth, was only two years old, but even at two feet three inches tall, he had complete command of the del Toro household.

Everything at Las Moras ran by his schedule. We didn't make noise in the morning until he was wide awake, and we didn't go to bed until he was settled in and completely asleep.

One of us—my mother, Doña Luz, or I—had to watch over him every moment of every day because you never knew what our little blond piojito might get into, and he liked getting into everything. Upstairs and downstairs, he was a locomotive, always going full steam ahead. And if you tried holding him down, he became an octopus, extending his long arms for things with which to pull himself out of your grasp: curtains, houseplants, furniture. Even when you carried him around, he would stretch himself out of your embrace to take things that didn't belong to him. He was fond of knocking precious artifacts off the coffee tables and shelves, an act that always made him burst into joyful laughter when the items crashed to the floor.

Even our family outings were on Wicho's timetable. We couldn't go out on picnics unless it was sunny with absolutely no chance of rain, because my brother had a weak constitution, and God forbid he should catch a resfriado. The world stopped spinning if he came down with a cold.

Wicho was born during a bitter hailstorm that swept over South Texas like no storm ever before. The wind of that storm had been so cold and so fierce, it brought down power lines and telephone wires all over the region. Papá had to drive all the way into Monteseco to fetch the town doctor to come deliver Wicho at home at Las Moras.

Doña Luz said that was why Wicho had always been so

sickly. He never quite got over that hailstorm. His constant drippy nose and rattling chest could attest to that. She claimed he carried the ghost of that winter storm in his lungs, and only time could heal him. The whole world stood still when Wicho caught cold. Every fireplace in the house had to be lit and maintained in winter.

Doña Luz wasn't exaggerating. When Wicho was sick, the phlegm kept him up at night, so he slept in fitful naps during the day. Unless, of course, he was running a fever, and then he didn't sleep at all, which was the reason she insisted we leave him with her when we went to see Tío Tomás give Mass in church on Sundays. We couldn't take a chance that he might catch something from a member of the congregation.

"Estrella!" my mother called from the porch again that late November afternoon.

"Coming!" I yelled back. Then I closed my journal and sat up.

Mamá put a hand out and waved me toward her. "What in the world are you doing out there?" she called. "Aren't you cold? Come on. Get in the house. I need you in here."

"Sorry." I ran up to the porch half-heartedly.

She didn't wait for me, so I had to rush up the porch steps and follow her into the house and on into the hallway. Sofía was standing outside the library, holding a napkin over her nose. Her eyes looked teary and red. "What happened?" I asked, but Sofía shook her head and kept a tight lip.

"Is he still in there?" Mamá asked. Sofía nodded and turned away to go up the stairs.

"Help me with your brother," Mamá said. "He's being very hard on Sofía today. He punched her in the face and made her nose bleed."

"Oh my god! Did you spank him?"

Sofía's footsteps became softer and softer until she was all the way up the stairs and out of earshot. I followed my mother into the study. "You should spank him. He can't go around punching people."

"Don't be ridiculous," Mamá said. "He's two years old. He doesn't know any better. Come on. Help me find him. I need you to give him a bath. He could use a good scrubbing."

"What?" I couldn't believe it. More babysitting duties! "You mean I have to do her job too? Don't I do enough around here?"

Mamá turned around and raised an eyebrow at me. "You mean like hide in the field all day?"

"Like peeling potatoes for dinner and washing dishes," I said. "I did that too. And I helped Doña Luz in the kitchen before I went out there."

"Wicho! Where are you? Come out here right now!" Mamá looked around the library for my brother, under the desk and behind the curtains. "Estrella, I need you to help me give him a bath and put him to bed. This room is filthy, and I have to clean it before I can write my editorial. I can't get anything done with all this mess everywhere."

"Do I have to?" I asked, trying to not to sound too whiny. She hated it when I whined.

"Yes."

Mamá dropped to the floor and looked under the couch. She scrambled on hands and knees around the love seat, then turned around, reaching under the massive sofa in front of the fireplace. Her hair bun flopped sideways and finally fell out of its tight constraint. Wicho squealed as she pulled him out by the legs. She grinned victoriously and pushed at her disheveled hair while holding Wicho prisoner in her arms.

"Is this what you called me in for?" I asked. "Really?"

"Yes," my mother said, standing up with a squirmy Wicho in tow. "Here, take him before he runs off again."

Wicho wrestled and pushed at my face. "No. No. Noooo!" he squealed.

"Stop it!" I yelled, pulling my little brother's chubby fingers out of my mouth. Then, looking at my mother, I said, "I can't do this anymore."

Mamá went over to the coffee table and picked through her cleaning box until she found a dust rag. "Do what?"

"Everything!" Wicho slipped farther down in my arms and kicked at my knee. I let him slide all the way down until he was standing in front of me.

"Let go, Trella! Let go!" he cried out, but I still held his arm. If I let him loose, I'd have to chase after him all over the house, and I didn't want to waste my energy doing that. I'd need it for the battle I'd be facing getting him in and out of the bathtub.

"Estrella, do this! Estrella, do that! I never get a break around here. I'm tired of doing other people's work."

"If you won't give him a bath, who will?" Mamá rested her knuckles on her waist, the dust rag on her hip. It was clean. She didn't need to dust. She was just doing it because she had other things on her mind. Political things. Newspaper things. Bookstore owner, business things. She had so much to worry about, she never had time for us—for me.

"I don't know." I looked out the window.

The sun was almost gone. I was missing it. The perfect sunset I'd been waiting to capture in verse was happening right outside our doors, and I was missing it. Again. "He's not my baby. Nobody asked me if I wanted a little brother."

My mother's hand dropped from her waist. Her brown eyes narrowed and her brows furrowed. I knew that crease between her brows. It was a dangerous crease. A crease you didn't want to see unless she was on your side, defending you. "Did you just sass me again?"

It was true. We'd been arguing a lot lately, my mother and I. But I couldn't help it. Ever since Wicho was born, she didn't really care about *me*. I was a nursemaid, a helping hand, the potty patrol, not a daughter. Every time my little brother needed to go to the toilet, I had to go with him to help him undo his pants and make sure he wiped before he pulled up his drawers. It was exhausting keeping up with him.

"I asked you a question, young lady." Mamá's stern voice pierced through my troubled thoughts, and I looked up at her again. "Is that any way to talk to your mother?"

"Umm . . . you in trouble, Trella." Wicho giggled, wrestled himself free from my grasp, and dropped to the floor. I looked down at him acting like an inchworm, squirming around on his back, but didn't say anything.

Mamá picked up the dust rag again and started to wipe down Papá's desk. "It's not like I'm asking you to do more than I do myself," she said. "Now stop sassing and go give Wicho a bath. He's been running under furniture all day, and he needs to get cleaned up."

I watched her tossing piles of newspapers into drawers and putting books back on the shelf behind her. Sure, she was a hardworking woman. She cooked and cleaned some, but more often than not, she was too busy to just be a regular mother. Most of my friends at school had housewife mothers who made flour tortillas from scratch and fed their families three times a day and washed the dishes afterward. They baked empanadas and joined forces and hosted posadas for the children in catechism at Christmastime. And when they had babies, they took care of them.

Not my mother. Mamá had to run her own business in town and write for her father's newspaper. She had to be the Texas version of Nancy Drew, always investigating something or other along the Río Grande border, never letting up on the politics in South Texas for even one moment. Not even to keep up with her children.

"I'm not sassing you," I said. "But maybe saving the world can wait."

Mamá tossed the dust rag into the wooden cleaning box sitting on the coffee table in front of her. She reached up and pulled the bobby pins out of her fallen twist. Pushing back at the hair on her forehead, she twirled her hair expertly into shape, a perfectly formed French twist, something she'd tried teaching me but I'd never master. Not in this lifetime. "I'm going to pretend you didn't say that," she said. Then she secured her hair with the bobby pins.

"Sure, go on pretending," I said. "Go on writing articles and speaking at women's conferences while the rest of us stay here, suffering, having to cook and clean and keep house because you're too busy being a heroine."

Mamá took a deep breath. "I don't have time for this, Estrellita," she finally said. "Now stop being difficult and get your brother to bed."

"No," I said. "You get him to bed. He's your kid."

A horrible feeling seeped into my heart the minute the words left my lips, and I felt absolutely ashamed of myself. I didn't quite know where they came from, those words, but they were out there, in the world, in the stuffy air in our house, in the distance between me and my mother, and I couldn't take them back.

Mamá's lips disappeared for a moment. Then she opened her mouth and said, "Look around you, Estrella." She pointed out the window. "Everybody's suffering. We're in a depression. Every person in this country must do more than they've ever done to keep their families together. Everyone is helping out as best they can. Everyone is making sacrifices. We're all doing more with less."

"I know we're in a depression," I said. "But that's not what I meant."

"I don't think you know what 'depression' means," Mamá said. "You think you have it tough because you don't have time to go outside and write poetry, and that's true. The world as you've always known it is crumbling, Estrella. But there is suffering everywhere. Real suffering. People in every state in this country have lost their homes to this depression, and those that haven't know they're next. Every morning they wake up wondering how they're going to keep a roof over their heads one more month, one more week, one more day. Hardworking fathers and mothers have lost their jobs and are standing in lines hoping the government will give them a few staples to keep their families fed."

"I know," I whispered. "I'm sorry."

"Forget dishes and laundry, Estrella," Mamá said. "There are kids out there helping their parents dig in the woods for roots to boil for their supper. And you're complaining about giving your brother a bath? You should be thanking God you live at Las Moras, where we can still afford to grow our own food and keep you and your brother fed."

"I do," I whimpered.

Mamá picked up the box with all her cleaning supplies. "Now stop being a martyr and help me by giving your brother a bath."

Feeling awful, I knelt to grab Wicho again. I was about to apologize to Mamá when Wicho stood up in front of me, swung his leg, and kicked my chin with his leather boot. He might have only been two years old, but he could really pack a wallop with those sturdy legs. The pain was so excruciating that I screamed out loud. "Ow! You little brat—come here!"

Without thinking about it, I reached down and grabbed Wicho by the leg. I flipped him over on his side and popped him a couple of times on the tush with my open hand. "Stop!" Wicho called out. "Stop! You hurting me, Trella! You hurting!"

"Estrella!" Mamá rushed over and pulled Wicho out of my grasp, wrapping her arms around him. He clung to her, crying into her neck.

"Trella hurt me! She hurt me!" he cried over and over again. "Why, Mami? Why?"

"I'm sorry," I said.

Mamá rocked Wicho in her arms. "Shh. It's okay, baby," she whispered to him in his ear. "It's okay. Mami's here."

"Here, let me have him." I reached for Wicho, but Mamá pushed my hand away.

"Just go get yourself ready for bed."

"Are you mad at me?" I asked.

Mamá didn't say anything. She just kept rocking Wicho. "Don't cry, baby. It's okay."

"Why are you babying *him?*" Tears pricked at the corners of my eyes. Once again, she was giving Wicho her undivided attention and pushing me off to the side.

"Stop it, Estrella," Mamá warned, creasing her forehead again. "You're upsetting him."

"Upsetting *him?* What about me?" I cried out. "He kicked me. Hard. And you didn't do anything to him."

Mamá stopped rocking Wicho and turned to me. "I'm

trying very hard to remind myself that you just turned fifteen years old last week," she said. "And that you don't quite yet understand that the world doesn't revolve around you. I hope to God nothing ever happens to make you regret you ever thought this was hard. Because your life isn't hard, Estrella. Your life is very easy. It's very simple. You don't have anything to worry about except homework and chores. I hope putting up with your little brother's kicking is the worst thing that ever happens to you. Now go to bed."

In my room, I lay in bed and crossed my arms over my eyes, completely ashamed of myself. In my mother's eyes, I was a spoiled brat, more rotten than Wicho, even, because I knew better—una fichita. That's what Sofía called me under her breath when she thought she was out of earshot. And she was right. I was rotten. In their youth, my mother and father had done great things. They had fought for the rights of the people of Monteseco. My parents had lived through a revolution, joined a rebellion, seen men hunted down and murdered for their beliefs, and they'd done everything in their power to defend them. They'd taken up arms, taken on the Texas Rangers and their posses, and lived to tell about it. It was very clear to me why my mother was so mad.

I was so mad at myself, so ashamed, I let the tears flow.

After a few minutes, I leaned over to pull my father's journal out of the top drawer on my nightstand. I caressed the weathered leather cover and opened it carefully, gently, so as not to disturb the yellowing pages too much. And I read through my father's familiar poems.

It was all right there in my father's own handwriting—the danger, the hardships, the struggles. My parents had fought injustices and lost family and friends in the Matanza of 1915. They had witnessed the death of my grandmother, Doña Jovita del Toro, a senseless, violent act which had caused everyone in my family great pain.

My grandmother's death had been a great loss for the people of Monteseco too. She was a hero to her community, even more so than my mother and father had ever been. She advocated for her people, the tejanos, who had suffered greatly at the hands of the Texas Rangers during the times of the Mexican Revolution. Yes, she helped the rebels, providing food and shelter to the families of those who had been murdered by rinches, but she only took up arms to protect her own family.

My grandmother's rebel name was La Estrella. That's why my parents gave me my name. And here I was, her only granddaughter, her namesake, complaining about chores and crying over getting kicked in the chin by a two-year-old imp of a brother. I closed my father's journal, shoved it away from me, and buried my wet face in my pillow.

My mother was right about me. I was a terrible sister and daughter. I had no sense of loyalty. I had no dignity. No shame. I didn't deserve the del Toro name. As I cried myself to sleep, I knew what I needed to do. I needed to grow up. I needed to start living up to my potential. I had to start earning the name Estrella.

Mr. Hernández's class roster at South Monteseco Mexican Secondary School as of November 1931

Student	Grade	
~~Lorenzo Alaniz~~	7	Picked up
Jose Luis Casillas	11	Absent
Estrella del Toro Villa	9	Present
Amalia Gómez	9	Present
Natalia Gómez	10	Present
~~Rolando Beltrán Jaramillo~~	11	Disappeared
Oralia Jiménez	7	Present
~~Crescencio Cristobal Hinojosa~~	8	Absent
~~Beatriz Huerta~~	7	Left with parents
Carmen Lascano	8	Present
~~Leticia Viramontez López~~	12	Left with parents
David Mendoza Uribe	9	Present
~~Aniceto Rodríguez~~	12	Disappeared
Alfonso Treviño	11	Present
~~Concepción Alambre Zertuche~~	10	Picked up, withdrawn

CHAPTER TWO

*A*ND THE ROCKET'S RED GLARE, THE bombs bursting in air!"

I raised my voice above the others, singing as joyfully and with as much power as my voice would allow. Singing was my delight. Singing filled me with love. It allowed me to let my spirit roam free.

It was my father's uncle, Tío Carlos, who taught me how to sing. He used to come stay with us at Rancho Las Moras when I was very young. He'd sit outside in the courtyard in front of the cement fountain, strum his guitar, and belt out one corrido after another.

One afternoon, he heard me humming as I examined a blue dayflower, and called me over. I was about six years old when he taught how to harmonize. I never stopped looking at nature, examining its beauty, and I never stopped singing either. In my mind, they were one and the same, nature and song, song and nature. They could never be separated.

When I sang a cappella in our high school's choir class, I could feel the earth moving under my feet, and I believed for a moment that I could levitate, that I could fly. My voice soared, and I soared with it. That's why I was grateful for our music teacher, Mr. Hernández, who closed down his music shop from two to four o'clock every afternoon to come teach us how to read music for the last hour of our school day.

Choir was the only elective class offered at our school. Other than recess, it was the only time in the school day that didn't revolve around books and what the school board considered *real* learning. The other school, the white school, offered many other classes besides reading, writing, and arithmetic. But not the Mexican school.

That afternoon, the school bell rang just as we came to the second line of the last verse. At the sound of it, everyone stopped singing.

Everyone except me, because I finished the verse. Standing at the front of our small, crowded classroom, Mr. Hernández nodded, smiled, and put his hands down when I finished.

At his signal, everyone started moving, scrambling for their books, bumping into one another, trying to get out of the room as fast as they could.

"Okay. See you tomorrow," Mr. Hernández said. "But don't forget to practice. The recital's in less than a month."

The students groaned and rolled their eyes.

I couldn't contain my joy at the thought. Why would anyone would be anything less than excited about having an honest-to-goodness recital at the end of the semester, our very first ever? I blurted, "Oh, come on, guys. It'll be fun! Just think, we'll be making history!"

My friend Amalia Gómez, normally a fervent, talkative girl, never afraid to say exactly what was on her mind, slumped her shoulders and let out a sigh. "Do we have to?" she asked.

"Amalia!" poor Mr. Hernández groaned. "You're my best alto. I need you on this one." He swiped his balding head with his folded handkerchief and put it back in his front shirt pocket.

I closed my book bag, pulled it over my shoulder, and walked up to Mr. Hernández's desk. "I thought I was your best singer," I said, looking back at Amalia and her older sister Natalia. Amalia and I were always competing. It was still up in the air as to which one of us would be valedictorian of our graduation class.

The verdict on our singing skills had not been determined because Mr. Hernández refused to have favorites, but I loved putting him on the spot about it anyway. I was confident it was me, but Amalia could hold a tune with the best of us.

Mr. Hernández cleared his throat and thumbed through the papers at his director's podium. "Well, Estrella," he began, "you are my best soprano, to be sure. But you two need to get over this competitiveness. It's not healthy." Then he turned to Amalia and asked, "What's the problem? You don't want to be in the recital anymore?"

Amalia shuffled her feet and groaned. "'The Star-Spangled Banner?'" she asked. "Why can't we sing real songs?"

"Like what?" Mr. Hernández asked. He leaned on his

18

podium and waited. "And don't say blues again, because you know how I feel about that."

Alfonso Treviño, a pragmatic, industrious boy two years older than me, took his time picking up his books, putting them into his book bag one at a time. It was clear he was eavesdropping on our conversation. "How about 'Mexico Lindo y Querido'? Or 'Cielito Lindo'?" he asked.

His suggestions came as no surprise to any of us. Alfonso loved the old-time Spanish tunes. He worked with his family in the fields outside of Monteseco, in Morado County, early mornings and late afternoons after school. In the evenings, he sat on his porch with the other campesinos clinging to the old way of life and sang the old-time songs.

Of course, asking Mr. Hernández if we could sing those songs at the recital was in jest. We all knew what the answer to that would be.

"Not funny, Fonso," Mr. Hernández said. "Don't forget your guitar."

Alfonso stood up, shrugging. "What? They're real songs."

Mr. Hernández shook his head and waved the papers in his hand in the air. "I know. But let's just stick with these songs for now, okay?"

Natalia, who was a lot quieter and nicer than her younger sister, grumbled. I leaned in and said, "It's not his fault. The school board won't let him."

"Is that true?" Amalia asked, putting her hands on her hips.

Mr. Hernández turned away from us and went to his desk. He put the sheet music in a folder and closed it.

"Stop pretending, Mr. Hernández," I said. "We know you love the blues as much as we do."

Mr. Hernández snapped his head up and turned to face us again. "Okay," he said. "But first, let's get one thing straight. The school board doesn't dictate what I teach. I teach music. That's it. That's what I was hired to do. You want blues? We can do blues."

"Seriously?" Amalia squealed. "You mean it?"

"Okay, sure," Mr. Hernadez said, lifting his chin and looking at us from behind the lenses of his round spectacles. "I'll bring in some sheet music tomorrow, and we can start practicing. But we have to give them what they want too. We'll start off with 'The Star-Spangled Banner'—"

"And then, right in the middle of it, we'll switch it up and start singing the blues!" Natalia cried out, her eyes glittering and her cheeks flushing as she jumped and clapped.

Amalia clapped too. "It's going to be great!"

"This is pretty radical, Mr. Hernández." Alfonzo grinned. "I didn't know you had it in you."

Mr. Hernández laughed, a loud, booming sound that reverberated all through the little schoolhouse. "Why not? A little civil disobedience couldn't hurt these days. They can take our jobs and send our friends away, but they can't take our love of music from us. We can't let them take our joy."

"Exactly," I said. *"The people must have some complicated machinery or other, and hear its din!"*

"You know Thoreau?" Mr. Hernández lifted his eyebrows and made a weird duck face, as if to say he was truly impressed. "I had no idea this school was so progressive."

I shoved my books inside my messenger bag. "Not school," I said. "My parents are activists. They make sure I'm well informed on anything that speaks to justice."

"Well, if letting you sing the blues at the recital helps you further the cause, I am happy to oblige." Mr. Hernández grinned and straightened papers at his desk.

"Thank you, Mr. Hernández," I said, remembering my meltdown at home from the day before. "You're our hero. A true rebel. Our parents will be so proud of us!"

"Oh, God help us all if I'm your idea of a hero," Mr. Hernández said. Then he lifted his hands and shooed us all out of the room. "It's time to go home. Away! Away! Your chores await!"

There was more groaning and grumbling as the rest of the students filed out of the room. "I don't care what it is," I said, still lingering by Mr. Hernández's desk. "'The Star-Spangled Banner' or the blues, I'll sing whatever you give us to sing at that recital. I love singing."

It was true. Like Amalia, I didn't really get the point of the patriotic songs the school board required us to learn, but a song was a song, and I loved singing too much to hate any of them. But getting to sing what we wanted, well, that was going to be transformative.

Mr. Hernández nodded. "And we're happy you do," he said. "You're my best singer!"

Amalia's eyes widened. "Aha!" she screamed, shaking a finger at Mr. Hernández.

"Soprano!" Mr. Hernández rolled his eyes and exhaled. His shoulders drooped, like dealing with us was taking the life out of him. "I meant my best *soprano!*"

"It's okay, Mr. Hernández," Natalia said, tugging on her sister's sleeve and pulling her away. "We already knew that."

Mr. Hernández guffawed and turned back to his desk, reaching for his briefcase.

I followed Amalia and Natalia out of the room. The girls turned left at the door, and I walked straight ahead, intent on getting to my mother's librería as fast as I could. Mr. Witherspoon, the bookseller from San Francisco, was probably already there. I couldn't wait to see if he'd brought the book about insects that I'd ordered for Wicho. He might get on my every nerve, but I still loved him. Besides, he was always willing to sit still for bug books.

Outside, the schoolyard was populated with a small smattering of students. A few years ago, the grounds would have been congested with Mexican kids walking home happily. Giggly girls would've walked alongside teasing boys. Their little brothers and sisters would have chased one another around the merry-go-round and past the swings, all the way to the fence and back, before finally rushing home. But now there were only a few students left in school. The younger ones fearfully ran up to meet their older siblings; friends formed grupitos and began strolling home together, talking excitedly; and fathers sat inside their ranch trucks, waiting patiently beside pink bougainvillea and red oleanders to collect their offspring.

"Estrella!" Natalia called out to me. I turned around as she and Amalia rushed to catch up to me. "You're not going out there alone, are you?"

"I'm not going very far," I said.

Alfonso shook his head. "Maybe I should walk her over," he said, turning to Natalia for approval. It was no secret to any of us they were sweet on each other.

"Maybe we should all walk you over," Amalia said. "That whole safety in numbers thing."

I knew why they were scared. Judge Burns, the head of the commissioners court in Morado County, had ordered a series of random raids and roundups in an effort to deport any and all lingering undocumented Mexicans in Monteseco. The whole thing had everyone on edge.

"No, I'll be fine," I said. "I'm just going across the street. My mother will be watching out for me. You guys go ahead. You don't want your mother to worry, Alfonso."

Alfonso pressed his lips together and nodded, keeping his thoughts to himself. Although his father had a worker's visa, he had been picked up in one of the early roundups, and hadn't been seen or heard from since.

"Okay," Amalia said. "We'll see you tomorrow."

I waved good-bye to them, and when they disappeared down the street, I cut through the yard with its bare brown grass and stopped to wait for a slow-moving truck to pass. Beside me on the lawn, two black grackles foraged for seeds. I liked to stop to watch strange and unique things in nature. There was something beautiful about these grackles, but there was also something fierce, something primitive, something that reminded me of what my mother always said, "el mas picudo siempre sale adelante," when she saw people willing to do whatever it took to get ahead. That's what I saw in those birds that day, the feral side of us.

So I stopped and studied those grackles and wrote about them in my journal. Their eyes were so clear, so alert. They watched everything. Even as one of them ate a grub worm, tearing and gulping, he twisted and turned his head sharply, looking from one thing to another, never letting down his guard, ready to open his wings, push off, and fly away in one swift, fluttery motion.

I kept my journal in my schoolbag at all times for that very purpose, to capture what I saw, the truthful beauty of a moment in nature. Mamá smiled the first time she saw my poems. She touched my scattered scribblings, like she was trying to feel the texture of the creatures and plants I'd written about, and said, "You have your father's heart." Then she swallowed hard and blinked like she didn't want to get emotional.

She's not an overly emotional person, my mother. She's loving and kind and generous. If I had to use only one word to describe her, I'd say she is *passionate*. She has two passions in life: our family and her work. She writes for her father's newspaper, *El Sureño,* but she also owns and operates her very own bookstore in Monteseco.

I put my journal back in my bag and ran across the street to meet Mamá. Librería Ave Negrados, like our school, is located south of the railroad tracks, on the Mexican side of town. It shares space with my grandfather's print shop. The librería is not just my mother's store, it is my haven. Other than Rancho Las Moras, it's my favorite place in the world. I could get lost in our bookstore.

That's why it made me so sad to know Mamá was thinking of closing it down. As much as she loved providing books for the community, giving them an opportunity to read, to educate themselves, she also probably couldn't keep it open one more month. It just was not financially feasible.

The depression was doing more than making our friends disappear and closing businesses all over town. It was sucking the marrow out of our lives.

ON THE GRASS

Two eager grackles walk on stilts,
raven heads held high. Their golden
eyes astute, foraging for generous
seeds to feast upon. Then, a grub worm,

fat and slippery, clutched in a black
bird's claw, ripped apart, torn open,
devoured by one who knows its creamy
yellow guts are more substantial.

CHAPTER THREE

*T*HE BOOK WAS SOLID AND WEIGHTY in my hands, its thick pages dense with words, alive with illustrations. Vibrant depictions of bunnies and deer pranced amid a flurry of butterflies and hid behind tall grasses, looking intently at their reflections beside water lilies in ponds and streams. It wasn't the book I'd been waiting for, but it was very beautiful, and I couldn't stop looking at it.

I put the book up to my face, pressed my nose against the center seam, and took in the woody scent of words on paper. The perfume of plot, the fragrance of fiction, the aroma of poetry filled my lungs, and I felt lightheaded, as if the air coming from the heart of that book were helium. If I took enough of it in, I could float up into the stratosphere.

Closing its pages, I caressed the leather face, admired the tight binding, and traced the golden script on its spine. When I thought of how far this book had traveled just to sit in my hands, I was overwhelmed with gratitude.

I was blessed from birth, born into a family who valued information and books so much it made sure they were accessible to everyone in the community.

My parents had transformed the front of my grandfather's print shop for *El Sureño* into a bookstore because they wanted the magic of books to enrich the lives of the people of Monteseco, the gente who lived on the border of Texas between Los Estados Unidos and Mexico.

The stained-glass door flew open and the bell above it tinkled, a light, airy sound that sparkled with the afternoon light filtering into the store through two large windows flanking door. I turned and caught sight of a slight girl moving briskly through the store toward me. I glimpsed the familiar eyes in her peaked face before she pivoted and rushed between aisles toward the back.

"Hello?" I called, but the girl dashed behind a display of ladies' journals, paperback books, and high-quality writing paper Mamá had put on a tall, slender table.

Mamá was busy talking to the new salesman, Mr. Witherspoon, so I put down my book and went to investigate. I hurried by my favorite section of our bookstore, the poetry section, and glanced up at the spines of books by Walt Whitman, Edna St. Vincent Millay, and Emily Dickinson. I didn't get very far down the aisle before a commotion outside the front door interrupted my search.

Mamá stopped talking. Mr. Witherspoon jerked and knocked over a stack of books on the counter. He squinted, pulled his spectacles off his ears, and cleaned them earnestly with a handkerchief. Mamá started to pick up the books, but abandoned the task when the screaming started immediately outside our shop door.

"Stay inside," she warned, pointing in my direction. She rushed down the aisle and out the door. I could see her through the wide window on the right, her hands over her brow, her long, dark hair blowing across her cheek in the breeze as she craned her neck, trying to get a better look at whatever was causing the pandemonium on Main Street.

Mr. Witherspoon walked over to stand next to me. He put his glasses back on, crunched his face as if to set them in place on the bridge of his nose, and blinked nervously. "What do you think is going on?" he asked.

"I don't really know." Remembering the girl who had rushed into the store right before the commotion ensued, I left Mr. Witherspoon's side and walked over to the tall table display. There, curled up into a small ball, was Cecilia, a girl from Colonia Calaveras who hadn't been in school for months. She was clutching the folds of her blue shawl around herself, but she didn't need it. Papá had stoked the furnace earlier, and it wasn't cold in the store.

"Can I help you?" I asked. The way she wrapped her arms around herself told me she was scared, so I reached out, offering my open hand to her, palm up. "¿Qué pasa, Cecilia? You're safe here. You don't have to hide." Immediately her face relaxed into a half smile.

"Are they gone?" she asked. She pointed at the window. "Los Rinches?"

"Rangers?" I asked. "No. There are no Rangers out there."

Cecilia ducked back down when my mother opened the door and came back inside. Mamá hurried around the desk, picked up the telephone receiver, and started dialing.

"What's going on?" Mr. Witherspoon asked, walking over to the window. "Why is everyone running around? Where are they going?"

"It's a roundup, Mr. Witherspoon," my mother explained. Then she spoke directly into the telephone. "Joaquín? Sí. Have you heard? They're doing it again. . . . No. . . . No. Not us. The whole plaza is cordoned off. They've got at least twenty people sitting on the ground with their hands on their heads. It's appalling—just appalling!"

I looked down at Cecilia hiding behind the display. She was visibly trembling. "Mamá?" I called out, but she was still talking to Papá on the phone.

"Sí," she said. "Rangers. Policemen. Sheriffs. All kinds of lawmen. . . . No. She's with me. In the store. Esta bien. . . . No. I promise. I won't. . . . Okay. Love you too."

Mamá took her keys out of her skirt pocket and waved for me to come to her. "Estrella, lock the door behind me!" Then she turned to speak to the book salesman. "You should go back to your hotel, Mr. Witherspoon. I have to go. We can take care of this later today or tomorrow morning, before you catch the train."

"And your father?" Mr. Witherspoon inquired. "Will he be back by then?"

"Yes . . ." Mamá's left eyebrow rose. Slight irritation laced her voice. "Yes, he will be. But I will be taking care of you. Like I told you last time, the bookstore is *my* business. I am the proprietor, even if my father and I share this building." Mamá handed me the key and turned back to the desk. She helped Mr. Witherspoon pick up his books, shoving them in his satchel and handing it to him, then put her hand on his shoulder and ushered him out. "Lock the door behind us, Estrella," she said again, turning to look at me. "And stay inside. Don't go anywhere. Lock the back door and pull the drapes."

She flipped the wooden sign on the window around so that the bold black words "SORRY, WE'RE CLOSED. COME BACK TOMORROW" faced the street. I watched her and Mr. Witherspoon walk down Progresso Street toward the general store and wondered what I should do about Cecilia.

If my grandfather, Don Rodrigo Villa, were not sick, I wouldn't be in this predicament. My güelito would know what to do to help Cecilia. But his health had been deteriorating in the last few months, and only the fact that my grandmother, Doña Serafina Villa, was escorting him on his monthly visit to his heart doctor in San Antonio kept my mother from closing shop altogether and driving him up there herself.

As I locked the front door, Cecilia crept out from behind the table and watched me pull the lacy beige curtains over the wide windows. I was about to tell her that we were safe in the store when another racket arose outside. Through the transparent lace, I could see people running everywhere. Men and women scrambled to get their families out of the streets and into their vehicles. Beat-up ranch trucks sputtered to life and took off. A group of young Anglo boys were yelling and throwing rocks at the people standing on our side of the street. I flinched and ducked to avoid the rock that broke through the window and came flying across the aisle, rolling on the floor until it stopped halfway down the store.

Before I could talk to Cecilia, another rock came crashing through the second window.

I panicked. "Come on!" I yelled at Cecilia, who was still hunched behind the display. When she didn't move, I ran over and grabbed her by the elbow. "We have to go. ¡Vámonos!"

"Where?" she asked, allowing me to drag her down the aisle of bookcases and display counters, past the printing press where my grandfather put together the daily newspaper, until we reached the back door.

"Give me your shawl," I demanded, grabbing my coat off the rack on the wall and holding it open for her. "Here. Put this on!"

She handed me her blue shawl, put her arms through my long overcoat, and started to button it up gingerly, like she didn't want to pull the buttons too hard lest she ruin it.

"Do you have a place to stay, somewhere safe to go in town?" I asked, helping her with the buttons and adjusting the lapels and collar around her neck.

"No. I live in the monte outside town." She pulled her hair out from under the collar and flipped it backward and out of her face.

I put on my mother's coat, knowing she would want me to borrow it. November wasn't usually a frigid month, not in South Texas, but for some reason, we were having a unusually cold spell, and the temperature was down in the low forties.

"In the woods?" I asked. "Where are your parents? Your mother and father, the rest of your family?"

"They're all gone," she said, wringing her hands. "Disappeared after the raids. Please, let's stay here. I won't be any trouble. I promise."

I shook my head. "No," I said. "There's no place to hide. We don't have an attic."

Cecilia blinked and looked around the print shop. "But they're out there. Please, I don't want to disappear!"

"It'll be okay." I said. "I know just what to do."

I locked the print shop, though little good that would do us with the front windows broken, and we hurried down the alley, stopping at every corner, looking both ways, making absolutely sure no lawmen were watching us from Main Street before we walked on and hurried over to the next block.

From the alleyway, I could see that the cross streets were in chaos. People ran everywhere, pushing pedestrians and store patrons as they went, trying to get around them. Screams and shouts came from Main Street, and people rushed out back doors and scuttled off toward the south end of town, where they could flee into the dense woods.

"Cálmate. Slow down a bit," I said. Cecilia was walking so fast she was almost trotting. The heels of her chanclas pounded the dirt and slapped back against her feet, making a rhythmic, punishing sound that sounded a lot like a whipping.

"Here, take my arm." I linked her hand around the crook at my elbow. "As far as anyone is concerned, we are just two primitas, going to the panadería for some conchas and semitas for the merienda."

Cecilia mimicked my smile. "Yes," she said. "Dos primitas going to get conchas."

"That's right." We grinned as we walked briskly, looking both ways and crossing yet another block toward Jimenez Bakery at the opposite end of the downtown strip on our side of town. "Señor Jimenez is very nice. Do you know him?"

"Yes," she said. "I know him. He used to send donas to the children at the colonia. His son delivered them at the end of the day. They would get hard by the morning, so we had to eat them right away."

"That's right," I said. "Day-old bread can get hard."

"But it's so good in the morning, dunked in cafecito." Cecilia grinned. "So we used to save it. It was all we had to eat until he'd come back to our house a few days later. But why do you take me there now? It's dangerous to walk so far right now."

"You'll see," I said, because it wouldn't have been wise to explain out there in the street where anyone could hear us that Señor Jimenez had a pantry underground where she could hide until the raid was over, maybe even until nightfall when my parents could come by and pick her up so we could shelter her at Las Moras. Normally, we helped people take refuge in my uncle Tomás's parish church if we knew there was going to be a raid and there was no time to move people out of town inconspicuously, but this raid had come too fast, and there had been no time to think, much less make a plan of action.

Cecilia and I were so wrapped up in our conversation, we didn't check the next intersection before we were already crossing. But by then, it was too late. Two deputy sheriffs were at the crossroads of Fresno and Main Street.

"Hey, you two!" one of the deputies hollered before he sprinted toward us. "Stop right there!"

Before we knew it, both deputies started running down Fresno, chasing after us as we ran down the alley toward the panadería. We were so close. I could see the wooden double doors of the cellar lying side by side, slanted against the ground on the side of the pink building two blocks away from us.

"Come on." I pulled on Cecilia's arm. "Don't look at them."

My arm almost popped out of my socket as one of the deputies grabbed at me, pulling both of us to a stop.

"Not so fast," he said. "Where do you think you're going?"

"Let me go. We haven't done anything wrong. We're going to the bakery." I pulled on my arm, trying to extricate myself from his grip even as I caught sight of his name tag. *Pittman*, the tag read, but it might as well have said "pit bull" on it, because his grip on my arm was like a vise, and it was clear he had no intention of letting me go. "You have to let us go. Our mother's waiting for us."

"Your mother, huh?" Pittman asked.

"Oh, yeah? And who's this? Your sister?" The second

deputy looked up and down at Cecilia and then back at Pittman before they both started to laugh.

My eyes lingered on Cecilia's dusty sandals and weathered feet. Her chanclas were not the only reason they wouldn't believe we were related. I have blonde hair and freckled skin, and although my eyes are brown, as deep and dark as my mother's, most people think I am Anglo. It is a curse, this hair and this skin. When we go out of town, I am forever having to explain I am Mexican American through and through.

"Hey!" The second deputy hauled Cecilia around by her arm. "What's your name, muchacha?"

Cecilia cried out. I wrapped my arms around her shoulders. "Let her go! You're hurting her!"

I read the second deputy's name. *Patrick.* He was young, severely bucktoothed, and as freckled and fair-skinned as Pittman. It was clear to me they were not from Monteseco, but part of the bigger picture, the deputy and Ranger squads recently assigned to Morado County to help local authorities enforce the recent city council ordinances regarding the removal of illegal aliens "hiding out" in our area.

"¿Cómo te llamas?" Patrick asked Cecilia. Then he put his hand on my shoulder and pushed, trying to pry us apart. "¡Dime! ¿Cómo te llamas, muchacha?"

"Let me go!" I screamed. Pittman wrapped his arms around my waist, hoisted me up in the air, and deposited me a few feet away from Cecilia, who was crying as Patrick dragged her down the street by the elbow. "Run, Cecilia! Run! ¡No te dejes—correle!"

"Ma'am?" Pittman held my arm in his grip. I writhed and twisted, trying to get away from him, but he was bigger and stronger than me. "Are you Mexican?"

"Am I Mexican? Of course I'm Mexican!" I practically spat the words in his face. "Look around you. This is Monteseco. Ninety percent of the population is Mexican. And why are you calling me 'ma'am'? I'm fifteen years old!"

"Sure you are." Pittman shook his head and rolled his eyes.

I was livid. "And I'm an American citizen. I have rights, you know."

"Tell it to the judge." Pittman twisted my arm behind me and walked me to Main Street, where he whistled for a couple of Rangers to come help haul me down the street.

We walked to where the trocas were parked just over the railroad tracks until we stood on the *other* side of town. I looked up at those buildings, trying to scan the perimeter for a place to run, but my spirit was dejected by every sign I encountered. I was more than appalled, I was horrified by the vile words written on business windows and doors. Every poster, every sign screamed hatred. "NO DOGS OR MEXICANS ALLOWED." "GO HOME MEXICAN!" "MEXICANS AND HISPANOS WILL BE SHOT! NO LOITERING!"

I couldn't take another step. I screamed, "Let me go! I want to go home! Let me go!"

No matter how loud I hollered, how much I strained my vocal cords, they ignored me. Before long I found myself standing in a well-guarded line next to Cecilia, waiting to be pushed up into one of the trocas with the rest of the gente being rounded up for repatriation hearings at the Morado County Courthouse on the far end of the white side of town, where the city council had its main offices.

I looked up at the people already loaded up, huddled together, looking lost as goats on the barricaded farm trucks that would take them away immediately after their "hearings" with or without their consent, whether they were US citizens or not.

Some of them were old, but most were young, not much older than Cecilia and me. While most of them were unfamiliar, people who moved about Monteseco at night looking for food or shelter, there were a few I recognized from my volunteer work at my uncle's church.

Among them were people I knew as squatters, who filtered in and out of the abandoned jacalitos beyond Monteseco, beyond even Colonia Calaveras, sleeping in ditches of neglected fields, hiding in the woods, and only risking a venture into Monteseco when the threat of death from starvation was too much to bear. Sometimes their desperation was so great, their hunger so strong, that they came out during the day to beg for donations and pick through trash cans for scraps of food to take back to their loved ones.

I knew them because my uncle Tomás did whatever he could to help them. He gave them bread he collected from Señor Jimenez, beans he begged off the grocer, and vegetables from his own garden, oftentimes going hungry himself to keep those poor souls fed.

As I watched two deputies shove Cecilia up into the troca,

the tears that had welled in my eyes earlier were long gone, replaced by a stark dryness that made it impossible to blink. A Ranger grabbed at me, and I punched him instinctively. Then I kicked him in the shin for good measure. Beside me, Cecilia did the same thing. She fought her assailants with all the strength in her little body. The lawman groaned, letting go of my arm to grab at his leg.

So I took off.

I ran as fast as I could, pumping my arms and elongating every pull of my legs, hoping to get back to the print shop and lock myself inside. I heard footsteps, and then Cecilia was beside me, running just as fast, her chanclas slapping furiously against her heels. I smiled at her. "This way!" I said, veering right at the corner.

However, we didn't get very far, because as soon as we turned the corner on First Street, I slammed right into a woman's chest. I knew it was a woman because I could smell her perfume as she held me tight against herself while we spun around in a semicircle until we had regained our balance.

"Let me go!" I screamed. "Let me go!"

"Estrella, ¡hija mia! It's okay, cariño," Mamá whispered against my temple. Her right arm was wrapped around my waist, and her left hand cradled the back of my head as she held me tight. "You're safe now. You're safe."

Dear Abuela Jovita,

Today I feared for my life. Darkness and ill intentions still feed the souls of men in your beloved Monteseco. Black-hearted men leap out of shadows, grasp and grapple with our gente and drag them off. Today, I met them face-to-face, was pulled in tight, wrestled with, and almost hauled away by those who would throw us into cattle cars, drive us to the border, and force us across to Mexico, back to what they say is the land of our ancestors, as if this America was not one land, one heart.

When I finally got away, when I stood trembling in Mamá's arms, my heart was a cardinal, a crimson flurry of feathered fright, fluttering inside my chest. In that moment, I thought only of you. I wondered if you felt it too. As you lay dying in Abuelo's arms, did you wonder how or why, as favored children of the sun, we are so often here all the stars denied?

I want to ride a horse in the moonlight and call out your name to the slumbering sun. I want to walk up to the horizon and climb onto the sky's crooked back. I want to take the stars one after another, and make my way through the winding roads of heaven until I find an answer to our plight.

I want you to hold my hand. I want you to show me how to be fearless. I want you to teach my heart to fight.

Love always,
Your granddaughter,

Estrella

CHAPTER FOUR

*T*HEY MEANT TO TAKE US AWAY," I told my father as I sat next to him on the couch in the sala, the family room at the back of the house where we gathered when it was only us, the familia. "Without checking my papers, without so much as a word to you, they meant to take me away!"

"Oh, I'm sure they would've contacted us," Papá said, caressing my hair and putting his arm around my shoulders to pull me in for a side hug. Across from me on the love seat, Cecilia was drinking a cup of Doña Luz's famous champurrado. I loved the chocolatey drink, but I was too upset to have any at the moment. "They would've had to call us. You're a minor."

"Yes," Mamá said, fawning over me, smoothing down my disheveled hair. "But it would have been awhile before you were out of their clutches, and that's what concerns me, that they are picking up children without trying to figure out where they came from. We have to do something."

She got up and began pacing in front of us, her hands balled into fists. "There are moral and ethical issues here that need to be addressed with our authorities. Our city council needs to be made aware that these so-called *lawmen* they've brought in are using unlawful tactics to enforce their new ordinances. These outside enforcers are coming into Monteseco without knowledge or respect of our community. They should not be allowed to haul people away indiscriminately."

"Are you going to print another editorial, Mamá?" I asked. "Can I write it? It happened to me. They didn't believe me when I said I'm fifteen. I can write about Cecilia too, tell her side of the story. How scared we were. How they hurt us, treated us like we were animals!"

Cecilia put the champurrado down. "No," she said quietly. "Please don't use my name. I don't want to make trouble. I don't want them to know where I am. I don't have papers."

"Oh no, Cecilia," Mamá said. "We would never do anything to put you in any danger. Estrella was trying to say we need to fight this, and the best way to change anything is to keep the people informed, to put things in the paper again and again until someone up above starts paying attention and does something about it. It's the only way to hold the city accountable."

"Well, not the only way," I said, turning to my father. "There is always rebellion. Right, Papá, like when you were young?"

My father scrunched up his face, like he didn't want to think about the things that had happened in his time, when Rangers used to hang Mexicans and leave them out in the chaparral. He lowered his eyes and said, "Let me see your arm."

I lifted my arms and showed Papá the bruises on my forearms and wrists. He swore under his breath. Then his jaw tightened and his lips almost disappeared. "Mauled and harangued and loaded up on farm trucks, como bestias," he said. "Disgraceful!"

Mamá continued to pace the length of the couch. "Yes," she said. "¡Como vacas o chivas! That's how they see us, Joaquín. We are nothing more than burdensome beasts, *the neighbor's cattle*, a nuisance to be driven off what they see as *their* land even though *we've* been here far longer. And now not even our children are safe?" She stopped and sat next to me.

"We have to do something, Papá," I said. "Something drastic and meaningful, like you did in your time."

"We *will* do something," Papá said, taking my hand and holding it between his, a frown marring his brow. "But not just in the paper. This requires more than an angry editorial. We can't let them pull one more person off our streets and haul them out of town. We are productive, hardworking people. We have the right to live peacefully and without prejudice in this country."

"I told them that," I said. "I told them I was an American citizen. That I had rights. But that stupid deputy, Pittman, told me to 'tell it to the judge.' Ay, Papá. He tried putting us in the back of a boarded-up truck. I was so scared. I thought I'd never see either of you again!"

Papá put his arms around me, and I clung to him. The tears I had been holding back were finally pouring down my face, and I let them run because I was so relieved to be home in my father's arms. He was my idol, my beloved.

Don't get me wrong. I loved my mother too. She was strong and smart and independent, but my father, el Señor Joaquín del Toro, was my hero.

He was a hero to a lot of other people too. His journal showed me how tumultuous a time it was during the Matanza, and Tío Tomás said it took many years for the people to recover from it. Some were still trying to recover, and the depression hadn't helped.

"You know, the Damas de Dios are coming over Saturday afternoon," Mamá told Papá.

"Yes," my father said, looking a bit perplexed. Then, something resembling a spark glittered in his eyes and he raised his eyebrows. "And if I remember correctly, they'll be bringing their families, ¿verdad?"

I had no idea what my parents were talking about, but something was afoot. I sat still as a campamocha on a jacaranda tree branch, hoping they would forget that I was listening, taking note of every subtle facial expression. The Damas de Dios was a group of devoted Catholic women, women of wealth and influence from all over Morado County. They prided themselves on taking care of the gente in our area by planning all manner of church events like Easter egg hunts, summer youth retreats, and rosary novenas for the recently deceased.

"I'm sorry, but why are the Damas coming over again?" Papá asked.

"To plan the Posadas," Mamá said, her eyes clinched on his. "We're hosting the whole thing this year, remember?"

Like my father, I had completely forgotten about the meeting to discuss the upcoming Posadas, the much-anticipated church event for nine nights leading up to Christmas Eve that commemorated the journey of Joseph and Mary into Bethlehem looking for shelter. How could I have forgotten? It was the most important church event of the year.

The ladies were coming over because they couldn't meet in town anymore. The last time they had a large public meeting, the Salon de Colores had been raided and more than twenty people had been arrested. They'd been tried quickly in closed chambers and hauled away the very next morning. Even though most of them were US citizens, neither they nor their families were given an opportunity to prove their citizenship in court. Family members were helpless. There was nothing they could do, no time to get papers to them, to hire out-of-town lawyers. Their families were simply picked up, tried, and deported, "repatriated" to Mexico. My parents were sure of one thing: the justice system in Monteseco was askew again.

My whole family had been incensed and done what little they could. My mother wrote scathing articles, and my grandfather printed them in *El Sureño*. My father even sent telegrams to our congressmen and senators, but the damage had been done.

"It's perfect, isn't it?" Mamá asked Papá. A tiny smile

formed on her lips. "Everyone who cares, everyone who knows what's at stake, will be here under our roof, all at the same time."

"That's true, and if we could all come to a mutual agreement based on our concerns, we could make plans to do something about this. ¡Mi amor! You are brilliant!" My father rubbed my arm and let me go to walk over to his desk. "That's why I married your mother, Estrella. She's the smartest woman I know."

"Come with me." Mamá put her hand on my shoulder and gently prodded me to get off the couch. "I need to give your brother a hot bath. And Cecilia should go upstairs and take a nap before dinner. Doña Luz, can you show Cecilia where everything is? She can take the guest room behind the stairs."

Doña Luz nodded. "Sí, señora."

Cecilia hesitated, but my mother smiled warmly at her. "Don't be scared, Cecilia. You're safe at Las Moras. Go with Doña Luz. She will make sure you get everything you need. You'll both feel much better once you've had a chance to wash up, rest, and put the memory of those awful lawmen behind you."

Cecilia clutched the cup of champurrado as she followed Doña Luz out the door. As my mother and I walked out of the room, she turned back to my father. "I'm going to check on Wicho, but I'll be right back," she said. "I've got a lot to say about what needs to happen tomorrow."

That's what I loved about my mother. Although she might

look like a lady, with her beautiful, long black hair curled and styled down her back and her red lipstick perfectly intact throughout the day, she's not afraid to get her hands dirty. She's not afraid to fight.

As I started up the stairs to my room, something odd and unfamiliar started to take root inside me. I wanted to believe that the incident in town was the only thing that had me so unsettled, but the truth was that the upcoming meeting with the gente had me worried.

I was sure my parents knew what they were doing. They would never put our lives in danger. But they'd never brought politics into our home either. They'd never held a public meeting in our house before. Ever. At least, not in my lifetime.

I paused at the landing and turned to face my mother. "Mamá?"

She stopped one step below me. "What is it? You look worried, Estrella."

I swallowed hard. "What if the lawmen come here?" I asked. "What if they raid the meeting and deport everyone at Las Moras, make us all disappear?"

"Oh, that's not going to happen," she said, putting her arm around my shoulder and pulling me into the safety of her embrace. "Believe me, sweetheart. Your father is taking the necessary precautions. We have men posted at the gates and all around the perimeter of Las Moras at all times. This isn't our first corrido, you know. Your father's had to protect Las Moras all his life. Trust me. We will never let anyone hurt us again. ¡No habrá otra matanza!"

I nodded, considering my mother's words, her conviction. As I walked down the narrow hallway to my room, I began to understand one thing. I had to stop being so scared. I had to stop letting fear rule my heart and my head and become more like my mother and father.

—*Copy of a notice procured from among the papers on Mamá's desk*—

Planning Committee Meeting for the Damas de Dios
Saturday, November 21, 1931

AGENDA

1. Friends of the Damas: responsibilities and duties
2. Posadas dates, times, and locations
3. Gifts and decorations; sponsorships
4. Music and entertainment
5. Food and refreshments; suppliers
6. Safety and security; nuestra gente viene primero

Chapter Five

Saturday afternoon, after I finished my homework on Mamá's desk, I went outside and sat on the porch with my journal on my lap. I went over a copy of the notice I'd taken from her desk, trying to think of something interesting to write about. The night before, I'd been unable to sleep, so I'd spent several hours poring over Papá's journal in my room.

His poetry had inspired me, and I'd decided to do what he'd done, to chronicle my life. I told myself I should keep a diary, with papers such as these, notices, pamphlets, and newspaper clippings with Mamá's writings. I'd also write poetry to document everything that happened to me from that moment on. I'd write poems about my struggles—well, what little struggles I had—starting with my near-abduction on Monday.

But that piece was still brewing in the back of my mind. I wasn't quite ready to put it on paper yet.

I looked for inspiration to the empty nest of a family of swallows that monopolized our back porch every spring. I wanted to capture the memory of one particular morning, when a giant moth had perched on one side of it and a huge spider on the other, but I couldn't get the poem just right. The memory was vivid, as fresh in my mind as that day, but I didn't know why it stayed with me, so the poem eluded me. I considered scratching it out, but I couldn't. The moth and the spider sitting atop the empty nest spoke to me of danger, of some deeper truth, so I just left the words sitting there until I could come back to them and figure it out.

Although I wasn't sure my writing would be that interesting to a wider audience. I had not encountered, much less overcome, ordeals such as my mother and father had faced in their youth. But I could write about the economic hardships our people faced. Mamá was right about one thing—there was suffering everywhere. Most people on the south side of Monteseco were starving or close to it. They worked hard, but their pay kept getting cut week after week. The government did very little to help. Mexicanos weren't allowed government aid. That was just for white folks.

But I didn't want to just write about the bad things in my journal. I wanted to document the positive things too. If I could perhaps capture the beauty of Las Moras, my love of nature, and the kindness of our people, their hearts and souls, their character as they were being rounded up and sent to Mexico, then the undertaking would have been well worth the effort.

I was so engrossed in my journal, I didn't hear the vehicles making their way down the road toward Las Moras until they were almost upon us. At which point I jumped up and started screaming for my mother. "They're here, Mamá! They're here!"

"Cálmate, muchacha," Papá said as he and Mamá walked out of the house. My heart was so full of excitement, I couldn't contain it. I was a bundle of nerves and energy, jostling up and down like a five-year-old. It was all I could do to keep myself from jumping off the porch and rushing out into the road to greet my friends arriving with their parents.

The caravan of cars moved slowly, making its way into the driveway and parking all along the front of the house like a slow caterpillar, raising a dust cloud as esposos drove the Damas and their children up to the main house in their nice, shiny vehicles.

However, it wasn't only the Damas and their families who came to Las Moras that day. Other families came too, families of women who were not associated with the Damas de Dios. The wives and children of campesinos drove up in their trocas. They parked their dusty work trucks farther down the driveway, toward the outbuildings.

"Welcome to Las Moras," Mamá said, her smile growing wider as she looked at the multitude of Mexican families getting out of their vehicles. A lot of them had brought metal folding chairs, which they took through the front door. The older children walked around the side of the house, heading out back to watch over the little ones while the grown-ups talked inside.

Mamá had made a comment about me joining the teens outside, but I wanted to be in the meeting inside. So when the time came, I sidled up to Amalia, Natalia, and Alfonso and asked, "Hey, I think we should go inside and help Doña Luz keep the cafecito going for the grown-ups. That's a lot of people for one old lady to serve, don't you think?"

"Okay," Natalia said. "I'll go if I can have some of those little fancy galletitas your mother puts out for her guests."

"How do you know what her mother serves her guests?" Amalia asked. "You've never been to any of her fancy-lady parties."

"What are you all talking about?" I asked. "My mother doesn't put on any fancy-lady parties."

"Oh, no?" Natalia asked, putting a hand on my shoulder. "What about that little non-quinceañera banquet she gave in your honor last week? That was some kind of fancy. I can still taste the apricot sauce on those pork chops."

"Oh, those pork chops were good!" Alfonso said. "All fat and juicy, and that sauce. That sauce was amazing."

"Okay, fine," I admitted. "My mother knows how to throw a party. But she's not fancy—she just loves good food. Doesn't everybody?"

"I know I do. Can I come help too?" Alfonso grinned. His wink at Natalia and her immediate blush told me he wasn't just doing it for the food. I didn't care why he wanted to tag along, as long as he did, because his presence in the house meant I would be even less conspicuous. With more of us moving around the room, I could blend in and pay close attention what was being said at the meeting. I was determined to find out exactly what my parents were planning.

"All right then, let's go," I said. "The meeting's about to start."

Without asking permission, we went to the kitchen and picked up trays of food and coffee carafes and headed for the library with them. I tapped Doña Luz on the shoulder and whispered, "I brought in some friends to help us." She smiled and looked genuinely appreciative for the unexpected assistance.

The gente talked, posing questions and criticizing the way Cecilia and I had been treated by the repatriation officers. Of course, we weren't the only ones swept up that day. Twelve people altogether were taken in and sent away, including the bakers, Don Celestino and his brother Ramon, who were born in Massachusetts. Copies of their birth certificates were lost in the move when their parents had come to Texas more than thirty years ago.

My friends and I walked around with the trays of bizcochos, handing out food and refilling the people's coffee cups. For a meeting meant only for women, there were a lot of men in the room. Farmers and ranchers, business owners and merchants of both genders were equally represented. Among the men sitting in our library that afternoon were Aurelio Molina, Don Hilario Torres, Don Ernesto Salazar, the owner of the farmacia, and Señor Carrillo, who had a cotton mill to the north of us. To the left of the men sat the women. Among them were Nina Pinkerton and Donna McKinney, the two white women who owned the clothing store and the diner. They were very upset because they were not only losing reliable workers to the repatriation, they were losing longtime friends, a concern many of the farmers and businesspeople had in common.

At the back of the room were the farm owners and their families. They had the most to lose.

"If all the people of Mexican descent in the valley were to disappear overnight, Monteseco would be sure to disappear too, and nobody wants that to happen," Don Ernesto said. It was true, and the presence of the gente in our library was a statement of commitment. More than that, their presence was an admission of fear, fear for their future and the future of their children in the country they claimed as their home. But even more telling, their presence was an act of rebellion against those who would interpret and enforce the laws that dictated where they belonged, which, as I'd learned from my father's journal, could cause the world to *flip upside down on its axis*.

When Mamá brought the meeting to order, I went to the back and stood in the doorway, holding a tray of bizcochos. I listened to *all* the conversations. The most interesting discussions were not taking place at the front of the room but rather in the conversations on the sidelines. While the women talked about printing editorials, writing letters, and sending telegrams to Austin, my father and the other husbands in attendance were having a whole other kind of conversation, a quiet deliberation, full of heated opinions.

"No, compadre," Señor Carrillo whispered. He was

hunched over on the edge of his seat, trying not to call attention to himself while still talking loud enough to make his vehemence known. "They can't tell us what to do, where to go, what time to go home. There are more of us than there are of them! We should be making our own rules. They should be following *our* laws!"

Hilario Torres sat back and stroked his mustache, taking Señor Carrillo's words into consideration before saying, "Well, now you're talking about calling for new ordinances, asking the council to ratify new laws, and we know from the history of this town that's hard to do. Look who's on the council. Not one brown face in the lot. Talk about taxation without representation."

"Ours is not the right to make the law but to obey it," Don Ernesto said, pushing his chair sideways to join the debate.

Aurelio Molina nodded. He patted his friend Hilario's shoulder, and then settled back to sip at his coffee. "You're right about that, compadre," he said. "These Anglos, they're holding all the marbles."

"Horse manure!" my father said. He waved his hand in the air, as if the idea was a fly he was swatting away. "We have as much right to request changes in policy and city ordinances as anyone else in this town. We're citizens of this nation, and we all have a vote."

I didn't get a chance to eavesdrop on the rest of their conversation because my mother, who had been talking at the other end of the room, stood very still and cleared her throat loudly.

"Do the gentlemen have a suggestion?" she asked.

My father and his compadres all tugged at their stiff shirt collars and dusted their lapels and shook their heads, but none of them would make eye contact with Mamá—except Papá, who grinned and said, "No, mi amor. We just think this situation calls for more action."

"More action," Mamá said, smiling politely. "What kind of action?"

Papá straightened up in his chair and cleared his throat. "Well, we were just saying that this required a call to action, changes in the town itself, the look and feel of it, and changes in our city ordinances."

"That's right," Hilario Torres said. He sat forward on the edge of his chair. "Why should we be forced to stay on this side of the railroad tracks while the Anglos get to go anywhere they like? We are all tax-paying citizens of Monteseco, are we not?"

Señor Carrillo stood up, his chest puffed out like a rooster. He put his hands on his waist and talked directly to the crowd behind him. "Somos humanos. We are decent, hardworking human beings," he said. "And we should be treated the same way we treat others. How would those white folks on the other side of the tracks feel if we started hanging up signs and refusing them service?"

"Why, I suspect they wouldn't like it very much," Mamá said, smiling. "So what do you suggest we do about it if you don't think letters and telegrams are going to make a difference? I hope you're not proposing we start acting like them."

58

"We need to meet with them," Papá said. "Demand to be heard at the city council meeting next month, present our position, have an honest and open discourse, let them know this is unacceptable."

"Sí," Señor Carrillo said. "We need to demand those horrible signs on that side of town be taken down."

"Exactly!" my father interjected. "We need to make city ordinances to protect our gente, and demand an immediate stop to the raids and roundups!"

My father's words riled up everyone in the room. They jumped out of their chairs and clapped. They complimented my parents and talked excitedly about going to the city council meeting to watch the proceedings.

But something felt wrong about the whole thing. I just couldn't see waiting until the following month to start making a difference. What about all the raids and roundups between now and then? Who was going to protect the people until that time? They couldn't all come live at Las Moras like Cecilia.

"No!" The singular word left my lips before I could call it back.

Everyone stopped talking. Papá turned his head toward me, his eyes open wide and his eyebrows raised, like he had just asked me a question.

"Estrella?" Mamá's voice was whispery, like she didn't know what to make of my outburst. "What do you mean, no?"

I swallowed and looked around the room. Almost every person had turned their attention to me. "It's not enough,"

I said. "We can't wait on this. Not a month, not a week. We have to do something now!"

"You mean, like call for a special meeting?" Hilario Torres asked. "We could. We should. It's our right as citizens, to demand an audience with the city council!"

"But we're not ready," Señor Carrillo said. "We have to get ourselves organized, make a list of concerns, businesses that need to take down their signs. There's a lot to do. We need time to plan."

"Forget the planning," I said. "We don't need meetings and lists. We need to do something right away. We need to get out there and stand up to them, chain ourselves to posts outside restaurants and hotels the way women chained themselves to machines and gates during the suffrage movement. We need to confront these businesses face-to-face. We need to protest now!"

My words had a completely different effect on the gente than the words of my father. The people started shaking their heads, letting out breaths in short, exasperated sounds. Some of them nodded and argued with one another. It was total chaos.

"That's ridiculous," Aurelio Molina said. "I can't afford to get arrested."

Nina Pinkerton's voice rose above the others. "She's not talking about rioting," she said. "She's talking about civil disobedience. You know, like Thoreau said."

"Who the hell is Thoreau?" Hilario Torres asked, and Nina rolled her eyes.

"Wait a minute! Hold on!" Papá yelled. He walked to the front of the room holding his hand high, trying to get everyone's attention. "Listen to me. Aurelio is right. We can't do anything rash. We can't afford to stir this pot until we know for sure what we're cooking. Let's sit down and get our bearings."

"But Papá," I said, "we don't have time."

"Then we'll make time," my father said. "Thank you, Estrella, for your suggestion. But it's time for the adults to talk." Then he turned to face the people again. "Forgive my daughter, ladies and gentlemen. She's young and passionate, and we've brought her up to always speak her mind."

I was so devastated—so humiliated—by my father's dismissal that I couldn't help myself. I dropped the tray of bizcochos I'd been holding on top of the nearest table and ran out of the library, down the hall, and out the front door.

Outside, the cold air slapped my face. I walked over to the edge of the porch and lingered there, wondering if I should just go to the back of the house and blend in with the younger kids, because it was doubtful my parents thought any more of me than that.

Natalia and Amalia came rushing after me first, followed by Alfonso, who crept up to stand next to Natalia.

"Sorry," Amalia said. She threw my braid over my shoulder and started rubbing small, soothing circles on my back.

"Are you mad?" Natalia squeezed my hand between hers.

I shook my head. The tears stinging my eyes were not

weepy tears. They were hot, furious tears. "I can't believe he did that," I whispered.

"I know," Natalia said. "My parents are always doing that to me too. Children are meant to be seen and not heard."

Amalia chimed in, "Papá always says, 'If I want your opinion, I'll ask for it.' I really hate that."

Taking a deep breath, I decided not to say anything else. As mad as I was, it didn't feel right to talk ugly about my parents.

"They're good parents," I finally admitted after a long silence. "I don't want you to think they're mean to me or anything. They love me very much. We're just having a difference of opinion."

The girls didn't say anything after that. We just stood there on the porch. Then Alfonso cleared his throat and said, "You're right, you know. To want to protest."

"I know I'm right," I said. "Why do you think I'm so angry?"

Natalia stopped rubbing my back. "So what are you going to do now?"

"Now?" I asked. The wind blew through the leaves in the trees in the front yard, and I put my foot onto the first step. I walked down the rest of the way into the yard and squinted as I lifted my face to the sun, letting it hit my face directly. "Now we take action."

To the City Council of Monteseco, Municipality of Morado County, Texas, United States of America:

Let it be henceforth known and acknowledged by all who read this document that our newly formed Council of Mexican American Citizens in this, our beloved city, has convened on this Sunday, November 22, 1931, to request the following ordinances be lifted from our township:

1. That no persons of Mexican descent should convene in public or private places, except in the service of God and in their places of worship for the sake of mass reverence or private veneration.

2. That all persons of Mexican descent retire to their homes and not move, loiter, or be seen in a public street or place of business after 6 P.M.

3. That no persons of Mexican descent carry weapons in public within the city limits.

4. That all persons of Mexican descent turn in their firearms, knives, and all manner of weapons to the authorities upon request.

5. That all persons of Mexican descent carry on their person and produce documents referencing their legal status in the United States upon request.

Furthermore, it is also requested that the ordinances below be approved and immediately implemented in our community.

1. That no manner of raids and roundup of persons of Mexican descent should be planned, executed, or condoned within the county lines.
2. That the protection afforded within city limits to all citizens of Monteseco be extended to the county lines so that all farm workers and field hands be safe at their work in Morado County.
3. That all signage, logos, and insignias denoting hatred toward Mexicans be taken down, painted over, torn off, burned, and/or otherwise made to disappear from our storefronts, restaurants, and public and private places of business.
4. That said storefronts, restaurants, and places of business, whether public or private, should open their doors to people of Mexican descent without derision, disdain, and/or mockery.

This we ask in the name of justice, for the sake of equality for all men, the security of our people, and in respect of and deference to the rights afforded to us as citizens of this country by the Constitution of the United States of America.

Sincerely,

Your friends and neighbors,

The Council of Mexican American Citizens of Morado County

Chapter Six

*W*HEN I GOT TO SCHOOL ON Monday morning, half a dozen or so of my friends accosted me in the courtyard. They surrounded me by the water fountain, asking all sorts of questions. They had heard from their parents about the outcome of the meeting, which was exactly what we had been proposing all along: a list of issues to discuss, a plan of action, and even a letter asking for a special meeting to discuss our community's concerns and only our concerns.

Although the young people of Monteseco who worked to help support their families were tired of the racism they had to put up with when they went to the other side of town, a few of them didn't join us by the fountain that morning. Not only did they not have the energy to protest, they were scared of saying or doing anything to endanger themselves and their loved ones.

But like me, my friends at the fountain that day were tired of having to step off the boardwalk or flatten ourselves against walls when an Anglo patron was walking toward us. We were the ones skulking down alleyways and using back doors just to put on aprons and cook the food and wash the dishes the white folks ate out of, while we weren't allowed to walk in the front door, order a meal, and eat beside them.

"What do you want us to write on the signs?" Gabriela Morales asked, holding a pencil over a small notepad ready to write down anything I had to say.

"I don't know. Things about our basic rights, like *We're Free to Walk Here—We're US Citizens,* that kind of thing," I said. "Think of the signs they had in the papers during the labor strikes a few years ago. Did you read about that?" I hadn't really thought about the specifics, what that would look like for us in our present circumstances, but I had read plenty of things about strikes over the last few years. My mother was always reporting on that sort of thing in *El Sureño.* Although I knew what we had to do, I really had no idea how to execute it just yet. "Just keep it simple. Write things that express how we feel," I said.

"Oh, I know. *Mexicans Are Not Dogs!* Oh, that's a good one. You should write that one down," Ignacio Torres said, tapping the top page on Gabriela's notepad.

"No," Alfonso said. "We don't want to use derogatory terms to refer to ourselves. We should keep it positive."

Gabriela scrunched up her face and scribbled on her paper. "I'll work on it," she said. "It's a bit rough, but it's got potential."

"I know, *We're in Service, But We're Not Servants!*" Amalia suggested.

"Oh. Yes. It makes us sound intelligent," Alfonso said. He was not as successful in school as the rest of us. He was capable of getting straight As, but grades didn't come easy to him because he didn't have the time for homework and study. Having to work the fields with his father before coming to school and then going back out there again after the final bell would make anybody's grades drop. But he and his family believed in the power of education, so sounding intelligent was very important to him.

I nodded. "Yes, I like that," I said. "I like that a lot. But we need to concentrate on signs that show we want them to stop the raids and the roundups. That's the bigger issue here."

Natalia suddenly jumped in place. "Oh. Oh. I have a good one. *Stop the Raids! Stop the Heartbreak!*"

"That's really good!" Alfonso said. He turned to Gabriela. "We should definitely make that sign. I know a lot of people are heartbroken because their family members who have no documents to prove they belong here are getting rounded up and sent back. It's not fair. Some of these people were born here, but they lost their documents long ago or just never got registered with the county. These roundups are not just breaking hearts, they're breaking up familias."

"What about the disappeared?" Natalia whispered. "The ones being dragged out of their homes at night because they angered the wrong person? The ones not being given a chance to prove their citizenship? That's happening too, you know. Talk about heartbreak!"

"Lawmen don't care if we're heartbroken," I said. "We

need to make political statements. Think about Gandhi and the salt march to the sea last year and write about our rights as citizens, because as citizens we belong in this country. The more political these signs become, the better. And stay away from making signs that demean us. So make signs about the way we see ourselves, not the way they see us."

"You mean, like those signs that compare us to dogs?" Pepe Lopez asked. "I'm tired of those *No Dogs or Mexicans Allowed* signs! I wish I could rip them all down."

Ignacio tapped Alfonso on the chest. "We should do that!" he said. "We should take down their signs and put ours up in their place."

"No," I said. "That would be destruction of property. We don't want to break any laws. We want to present ourselves in the best possible light, as good, productive, law-abiding citizens. Remember, whatever happens, we're not just representing ourselves. We're representing our parents."

"That's why we need to make sure the slogans on the signs are all not just appropriate, but also grammatically correct," Gabriela said, swishing her pencil between us to accentuate her point. "I've won the spelling bee three years in a row, so everyone needs to give me all your ideas for the rest of the day, and I'll write them out. I'll punctuate them and everything. Then and *only* then can you all make the posters. Got that?"

"Got it!" the whole group agreed. Then, as if suddenly realizing they hadn't cleared it with me, Amalia asked, "Is that okay?"

I smiled and shrugged. "Sure," I said. "That sounds great. Who's making the signs? And where?"

It took two more meetings, one at lunchtime and the other at recess, to get fully organized, so that on Wednesday, at exactly six-thirty in the morning, eight teenagers skipped school and joined me at the sugar mill, where we picked up our signs from Alfonso and his uncle Josue, who was a carpenter and happy to help put together the picket signs. As soon as we had our slogans, we started to walk in solidarity down Main Street toward the other side of town.

We didn't say anything. We just walked side by side in groups of three, letting our picket signs do the talking. At first, no one said anything. It was early, so the streets were almost bare, and the few people on our side of town who saw us shook their heads and went about their business. But that changed quickly.

"What in the world . . ." Donna, who was my mother's friend and ardent supporter, came out of her café and stood with her hands on her ample hips, just watching us pass by, a smile on her wide, ruddy face. "Hey!" she yelled. "Hey! You got one of those signs I could use?"

"Yes! Yes, we do! Hey, Fonso!"

Alfonso was hauling a huge brown sack full of extra signs on his back.

"Give Donna a sign!"

Donna wasn't alone in her commitment to our cause. As soon as she saw us, Nina Pinkerton ran across the street and joined us. And then Mr. Morales came out and just walked among us. He said he had arthritis in his fingers real bad, so he couldn't hold a sign, but his legs worked fine, and he was happy to walk with us. Before we knew it, we had almost fifteen grown-ups picketing with us.

Walking through our side of town was a breeze, a pleasure. There was pride in every step we took, and we smiled at one another, still letting our signs do the talking for us.

However, as soon as we crossed the tracks and entered into Anglo territory, things changed. The barber, Mr. Jenkins, stopped sweeping the porch in front of his shop and stared at us. Leaning on his broom like it was a walking stick holding him up, he watched us go by. Then he rushed into his shop and flipped the sign in the window to read CLOSED, disappearing into the shadows of his business.

The grocer's wife, Mrs. Stella, was shocked when she saw us walk by. She had been writing out the day's specials on the portable blackboard beside the door, but she stopped to tap on the window and wave for her husband to come outside. The grocer, Old Man Rice, was not amused. He tightened his jaw and shook his head as his wife talked to him in hushed tones.

Somewhere, a phone rang, then another and another, and more and more people started coming out to look at us walk by.

Finally, we were standing in front of Louie's Hotel & Restaurant. We'd settled on stopping in front of Louie's place for two reasons. His was one of the many businesses that allowed Mexicans to work inside but refused to let them register as guests, much less sit at the restaurant and eat a meal in sight of their white clientele.

But most importantly, the commissioner and his cohorts, city councilmen and the like, met for coffee there every morning, in full view of the street. They were the reason the raids were happening. They were the ones who needed to see our signs.

After a few minutes of us standing there, just holding our signs in silent protest, the owner himself, Mr. Louie Chambers, drove up to the hotel. "I've called the cops, I'll have you know," he called out, ambling toward us, knees bowed out. He waved his hat back and forth, trying to make us move out of his way. "I don't know what you want with me, but I've done nothing to you people but be nice to you. I've given you jobs, lent you money for med'cine when you couldn't afford it, let you take home the leavings from the kitchen. Ain't fair what you're trying to do to me. Ain't fair at all."

"Leavings are for dogs!" Donna said. "Not humans. You should be ashamed of yourself."

"We have to be silent," I said, turning around to look at Donna. "Let the signs speak for themselves."

"But I'm right, aren't I?" Donna asked. She put her sign on her shoulder with her left hand while she rested her right fist at her hip.

I grimaced. "Yes," I admitted. "But we can't argue with them. Arguing is aggression. We have to remain passive. According to Gandhi—and my parents—civil disobedience means we don't talk back and we don't get sucked into debates with our oppressors."

"Talking—even trying to make our point—creates conflict," Nina told Donna in a friendly tone of voice. The two women weren't just commercial neighbors on Main Street on our side of town, they were best friends.

"And we're not here to cause trouble," I said. All around me my school friends nodded. "We're here to stand up for our rights."

Donna raised her eyebrows. "Oh!" she said. "I didn't know that. Learned something today. Thank you."

"You're welcome," I said, and then I put my finger to my lips to let her know we couldn't even talk to one another. "We have to be completely silent if we don't want to get arrested."

No sooner had I said that than two police vans turned the corner, their sirens wailing as they drove right up to the hotel and parked in front of us. The chief of police, Kurt Hoffmann, and about ten other officers rushed out and formed a line directly in front of us, their hands hovering over their clubs.

"You people have to clear the street," Chief Hoffmann said. He waved his hands, like he was trying to scare grackles away from a pumpkin patch. "Come on. Let's go. 'Nuff of this nonsense."

Old Man Rice crossed the street and came over. "Those kids ought to be in school, Chief!" He stood next to Mr. Chambers. "I don't know why they's trying to harass Louie like this. He ain't done nothing to 'em."

Alfonso squeezed past Donna and Nina to put his sign at the forefront. "Don't say anything," I whispered.

Alfonso waved his slogan side to side, like it was a small flag: WE NEED RIGHTS, NOT ROUNDUPS!

Natalia and Cecilia beside me started doing the same thing. They waved their slogans side to side and up and down. The words DOWN WITH DEPORTATION! and REPATRIATING US CITIZENS MAKES NO SENSE! were written in red, white, and blue.

"Go home, Mexicans! Go home, mojados!" Phillip Rice, the grocer's youngest son, yelled. He left his mother's side and came down the street toward us.

Alfonso started to lose his temper. "Little—"

I put my hand on his arm, and he stopped himself from finishing what he wanted desperately to say. Pressing his lips tightly together, he forced the air out of his lungs through his flared nostrils.

I also had to bite my tongue and swallow my rage at Phillip's degrading words, especially when I was holding up what was, in my opinion, the most important slogan of all, a sign that said, I AM AMERICAN! I HAVE RIGHTS! in great big red, white, and blue letters.

However, no matter how high I held my sign, how much I waved it and moved it up and down, other white people left their businesses to come and stand in protest against us. No longer intimidated, they stood behind the line of policemen, yelling things like, "Arrest them, Chief! Arrest those Mexican dogs!" "Get those bean eaters!" and "Run those filthy dogs outta town!"

I tried ignoring them, tried staying quiet, but I couldn't help it—my heart hurt, and the only thing I could think was that there had to be *something* we could say, *something* we could do to vocalize our rights.

I thought about my family, who had been here in this country, on this very piece of land, for eight generations on my paternal grandfather's side. I thought about my mother and father, who fought for their land and home fearlessly. And I thought about my deceased grandparents, Jovita and Acevedo, and my beloved great-uncle Carlos, who—up until he passed away two years ago—used to come over from Brownsville and play his guitar for us, singing his famous corridos. It was his way of remembering, of documenting the struggles our family, friends, and neighbors had overcome as they'd fought for their rights all along the Río Grande borderlands.

I thought of my father's courage the day he stood on a barrel in the center of town and spoke to the people from his heart, and then I thought of my sign again. I opened my mouth and said, "I am American! I have rights! I can speak my mind! I can speak my heart!"

Amalia and Natalia turned to look at me, and I said it again, "I am American! I have rights! I can speak my mind! I can speak my heart!"

"I can speak my mind! I can speak my heart!" Alfonso repeated, chanting with pride.

Before I knew it, everyone was chanting the words. "I am American! I have rights! I can speak my mind! I can speak my heart!"

At first, we didn't sound so good. But that didn't matter, because we were doing it together. With every word we repeated together, we gained momentum, and soon we were all synchronized, our voices perfectly tuned with one another.

I only wish the moment had last longer, because we were just getting started when Chief Hoffmann took out a whistle and blew. Then all the other policemen pulled out their clubs. They stepped forward in unison, a wall of attackers with a club in one hand each and the other grabbing for us.

I screamed. The first blow made contact with my right temple as I twisted and recoiled from it. The second blow got me directly on my shoulder, and I went down, dropping my sign and hitting the ground hard with both hands. The bottom step of the wooden porch in front of the hotel scraped my face as I fell.

I don't remember much else about the incident. Only that I rode in the back of a police van with my head lying on Amalia's shoulder. She said I had a gash on the side of my head above my ear. I couldn't tell. She wouldn't let me touch it, but kept her handkerchief on it, taking turns with Natalia to press on it. The last thing I remember was sitting in a jail cell with Natalia and Alfonso beside me, my head on Amalia's lap.

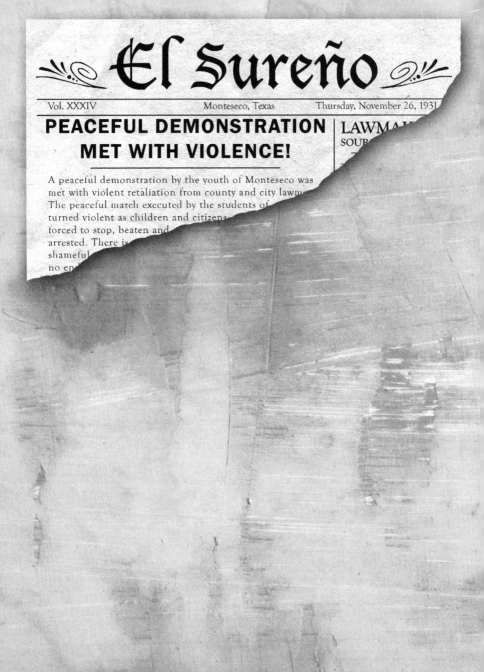

El Sureño

Vol. XXXIV   Monteseco, Texas   Thursday, November 26, 1931

PEACEFUL DEMONSTRATION MET WITH VIOLENCE!

A peaceful demonstration by the youth of Monteseco was
met with violent retaliation from county and city lawm
The peaceful march executed by the students of
turned violent as children and citizens
forced to stop, beaten and
arrested. There is
shameful
no en

LAWM
SOUR

CHAPTER SEVEN

I WAS RELEASED NOT LONG AFTER, AND my parents took me straight to the doctor. According to Dr. Analiz, the Mexican doctor who had an office on our side of town, I had a concussion, but I'd be all right. Both the laceration and the concussion just needed time to heal. Mamá kept me home from school for a few days, and I was strictly on bed rest with orders not even to read or write anything. So I was still home when we received news of the special city council meeting.

The Monteseco City Council only met once a month. However, thanks to a phone call from Mr. Rogelio Mendez, a prominent lawyer from Brownsville and my father's personal friend, the people of Monteseco had been granted a special meeting scheduled first thing Friday morning, during normal business hours, which meant most of my friends would have to miss school if their parents wanted them to attend.

It was clear as we waited outside the courthouse that the town had become even more divided since our arrest. Even though nobody had been officially charged, the incident had left everyone feeling vulnerable. While the Mexicans felt their rights had been trampled by the brutal treatment at the hands of Chief Hoffmann, the Anglo people felt threatened by what they had begun to refer to as "another uprising."

The division wasn't just evident in the discriminatory signage that had more than doubled since the protest; you could actually feel the discomfort and aggression coming from the glares of the people who lived on this side of town.

Anglo folks crossed the street to avoid us as we stood on the sidewalk outside the courthouse, and their faces were strained, overwrought, like the sight of us was something to be scared of. That's why my parents and grandparents decided to stand outside the courthouse and wait for the gente to arrive. They wanted to make sure every Mexican who wanted to attend the meeting made it all the way inside the courthouse. As soon as anyone drove or walked up, my parents called out to them, shook their hands, thanked them for coming, and quickly ushered them inside.

However, things were very different when the Anglo members of the city council drove up to the courthouse. They nodded to us as we stood on the sidewalk, but they didn't smile. The men just walked on by, like we weren't worth their time. The white women of prominence who came to watch the proceedings were even more dismissive. Most of them averted their eyes and busied themselves with taking off their gloves or looking down at their shoes as they walked by. Some of them, however—the wives and mothers of city councilmen—were not as subtle. They raised their eyebrows at us and put their gloved hands up to their noses as they walked by us, like our presence there was infecting the very air they breathed.

The same tension afflicting my parents was also present in my grandfather Rodrigo's shoulders and back. He shifted from foot to foot, adjusted his tie, pulled at his shirt collar, and took his gray felt hat off to fiddle with its thin leather band.

I took his hand and squeezed it between both of mine. "I missed you," I said. "You didn't come to the meeting and you missed brunch last Sunday. Is everything all right?"

"Yes, yes. I'm fine," Güelo Rodrigo said. Then he cleared his throat and patted my hands. "I just have to take things easy. I'm not a young man anymore, corazón."

My mother put her hand on my grandmother's elbow. "Mamá, it's cold out here. You and Papá should go inside. Save us a seat at the front."

"That's a good idea." Güelita Serafina turned around to face us. "Come on, you two. Let's get inside. I need to sit down."

The whole thing was a strange experience. I had never been to a city council meeting where my father was going to present a proposal, much less a loaded one. But Sheriff Caceres was present, which made us all feel safer. I only wish he'd been around when Chief Hoffmann and his men had started beating on us. Then maybe I wouldn't have gotten hurt.

As my parents made their way into the boardroom, Papá stopped to shake Sheriff Caceres's hand. My father had a lot of respect for the sheriff; ever since he'd taken over as sheriff, he'd made it very clear to everyone in Morado County that he would always look out for the gente of Monteseco. He tried making sure the racial conflicts didn't seep into the justice system, but his care could only extend so far. He was powerless to stop the roundups. The federal mandate to repatriate Mexicans was ambiguous, he'd told my father a few days ago. It gave local authorities too much leeway in the execution of the plan, and the best Caceres could do was keep things civilized enough to avoid another matanza.

When the board sat down and the meeting began, we listened attentively, waiting patiently for my father to be asked to speak. My parents sat to my left, with my father taking the aisle seat, ready to spring up to the podium. He would read the proposal that the gente of Monteseco had drafted the night before with the help of a LULAC lawyer in our sala.

My grandparents sat to my right, with Güelo Rodrigo between me and my grandmother. Güelo Rodrigo held my hand like he was trying to give me courage, but I could feel the weakness in his grip, the frailty in his fingers. He was getting thinner too. His cheeks had become a bit gaunt in the last few weeks, and I worried that he might not be able to make it through the whole meeting. What if they took a long time to start? What if they brought us here under false pretenses with the intent of wasting our time?

To my relief, after the initial welcome, Councilman Jones looked at the itinerary and cleared his throat. "Well, let's get the unpleasantries out of the way first, shall we? Gentlemen, I hear we have some kind of proposal on the agenda." He chortled, something akin to the sound a pig makes when it smells a fresh puddle of mud.

"Yes," my father said, standing up and walking over to the podium without being called. "Concerned citizens, councilmen. First of all, thank you for taking time out of your busy schedules to be here today, and for granting us this special meeting so that we might present you with a list of ordinances we'd like to see brought into effect for the betterment of our community."

"Well, then, get on with it, man," Councilman Jones said, waving his hand as if to push foul air aside. "Let's get down to business."

Without wasting another moment, my father put the documents he'd been holding in his hands on the podium and addressed the city council. "Gentlemen, as you well know, I am a son of Monteseco. My family and the families of friends and neighbors have lived here for a long time, generations and generations. So it is with this, my right to live and speak for my fellow citizens, that I ask you to listen to and acknowledge our concerns, weigh our proposal fairly, and give it your full consideration."

I sat quietly, listening to every word coming out of my father's lips as he read from the document that outlined our community's grievances, even though I knew the speech by heart because Mamá and I had spent hours being his audience as he practiced delivering it last night.

When my father was almost done reading his closing remarks, the audience began to stir. The talking started at the right side of the room toward the front, where the Anglo citizens were sitting, and quickly spread. Men turned to their friends and spoke vehemently to one another.

At first, the wives listened to their husbands, but then they too turned heads and twisted torsos to speak to their friends. The whispers and hisses and frowns grew until the whisper became a sonorous buzz that permeated the air.

"Listen to them lose their minds. You'd think we were asking them to slaughter their firstborn!" Mamá said, looking at my grandfather. "¡Parecen avispas desquiciadas!"

"Order! Order!" Councilman Jones called out. He pushed back his chair and stood up to get the people's attention. Then looking at my father, he said, "Well, thank you very much, Mr. del Toro, for your very . . . *passionate* proclamation. Of course, you know that this is not something we can make a decision about today. The council has to meet privately to discuss the ordinances you and your people propose, give— what did you say? *Weight?* Yes, we need to weigh the merits of your plan . . ."

The councilman's words shocked me. "Why do you need to meet in private?" I asked. I stood up and started moving past Mamá.

She didn't move her knees out of my way, but she didn't have to. I squeezed right by her as she reached up and touched my arm. "Estrella. What are you doing, m'ija?" she asked.

"What does it look like I'm doing?" I asked. "I'm going up there to ask questions."

"Don't!" Mamá said. Her hand on my arm was a command,

but I was too angry to let her hold me back. "Let your father handle this. He knows what to say."

My mother's voice was gentle, genuinely concerned for me, but I didn't listen. I walked down the aisle, stood beside my father at the podium, and said, "We brought these matters here so we could discuss them today. What do you mean, you need to meet in private? We are citizens here; this is our town. We have a right to hear what you have to say when you make these decisions."

"I'm sorry, Mr. del Toro, but you'll have to make your daughter go back to her seat. This is a serious meeting, and your child is not on the agenda."

"I don't give a hoot about your agenda," my father said, putting his hand on my shoulder. "My daughter is exactly the reason we're here today. She and her friends had the presence of mind to stand in protest against the very things outlined in our proposal, and for that they were beaten and arrested right here on this street, just a few yards away from those doors."

"You have no right to bring that up. That's not what this meeting is about," the councilman said, ruffling the papers in front of him, refusing to look at us as he spoke.

"Why not?" I asked. "It's your fault it happened."

Councilman Jones dropped the papers, put his hands on the table, and leaned into it. "Young lady, you have no right coming in here making these accusations."

"My daughter has every right to speak her mind," my father said. "You and your friends, the white citizens of

Monteseco, have taken over this town and turned it into a vile, abhorrent place."

"I beg your pardon," Councilman Jones began.

My father didn't let the councilman finish. "The signs outside your businesses are nothing compared to the hatred and animosity that permeate our streets. Now, we all know Monteseco has had its problems," he continued. "As people from different backgrounds, different cultures, we've had our differences, but in the end, we were always a community, a pueblo full of decent people, working toward a better future for our children. But this intolerance, this lack of concern for our laborers, our immigrant friends and family from the other side of the border, and now even our own children have made it impossible for us to remain silent."

"So you think protesting is the answer?" the councilman asked. "You think sending children to riot in the streets is right?"

"My daughter and her friends were engaged in a peaceful demonstration, just as the founding fathers did, just as the suffragists did fifteen years ago. It is their right as citizens of this country." My father lifted his chin and put his arm around my shoulders. "They had the courage to do what they felt was necessary to stand up to the injustices they see in their world. You know as well I do that this situation is dangerous. This side of town has become a viper pit. Not even the buitres will descend on your streets for fear of falling prey to the raids and the disappearances plaguing our working class."

Once again, the citizens of Monteseco broke out talking,

only this time, the buzz was alive and moving through the entire room—not just the Anglos, but every person.

"Stop it! Stop it!" Councilman Jones roared. His hair billowed like a limp cloud of orange cotton candy on top of his head, flopping over his forehead. He pushed it away with a disgusted swat of his hand. "You, sir, have no right to come here and call us vipers. Your disrespect for this council, for some of the most productive, most hardworking citizens of Monteseco, is beyond disgraceful—it is downright reprehensible. Now, I know you have a right to speak, and we've heard what you have to say—"

My father let go of me and put his hands on either side of the podium. "Oh, you haven't begun to hear what I have to say. My daughter is right about one thing. This is an open meeting. We have a right to be present and hear what you have to say when you and your *city councilmen* discuss our proposal."

"That's quite enough!" The councilman's voice reverberated through the room as he stood up. "I refuse to have the whims of a child, let alone a female child, dictate my actions. I suggest you have your daughter sit down before I have her hauled away again. Caceres! Either escort this girl back to her seat or arrest her. We have no more time for shenanigans!"

"No!" my father said, pointing a finger at the city councilmen sitting before him. "We will not be hauled away. We will not be silenced. Not today! You say you feel disrespected? Well, what do you think we feel when we are not allowed to sit next to you in a shop and order something as simple and fundamentally necessary as a glass of water? Water! Which is supposed to be free! How do you think we feel when we walk down the streets and see sign after sign proclaiming your contempt? We work just as hard—no, that's not true. Every single one of our campesinos works harder, longer, and for much less pay than the lot of you put together. And for what? To what end? They pick your vegetables, your fruits, your grains. My gente dig the irrigation systems that give you clean food and water from the very soil which was stolen from their ancestors, food and water which you gladly take, and what do they get in return? Hate. Hate and intolerance and now fear. Because that's what the raids have brought us, a foul, fetid fear that taints every breath our workers breathe. Now the question still stands: What are you going to do about it? How are you going to undo these injustices?"

The councilman didn't answer right away. He sat down, pushed the puff of orange hair farther back on his head, pulled on his coat, straightening it on his frame, and then looked straight at my father. "Well, Mr. del Toro, the answer is simple," he said. "There is nothing we as a council can do to help you. The ordinances you call for are not within our domain."

"What do you mean?" I asked. "You make the laws, don't you?"

Councilman Jones ignored me, but continued to speak to Papá. "We can't tell the business owners of Monteseco who to serve. They are free agents, and as free agents they have the right to decide what happens in their places of business. If they don't want to let dogs or birds or unicorns come through their doors, that is for them to decide. As for the raids, well, those commands come straight from our nation's capital. You're a smart man. You know that, del Toro. We have no choice. We have to comply with the law, to collaborate with those authorities who come into our community and take the necessary actions to preserve the laws of our land. So as you can see, there is absolutely nothing we can do to help you today."

"Preserve the law of the land?" Papá asked. "How is it the law of the country to deport American citizens?"

Councilman Jones pressed his lips together and shook his head. When he finally spoke, he spoke slowly, as if measuring every word. "Those citizens who've been removed were a liability to our country. As the governing party in Monteseco, we reserve the right to take action whenever we find a threat."

"What you are doing is unconstitutional!" Papá said. "We're humans, not dogs or cattle or any other kind of beast, and we demand that you start treating us as such. We might not have the opportunities your education has afforded you, but in the eyes of God, we are part of the human race, and we will no longer permit you to demean us. We demand fairness and equality and respect in the city our fathers and grandfathers created. Monteseco is our inheritance, our legacy, and we aim to take it back by any means necessary."

"Are you threatening to strike, Joaquín?" Mr. Shearn, the city barber, stood up at the council table and leaned in so his belly shoved the papers in front of him forward. "Because we're not putting up with any more of your shenanigans!"

"If that's what it's going to take," I said, answering for my father. "We'll march all the way to Washington if we have to."

Papá rolled his shoulders back and turned to smile at me. "If that's how you choose to perceive this," he said. "Then, yes. Yes, we are."

This time the room exploded. People stood up, shouted, yelled, cursed, and then the Anglo citizens of Monteseco practically trampled one another as they left the courthouse.

From my place at the podium, I saw my grandmother wrap her arms around my grandfather while my mother stood up and blocked them from the mad mob exiting the building. The tejanos sitting on our side of the room didn't budge. On the contrary, they put their hands on the wooden frames of the chairs in front of them and remained firmly planted in their seats.

Papá patted my shoulder as if to say, *I'll take it from here*, and then he turned to address the city councilmen. "Understand," he said. "We came here to talk, to lay our cards on the table, but your refusal to validate our concerns has given us no choice but to get tough."

"Do me a favor, del Toro," Mr. Jones said. "Take your people and get out of our chambers. We have no use for you and your kind."

My father's face turned bright red. "Your chambers?" he called. "Who do you think erected this building? We did, with our brown arms and brown hands. We built this town from the ground up. This is no more *your chambers* than Monteseco is *your town*."

From his seat beside my grandmother, my grandfather raised his hand and hollered, "We will not leave this meeting until you honor our requests!"

"This meeting is closed!" Mr. Jones said, and to punctuate the statement, he took the papers in front of him and shoved them in a leather case he pulled up from under the table. "Done. Finished. We've wasted too much of our citizens' time already. Now I don't know about you, gentlemen, but I need a strong cup of coffee to wash down the bad taste in my mouth. Shall we?"

At his words, the city councilmen stood up. They filed out silently after Councilman Jones through a door behind the table, their own personal exit, their only means of escape.

Dear Abuela Jovita,

I have been thinking a lot about you today, because today we stood together, Papá and I, and spoke of justice for our kind, demanded it of the whites, but no one cared. No one listened.

I need you to show me how you did it, how you fought for your gente without being overwhelmed by fear, without the rage that blinds and makes us say rash things to those who would raise their batons and crush our skulls.

When that happened to me, when the officer's stick rained blows upon my forehead, I saw flashes of light. The fire of white relámpagos ran across a moonless sky, and I was alone with the shadow of death breathing into my lungs. Cloaked in black blood, she stood over me, waiting for me to make a move, to stand up or die. I thought I might perish. I feared I might. My only regret as I lay motionless was that I might have compromised my familia.

pray for us, Abuelita. Pray that we might find a way to banish the madness that lingers in every dark corner of our town. Pray that we don't disappear into the night.

Love always,
Your granddaughter,

Estrella

Chapter Eight

*T*HERE IS NOTHING MORE CONFUSING OR frightening than waking up to the smell of something burning. I lifted the lid of the kerosene lamp, lit a match, and twisted the knob until there was enough light to illuminate my room. There was smoke everywhere, enough of it that it stung my eyes and I had to fight to keep them open.

I grappled with my bedspread, kicked at the heavy woolen material, threw it off me, and jumped off the bed. I tripped over my shoes in the middle of the floor, but I didn't have time to drop to my knees and scramble around looking for them. The smoke was clogging my airway. Besides, wasn't smoke always thickest at floor level, or was it lighter because it rose as it filtered into the room from under the door? Should I be dropping to the ground and crawling? And where should I crawl?

There was no way of knowing where exactly in the house the smoke was coming from, and I panicked. "Mamá? Papá?"

I called out, but my lungs took in too much smoke, and I started to cough.

"Papá?" I called out again. When I didn't get an answer, I panicked. What about Wicho? He was too small to get out of the house by himself. What if the fire had started near my parents' room and they were trapped? What if my parents had succumbed to the smoke? What if they were passed out somewhere in the house trying to get to us? The thoughts burned through my mind, and I froze momentarily.

Coughing, I decided I needed to move, to go find them. But how? Door or window? I thought maybe window since it was the most direct route to the outdoors and I could crawl the length of the first floor roof ledge and look into Wicho's room. However, there was the eleven-foot drop from there to the ground to consider, and how would I get Wicho down with me? What if the fire had reached the roof of the first floor directly outside my window? Then all bets would be off, and I'd have to get back to the other side of the room, to the door. Did I have enough time?

Instinctively, I put my hands flat against the wall and used it to orient myself as I made my way to the door. What was it Papi said about touching a doorknob if there was ever a fire at Las Moras? Just hold my hand over it, feel for heat before trying to open it.

To my relief, the doorknob wasn't hot. In fact, it was cold, very cold, as it should be in November. I twisted the knob and the door flew open, yanked out of my hand so violently I almost fell before I let go.

"This way!" I didn't recognize the voice, couldn't place the strange timbre, the deep resonance, the unusual accent, except to acknowledge that it belonged to a man whose extended hand reached for me in the darkness. "Come, señorita, give me your hand. We don't have time to waste!"

My frightened, fevered mind switched to primal mode. I looked at that strange, meaty hand and panicked. *La Mano Pachona*, my feral mind screamed. *Run! Run the other way!*

No, my rational self said from somewhere in the back of my mind. *There is no such thing as an evil corpse's detached hand reaching out for you in the dark. No such thing as a hairy, immortal appendage trying to drag you away and pull you down to the depths of hell where all manner of evil things lurk to devour you. No. Such. Thing.*

But if it isn't some evil thing, then he must be an intruder.

His voice told me he didn't belong in the house. Nobody I knew talked like that, with that strange foreign accent. But there was more to it. Something deep in the pit of my stomach said I couldn't, shouldn't, trust the man behind that hand.

"Mami! Papi!" I called out in the darkness, resisting the outstretched hand. "Sofía! Doña Luz?" *Where is everyone?*

The outstretched hand shook, opened wider, reached for me. "Señorita, por favor!" The hand groped in the dark, grabbed at my sleeve.

"No!" I screamed and ripped my sleeve out of its clutches.

I pushed hard at the fearsome thing, shoved it out of my way, and rushed out of the room. I stumbled on weak knees, clinging to the wall as I made my way down the hallway toward my parents' room, knocking down several small family portraits.

The fearsome thing followed me. "Get away from me!" I screamed. "Mamá! Papá! Where are you?"

My eyes watered profusely from the smoke, and I was too scared to pay any attention to the frames I knocked down as I struggled to stay one step ahead of the thing that stalked me.

"Mami! Mamá!" I called out.

Then I was caught, engulfed in a strong embrace, trapped against a man's chest.

"Estrella, hija! Thank God."

Papá's voice was in my ear. He pressed a kiss upon my head. "She's okay!" he called out. "I've got her, Dulceña!"

Mamá's voice came out of the smoky shadows. She crept over to my father and reached out to touch me. "Estrella, corazón!" She hugged me to her with one arm. I felt the bulk of what must have been Wicho, bundled up like a tamal and cradled safely in her arms.

"This way, señor." The man who followed me called out again from the dusky murkiness of shadows and light created by the fire down the other end of the hall by the banister. "The left wing is too far gone. This is the only way out."

Without questioning who the man was, my father put his hand on my shoulder and pushed me forward. The smoke was so thick I couldn't see anything as we moved away from the fiery left stairwell to the right side of the house.

Rounding the corner, we came upon the staircase. Doña

Luz, Sofía, and Luz's husband Manuel were standing at the bottom of the stairs, right in front of the open front door, looking up at us. "Oh, thank God you're safe," Doña Luz called out. "Manuel was about to run upstairs to look for you."

As we took the stairs, we could see the fire raging to the left, consuming the walls, eating up our furniture, blowing its fiery breath upon the heavy drapes until they billowed feathery crimson flags that blew great puffs of black air toward us.

"Is there anyone else in the house?" the strange voice of my stalker called out from behind us.

"No," Papá said. "It's just us upstairs."

"Good," the man said. "Let's go."

We rushed forward, reached the landing, and headed out the front door behind the man whose outstretched hand had frightened me out of my wits.

Outside, there was pandemonium. A huge part of our house was engulfed in flames. The fire licked the edges of windows and doors and spewed up black smoke into the night air. Everywhere we looked there were Rangers, police officers, and deputies. To the left of us, Rangers and lawmen grabbed at our campesinos and their families, pulled them away from one another and made them get into the backs of boarded-up field trucks. Babies wailed, children cried, and women clung to them as they were being loaded up. Husbands were pushed away roughly, sent to the next truck if they didn't fit.

More frightening still was the strange sight of so many lawmen standing with rifles at their sides, watching menacingly while the rest of our workers were rounded up.

Doña Luz's eldest daughter, Juanita, and her husband, Guillermo, stood huddled together far off to the right of us, partly hidden by the anacahuitas, holding a bundle of items in their arms. As soon as they saw us, they waved. We rushed over to them. "Señora! Here, my mother got your coats and shoes from the hall closet for you," Juanita said. Mamá unfolded my red tweed coat and handed it to me while Doña Luz held Wicho so that my mother could slip into her soft gray winter coat.

"Oh my god," Mamá said. "You didn't have to do that. What about your things?"

"I couldn't think what else to get," Doña Luz admitted. "Otherwise, I would have brought the boy's things too."

"He's got his shoes on," Mamá said. "And his coat. I made sure of that."

Sofía held out my father's working boots for him and said, "I got a pair of boots for you, señor, but I didn't see your coat. The fire was spreading, and I couldn't go back upstairs. I got your schoolbag, Estrellita. It was in the closet too."

My father took my schoolbag and his worn boots and stared in disbelief at them. "Thank you," he said. He handed me my bag and leaned down to slip his feet into his boots. My mother put on her coat and helped me button mine as I clung to my schoolbag, thinking that of all the things I would have saved, my schoolbag was at the top of my list. It had my journal with my poems and letters in it. Other than the guitar my uncle Carlos had given me before he passed away two years ago, the journal was the most precious thing I owned.

"Papá?" My voice trembled as it left my lips. "What's going on?"

"You're being raided," the man who'd led us out of the house told us. He put his hands on my father. "Are you Joaquín del Toro?"

"Yes," my father said. "Who are you? And what were you doing in my house?"

The man reached into his pocket and pulled out a thin black wallet. He opened it and showed his badge to my father. "Tobias Williams, with the Morado County Sheriff's Department," he said. "These are my colleagues, Ernest McCoy and Simon Pearson, here to escort you."

"Escort us? What are you talking about? We haven't done anything wrong. Did you do this?" Papá asked. "Who started the fire? Where is Sheriff Caceres?"

"Joaquín del Toro, you are under arrest for violating county ordinances and conspiracy to commit treason."

My father's voice changed then, and I could tell by the lowered tone he was as surprised as we were. "You're not going to get away with—"

Papá didn't get to finish his thought. All at once, Ernest and Simon descended upon him, holding him still and hand-cuffing him. "Don't fight," Tobias said. "It's better for you if you don't fight."

"Why are you doing this?" my mother asked, shielding Wicho's eyes from the horrible scene taking place in front us. But Tobias didn't answer her. Ernest just started walking away, hauling my father by the arm.

"Papá!" I screamed while Mamá held me tight.

"Don't worry about me," my father said as they took him away. "Just do as they say. We'll be all right. I promise."

"Papá! No!" I cried out, but the men walked fast, rushing him through the yard into the garden.

One of Tobias's colleagues waved at us. "You too, señora," he said. "Walk. Don't make this difficult on your children. Just walk that way. I'll tell you when to stop."

"Where are you taking us?" I asked.

Mamá didn't wait for them to answer me, or perhaps she knew they had no intention of answering me. They couldn't be from the sheriff's office of Morado County. Sheriff Caceres would never have stood for this treatment, the burning of our home. She put her hand on my elbow and turned me in the direction the two other men had taken my father.

I turned around and saw that Doña Luz, Manuel, and their family were being loaded into a truck. Manuel had to pull Doña Luz up while Juanita and her husband pushed at her gently. Doña Luz's hands slipped from Manuel's grasp, and she fell sideways. Juanita tried to keep her balanced, but Doña Luz slipped and crashed to the ground. She screamed as she fell and grabbed at her leg.

I broke away from Mamá's grasp and ran toward Doña Luz. Juanita was behind her, holding her up against her lap, while Manuel looked at her leg. Blood was gushing out of a laceration that ran from high above the inside of her knee halfway down her calf. Doña Luz whimpered and held her skirt down in an attempt to be modest even as she writhed in pain. I tried leaning down to help, but the officer in charge of loading the truck put his arm out across my shoulders and stopped me.

"Stay back," he said.

"She needs to go to the hospital," I said to Manuel, who had taken off Doña Luz's apron and was using it to wrap her leg.

One of the deputies who'd stayed with Mamá, either Tobias or Simon, pulled my arm. "Come on, señorita, we have to go."

"No," I said. "I can't let you load her back up and haul her away like that."

Juanita looked up at me. "It's best if you do what they say," she said. "We'll take care of Mamá."

Doña Luz waved her hand to get my attention. "Listen to Juanita," she said. "Stay with your family, Estrella. We'll see you when we get there."

"But you're hurt," I said, fighting to hold back the tears that were burning in my eyes. Doña Luz had always taken care of me. She had put aloe vera on my hand when she was teaching me to make tortillas and I burned my fingertips on the comal. She had pulled espinas out of my feet when I ran around barefoot in the yard every summer. She made sopitas for me and brought them to me in bed when I had a cold. Besides Mamá, she was the most important woman in my life. I couldn't leave her side, not while she was bleeding like that.

"Come on!" Tobias yanked me back again.

The officer in charge of loading the truck patted Tobias on

the arm. "Be careful, will ya! You don't need to be so rough. She's just a kid." Then he turned to talk to me. "You should listen to the señora and go with your mamá," he said. "It's better if your family stays together."

Everywhere, people looked terrified. Their faces were pale and not just from the cold November wind. There was susto in their pallor, pain in their round eyes, and worry in their furrowed brows. Fear roared and crackled and burst into flames in our ears, and we knew the future was burning down, collapsing before us, devouring our home and our livelihood. Worst of all, there was nothing we could do to stop it.

I let Tobias escort me back to where Mamá was being detained in the garden. She pulled me in for a side hug. Wicho lifted his head off my mother's shoulder and looked at me. He reached out and patted my face. "Trella," he said, and I kissed and rubbed his hand, trying to warm up his cold little fingers.

"Please don't do that again," my mother whispered against my forehead. "Wait with us. We'll get it all sorted out soon enough."

As we passed the garden's walkway, where the bougainvilleas and cenizos and anacahuitas created a natural canopy for an afternoon stroll, we saw two dark sedans idling with their parking lights off. My father was sitting in the car parked in front, but we were being directed to the second car.

Ernest stepped away from the first car and joined us. "We're all set. Let's go, ladies, get in the car."

"What if I don't?" I asked Tobias.

"Estrella!" Mamá's whisper was a plea to stop being obstinate. The three men flanked me and my mother, surrounding us. Simon took hold of my arm, and I walked forward obediently, because that was what my mother expected from me. For now.

The last I saw of my home was from the back seat of that sedan as we crested a hill near Arroyo Morado, our house blazing in the distance as my mother sat beside me, silent.

El Sureño

| Vol. XXXV | Monteseco, Texas | Saturday, November 28, 1931 |

FIRE AT LAS MORAS!
AUTHORITIES BAFFLED!

—The People Demand Answers —

A fiery inferno, owners missing, and all the authorities of Monteseco can say is an investigation is under way. They don't know how the fire started, only that more than thirty Mexican campesinos on the premises at the time of the fire were arrested and hauled away in yet another so-called roundup for the purpose enforcing the repatriation This state of affairs not be tolera

DESAPARECIDOS!

This paper's most ardent contributor, Monteseco's most beloved daughter and family—
Vanished!

This paper's founder and grieving father South Texas reporter, Dulceña del T a reward of 10,000 dollars and her family, husb daughter son

CHAPTER NINE

WE TRAVELED BY NIGHT FOR HOURS, huddled together, Mamá, Wicho, and I, in the back seat of the black sedan. In the front seat, Ernest and Tobias were silent. Their shadowed faces under their felt hats were lean, tough.

"Monteseco is that way," I said, pointing to the right when our driver missed the turn in the road. Then, as if it wasn't strange enough that our driver just kept driving straight through the intersection, taking us away from Monteseco, he was taking us away from Papá, whose car had turned while we continued straight. "What are they doing?" I asked. "Where are they taking Papá?"

Mamá shifted a fussy Wicho in her arms. "Why aren't we going with the other car? Why are you separating us?" she asked, looking at the man in front of her.

Tobias pulled his hand up to his face, flipped the sleeve of his coat back, and looked very closely at his watch. "Hurry up. We're behind schedule."

Mamá broke down then. She put a hand on the back of the driver's seat and sat forward as she asked again and again. "Where are they taking him? Please, please, just tell me where they're taking him. I need to know what's going on."

"I thirsty," Wicho whispered, reaching up to touch my mother's face. "Mami, I thirsty."

"I know, sweetheart. We'll be there soon, and you can have something to drink then." My mother took Wicho's little hand and kissed it, rubbing his palm with her thumb.

"Try to get some sleep," Tobias said after a long pause. "It's going to be a long ride, ladies."

I didn't want to sleep. I wanted to go back to Las Moras, back to my bed, back to the safety of my father's arms. But there was no going back. Las Moras was burning, and the road lay blank and bare on the narrow moonlit path before us.

Out my window, the scraggly, thin torsos of phantoms and ghouls sprouted from the trunks of mesquites and huisaches, and once at an intersection, a ghostly lechuza screamed and dove past us. Its white wings flapped powerfully, the sound of muscle and feather sending a chill up my spine as it echoed in the dark.

A long way from home, after many hours on that dark, unsettling road, I laid my head against the glass of my door window and drifted, allowing myself to float somewhere between wakefulness and sleep. But even as my eyes closed, I saw something white and small come into focus in the woods.

As we drove by, a ghostly figure appeared in the bushes. Her white-veiled head swiveled, and she looked directly at me. It was the Santa Muerte. I craned my neck, unable to take my eyes off the specter. La Santisima, waiting in the darkness, biding her time. Was that what awaited us? Was death at the end of this road trip?

A sick feeling overcame me, and I thought I might throw up. *No*, my mind whispered. *You're hallucinating. The smoke must have warped your thinking. Stop giving into the fear. Concentrate on what's real. Concentrate on Wicho and Mamá. They need you right now.*

As if he'd seen the fearsome sight too, Wicho suddenly let out a long, loud wail. He cried and cried, his body quivering as my mother tried to shush him back to sleep. "Here," I said. "Give him to me. Your arms must be tired by now. Come here, tlacuachito," I said, coaxing him with his special pet name, the one I'd given him when he was born because he'd had a sprig of fuzzy, light hair and his skin had been so transparent, he looked as ugly as a baby possum. Of course, that had all changed. The fuzz had fallen out, and he'd grown a gorgeous head of hair, dark and rich as mahogany.

Mamá hesitated, but I took Wicho from her shoulder, kissed him, and cradled him gently in my lap. Wicho's short, tormented sobs quieted as I sang his favorite lullaby, "Doña Blanca."

My little brother giggled when I tickled him as the song came to an end. "¡Otra vez!" he squealed, and I started humming the tune again.

"Thank you," Mamá said. She rubbed her shoulder and took a long, deep breath that told me she was exhausted.

"You should really try to get some sleep," I whispered when Wicho started to drift off in my arms. There were dark bags under Mamá's brown eyes, and she furrowed her brows and bit her lip.

"I can't," she whispered. Then she looked out the window, past me, and let out a shaky sigh. "Not until we get where we're going. So I can call your Tio Tomás. Ask him if he heard what happened. He needs to know what's going on. He can get our lawyer and get this all sorted out."

I didn't want to take Mamá's hope away, so I didn't share my misgivings about her plan, but I doubted we would be allowed to call anyone. From the way we'd been treated so far, I knew exactly what was going on.

We were being vanished.

We were on our way to becoming more of the many who had simply disappeared from our community. *You need to be ready for anything,* I told myself. *You need to be ready to escape. Kick, punch, and run if you have to. You need to be ready to fight, like your grandmother fought, fearlessly, without overthinking it, without regard for your life.*

After all, this is your fault, isn't it? a guilty little voice inside me whispered. *You're the reason your family is being evaporated. You did this to them.* The terrible truth of it took my breath away and replaced it with a wrenching pain, a sleek arrow of truth that shot through me and wedged itself right in the center of my heart. A wounded little noise left my lips involuntarily.

"Estrella?" Mamá put her hand on my arm. "Are you okay?"

I coughed and cleared my throat. The last thing I wanted

to do right then was cause my mother any more distress than I already had. "Yes," I said. "It was just something in my throat. I'm all right now."

To my relief, she relaxed. A few minutes later, she laid her head sideways on the back of the seat. "I'm just going to rest my eyes," she said quietly, so as not to unsettle Wicho, who had finally fallen asleep in my arms.

"Okay," I said.

Tobias turned back to look at us. His eyes glistened in the darkness for a moment, and then he went back to facing the front, looking at the empty road ahead of us.

Mamá tried to rest, but after a while, she gave up on it. "Can we stop for a while? I need to relieve myself, and I'm sure my children need to as well," she said.

"What do you mean?" Tobias asked.

My mother put her hand demurely over her chest and stared at him, unblinking.

"Oh. Oh," Tobias said, turning to look at Ernest. "We should stop. They need to make water."

Ernest thought about it for a second and then slowed down, driving into a small patch of low grass and dirt off the side of the road. The men got out, but they kept their shooting hands in their coats. Mamá stepped out of the car with Wicho and started walking gingerly into the woods.

"You wait here," Ernest said, taking my elbow and pulling me back.

Mamá, who had started moving toward a thick oak tree, stopped. "What?" she asked. "Why?"

"You can take turns," Ernest said. "That way, you don't get any ideas about taking off."

"Where would we go?" my mother argued. "Look at us. We're out in the middle of nowhere. There's absolutely no place to go."

"Are you going or not?" Ernest asked, waving his gun toward the darkened woods.

Mamá put my brother down and straightened up, rolling back her shoulders. "Not without my daughter, I'm not. No."

"Come on, Ernest. What's the harm? They have the boy. They ain't gettin' very far," Tobias reasoned.

Ernest turned his face away and tapped his gun against his thigh as if he was losing his patience. "All right," he said. "Make it quick. And don't make me come after you."

When we first started out, we could see all right, but as soon as we got into the brush, we couldn't see more than a couple of feet in front of us. To make things worse, the moon was thin and frail, so it didn't offer much in the way of illumination.

"Hurry up," Ernest yelled from the side of the road. "We don't have all night."

"Stay close to me," Mamá said, pulling my hand to drag me behind a tree. Then, putting Wicho down, she pulled down his pajamas and told him to go wee-wee. Wicho rubbed his eyes and whined, but complied. Pulling his pajamas back on, Mamá said to me, "Go on, take your turn. I doubt we'll stop again anytime soon."

I didn't want to have to relieve myself in the woods. But

as I stood there, listening to my body, I knew that I shouldn't wait. Mamá was right—there was no telling when the opportunity would present itself again. So I fought my way through the weeds and did my business as quickly as I could. Then I walked back to Mamá's side, completely mortified by the whole thing.

As we made our way back out of the brush, Mamá leaned in and said, "Listen. If you get a chance, I want you to run. You understand?" I nodded and looked past my mother, at the men giving us their backs. They were too busy talking to hear what my mother was saying to me. "I don't want you to worry about us. You just get to a phone and call your Tio Tomás. Tell whoever you can reach at the parish what's going on."

"I will," I said. We got out of the brush and stepped onto the road.

"Get in the car," Ernest demanded, and we did.

"You go first, Ernie," Tobias said, dropping his cigarette on the dirt road and crushing it with his foot. "I'll watch them till you get back."

As Ernest took his turn in the woods, Tobias lit another thin cigarette. The light smoke coming from deep inside his lungs mixed with the coldness of the chilly winter air, creating an odd-shaped haze that lingered like a phantom and crawled into the open windows of the car. From inside the car, I watched those white slivers of breath dissipate while I sang Wicho another Spanish lullaby.

"You got good pipes," Tobias said. "You take lessons or something?"

"No," I said. "My great-uncle Carlos taught me." My mother's elbow at my side told me to stop talking to them, so I didn't go into any more detail.

Wicho wiggled and sat up on my lap. "I hungry, Mami!" he wailed.

"I know, chiquito," my mother said. "We're almost there, corazón. We'll get you some papa soon. Okay?"

Ernest came out of the woods and ran across the road. "Let's go," he said, waving at Tobias to jump into the car. Tobias dropped his cigarette butt and put it out with the tip of his dark dress shoe.

As we set out again, I looked at the bare road before us and wondered what lay ahead. Would I even have the chance to stay in the country, or was I about to become an immigrant in our ancestral land, a place as foreign to me as home was familiar?

Dawn brought with it a winter storm. Rain poured down in long, bleak sheets the color of thin cement. As the rain fought the daylight for attention, Mamá rested beside me. Wicho lay scrunched up on the seat between us, folded over awkwardly and snoring quietly. We drove over a small bridge that jostled us around in the back seat, but Wicho didn't wake up. Mamá stirred, but she didn't open her eyes.

A swollen creek ran under the precarious bridge, treacherous and vindictive in its mad rush to flow, to gain ground. Farther ahead, across a road, a herd of cows moved away from the creek through the blurry rain in slow progression. They knew better than to panic. Their migration was temporary, so they took it in stride. Worried that we might never see home again, I reached down by my feet, pulled my journal and a pencil out of my backpack, and scribbled a quick little poem.

As I continued to scribble, I let silent tears fall onto the paper, swiping them away discreetly. When I was done, when the page was stained with my fearful tears and my crowded words, I put it away. I closed my eyes and spoke to my abuelita Jovita. Then I said a silent prayer for protection. I prayed for intervention, for deliverance, because I had a feeling only something otherworldly could save us now.

ACROSS THE ROAD

Cows migrate in unison, slowly, quietly,
Plowing against the forceful rains.
Heads hung low, resigned, they keep
Their eyes to the ground as if in prayer.

They do not wait for the waters to rise,
The lip of the creek to curl up cynically,
Swallow them up, drag them downstream.
They walk steadily, calmly, don't look back.

Chapter Ten

I MUST HAVE FALLEN ASLEEP TOO, BECAUSE it was morning when we finally came to a stop and I opened my eyes. There was hollering and crying coming from outside. I leaned over and looked out the window. We were crossing the border in Mexico, on the other side of El Paso. Why they had brought us here, clear across the state, was a mystery to me.

I knew we'd passed through El Paso because of the sign overhead, over the arch of the international bridge between Chihuahua and Texas, which read *¡Bienvenidos a Ciudad Juárez!* But the sight before me wasn't very welcoming. Hundreds, maybe thousands of people clogged the streets, some in cars, others on foot, all making their way through a gate to a fenced-off section of the sidewalk.

Everywhere I looked men, women, and children dressed in all manner of clothing—from filthy rags and threadbare dresses to fine coats and warm hats—stood in line. They held on to their belongings, looking lost and confused.

"What are we doing here?" I asked Mamá, who was peeking at the scene outside the car with her hand on my shoulder.

"This is it, ladies," Ernest said, opening the door and getting out of the car. "Our final stop. You're free to go now."

"You can't just dump us here!" my mother said. "We don't have our papers. You have to take us back! We need our documents!"

Tobias opened the door and let himself out. Then he came around and opened the door for us. "Come on. Don't make this more difficult than it already is," he said. "Time to get out."

When I stepped out of the car, the sunlight assaulted my eyes and I cringed. Wicho covered his eyes with his little hands and said, "Too bright."

The light had us perplexed, but only for a moment, because no sooner had we adjusted to the sunlight than Ernest handed me my bookbag, and they both got back in the car and drove off.

As I watched them disappear down the street, a group of uniformed guards came over and started hollering for us to get moving.

"Move along! Let's go!" the first guard said in Spanish.

"Get your things together! Let's go! Let's go," another guard hollered, pushing me and my mother, trying to make us get through the gate.

"Where are you taking us?" I asked the second guard in Spanish.

The guard regarded me through narrowed eyes. His dark

mustache twitched and sighed. "Where else?" he asked. "To processing."

"Processing?" I asked my mother. "You mean, deportation? Now? Just like that?"

My mother's lips trembled, and she shifted Wicho in her arms. "No," she said. "There's got to be more than that. Come on. Let's see what they have to say."

"Let's go! Get going! That way!" The guards waved batons in our faces and shoved us into line as they hollered. "Today! Today! Today!"

I wanted to scream at them, shove them back, but I was afraid—not for myself, but for my mother and little brother. What would these men do to them if we didn't do what they asked? I moved when they told me to move, letting one vicious guard after another herd us like goats. But I dawdled, staying as close to Mamá as possible at all times.

"Look for your father and anyone else you might see from Las Moras," Mamá said, scanning people's faces as they walked by. Her hair was disheveled where it had slipped halfway out of its French twist. Her face was pale, her lips bare of lipstick, but she didn't lose her decorum. She still looked like the doña she was, the lady of the house at Las Moras, as we moved forward, keeping an eye out for my father.

After we were sure our family was not among the repatriates on the street around us, my mother sidled up to one of the younger, less aggressive repatriation officials and asked, "Excuse me, can you tell me where I might go to talk to someone about our situation?"

The official pointed at an old sign hanging off the side of a building behind us. "That's the customs house over there. They will show you where to go. Just stay in line. Follow the others."

"Oh my god!" Mamá's face went suddenly pale. "How am I going to get in touch with your uncle Tomás? God only knows where they took your father! And your güelitos. What if they took your güelitos? They could be anywhere along the border. There are repatriation stations all along the Río Grande, all the way up to California."

"California!" The thought of never seeing Papá again was enough to make the coldness of the November air chill me down to the bones. I shivered. "No. They wouldn't do that, would they? Send them all the way up to California? That's insane. Why would they do that?"

"They didn't need to bring us all the way out here either," Mamá reminded me. "They could have sent us through Reynosa or even Laredo, but they didn't. They intentionally separated us!"

"They're probably just trying to scare us," I said. "He's gotta be here somewhere. We just need to find him."

"Let's go! Let's go!" A guard was coming down the line, making sure we all moved along. "We don't have all day! Move!"

Wicho stirred in my mother's arms. Then he started fussing. "I hungry."

"Yes, I know, chiquito. Don't worry, we're here. We'll get something to eat soon," Mamá said.

As we walked, I continued to scan the line of repatriates, looking for my father. But there was no sign of Papá, or of Doña Luz or her family, no sign of even one campesino from Las Moras. They'd truly separated us from everyone we knew and loved.

Mamá rubbed Wicho's back softly as we inched forward, moving up a few steps at a time. "The line is moving fast," I said, and she nodded and hummed a soft arrurrú under her breath. She wasn't much of a singer, not like my uncle Carlos, but I wasn't in the mood to sing Wicho any lullabies, so I just stood in line beside her.

As we got closer to the customs house, I saw that the people in front of us had to walk on trays. "What's going on?" I asked Mamá.

"I don't know," she said.

The trays were full of a strange, strong-smelling chemical liquid. "Excuse me." My mother turned to look at a guard standing beside the trays, making sure everyone stepped into them and soaked their shoes through before they proceeded to customs. "What is this?"

"Disinfectant," the guard said, waving us forward. "Let's go!"

My mother hesitated for a moment. A well-dressed man in front of us turned around and pointed at his soaked shoes. "So we don't infect their livestock," he said.

"Imagine that!" the woman behind us said, shaking her head.

"Us? Infect their livestock?" I asked the guard in Spanish. "When would we get an opportunity to do that?"

"Estrella," Mamá hissed, shifting Wicho in her arms.

The guard pointed at my little brother. "Him too," he said.

"Him? He's a baby!" I said.

The guard tapped the ground with his baton and waited.

My mother put my brother down with his feet on the trays. Wicho was startled, but only for a moment. He started to whimper, the usual beginning of a temper tantrum.

But then my mother stepped into the tray with him and said, "Oh, this is fun!"

She stomped in the disinfectant like it was a rain puddle and laughed the way she laughed during playtime with Wicho.

I threw my arms up. "This is stupid," I said to the guard. "I'm not doing it."

"Estrella, por favor," my mother begged in a tired, almost resigned tone of voice as she stepped out of one tray and into the next one.

"But my shoes!" I cried. "They'll be ruined."

"Don't be difficult," Mamá scolded, her brows knitting together again.

I sighed and stepped onto the tray. The liquid rose over my ankles and soaked into my socks and shoes. I could have cried for the inhumanity of it. To think we were being treated like infectious beasts made me want to lash out at the guards.

As we walked through all the trays, I glared at the back of my mother's head. "I hope Wicho doesn't get sick," I said. "Because that's poison we just put on our feet."

"Mind your tongue," Mamá whispered sharply, right in my ear. "You shouldn't even think such things, much less

❧ 119 ❧

speak of them. Concentrate on our mission. There ought to be a phone I can use in the customs house. If there is, I'll call your uncle Tomás first. If he answers, he can call Güelo Rodrigo's lawyer down in Brownsville, see what he can do to help us."

"Do you think they'll really let us use the phone?" I asked. "Can we call the United States from here?"

Mamá didn't have time to answer me, because we had reached the door to the customs house, and a soldier was waving us in. "Come on," she said. "Let's see what they have to say."

The customs house was noisy and crowded. Everywhere I turned, there were men, women, and children standing huddled together in front of the many little desks where official-looking clerks dressed in khaki uniforms sat asking questions, scribbling, and stamping papers.

"Where do we go?" I asked.

Mamá's eyebrows knitted together. She shifted Wicho to her other hip as she glanced around for an available clerk.

"This way!" a middle-aged male clerk called out in English. He waved to us from his desk. His nameplate read ALFONSO MOLINA. "I am here to process your family. You are the next. Come. Come."

We hurried over to the desk. My little brother squirmed and then, lifting his head, he sneezed and started to shriek, sounding as if he'd just been bitten by a scorpion. "I'm sorry," my mother said over the sound of my brother's crying. "He's hungry and cold and wet and tired! I was wondering, is there a phone I can use somewhere? To call my brother-in-law on the other side?"

"No. No telephone, sorry." Alfonso Molina opened the drawer to his left and pulled out a fresh form without looking at us. He extended his right arm and shook it a bit, like it was cramped. Then he dated the form, cleared his throat, and lifted his head. "Where is your husband?"

"My husband?" Mamá was as perplexed as I was. She thought about the question for a second, and then answered, "I don't know." She rocked Wicho, who calmed down a bit.

"You don't have husband?" Señor Molina asked.

My mother's eyes glazed over for a second, and she didn't speak, so I elbowed her. "Yes," my mother said. "I do have a husband. I just meant he's not here. With us. That's why I need to use the phone. I need to speak to his brother. He can get in touch with our lawyers."

The clerk pressed his lips together and made a weird smacking sound before he spoke again. "¡Ay! No husband is a big problem. He is necessary here. To make things go smooth, we need to talk to head of household, to husband."

"You don't understand," Mamá said. "We were illegally deported. We don't belong here. I just need to make a phone call. I need to call my brother-in-law in Monteseco to come get us."

Señor Molina sighed. "Illegal?" he asked. "No. You are here by lawful agreement. Between our countries. You are repatriating. Just fill out form for to get Certificate of Residency as well as you can. We try our best, ¿verdad? To make this fast, but without your husband, this will take time. Do you have deportation papers from the United States? I will need it now."

"That's what I'm trying to tell you," my mother said, her lips tight, forcing a nervous smile. "We don't have any papers. We're US citizens, born in Texas, all of us. We had birth certificates and passports at our house in Monteseco, but there was a fire last night. We were raided and we didn't have time to get them. The house was burning too fast. We left without them. But if you just let me use the phone, I'm sure my brother-in-law can get copies of our birth certificates to help clear this up."

"No phone!" the clerk said, chopping his hand across the air in a quick motion.

"What?" I asked. "Then what are we supposed to do?"

"We fill out papers here, send them back to the United States for process," he said, waving his hand in some secret sort of sign language only he was familiar with. "Your name, please."

"No," my mother said. "No names. There has to be another way. Who's in charge here? Who runs this place? Someone has to run this place?"

Wicho started screaming again, and the clerk rolled his eyes. "Díaz!" he screamed, turning his head to the right and calling out to someone behind him. "Díaz! We have another *special one*! Come! I have no time for this!" Then, standing up and looking past us, he yelled, "Next!"

A young uniformed clerk stepped away from his desk and

came over to us. "Hello, señora, I am Sargento Romero Díaz. Would you please to come this way?" he asked, putting his hand on my mother's arm and opening his other arm out to show us the way.

Sargento Díaz led us to a smaller desk at the far right corner of the room. We sat down side by side, my mother and I, with Wicho howling uncontrollably.

"Oh, he is very upset, el niño, ¿verdad? Well, no matter. How can I help you today?"

Cuddling Wicho against her chest, Mamá explained our situation as Wicho wailed. Sargento Díaz listened quietly. His small, dark lips were pursed into a tiny little knot as he waited patiently for my mother to finish telling her story.

"I see. I see," he finally said. "Unfortunately, we do not let people call Los Estados from here. International calls are very costly. Even I am not allowed to make them. If we were to let you call, we would have to let everyone else call, and that would be muy expensive, you understand? So no, I can't lend you the phone. But I can look into your case. Find out if we have a paper trail, perhaps a name of the institution or court who processed your paperwork in your city or county."

"You can get information from our city?" Mamá asked. "Because my brother-in-law would be happy to help. He's a priest there."

"In some cases, yes. Yes, we can find out how you came to us," Sargento Díaz said. "I have your name here in my notes, señora, and your address. All I need to know now is your birth dates; perhaps we can look you up by your birthdates.

And you say, you have no form of identification on you? No baptismal certificates, records of communion? Nothing in your purse to help me?"

"I don't have my purse," Mamá said. "Weren't you listening? We've been abducted! The lawmakers of Morado County sent the sheriff's department to get us. They raided our property and burned down our house! I have nothing! No purse, no birth certificates, no house—nothing! We've got nothing!"

It wasn't the first time I had ever seen my mother lose control of her emotions, but it was the first time I had seen her cry in public. She was strong-willed and passionate, but she was always even-keeled. To see her lose her poise made me want to punch the sergeant's pursed little lips right off his face.

"I am sorry," Sargento Díaz said. "I did not mean to make you upset. It is just that it will be difficult, especially because your husband is not here to verify your identity, that you are who you say you are. Difficult, but not impossible. Here, here is your case number. I will look into this and call you back in here when I have something to say. Don't cry, señora. We will find a way to help you soon."

I didn't believe him. Why would Papá's word verify Mamá's identity more than her own? But I needed Papá here even if they wouldn't believe him either.

"Thank you," Mamá said, ignoring his insult. "How long do you think it will take?" She wiped her tears away and took the single sheet of paper the sergeant was handing her. She folded it twice to create a small square and shoved it in her coat pocket. "To sort this out, I mean. How long?"

"Without papers?" he asked. "Hard to tell you. Days. Weeks . . . maybe months."

"Months!" I cried out, the words leaving my mouth before I could censor myself. "Are you crazy? We can't stay here for months!"

Wicho stopped sobbing. He blinked, looking up at me.

"Yes," the clerk said. "If your father was here, it would be so much easy to process you."

"Why?" I asked. "Why would it be much easier if my father were here? It's not like he would have papers either."

The sergeant looked at my mother, cleared his throat, and said, "Forgive me. I meant no disrespect. It's just that here everything goes through the head of household. It is just the way we do things. All paperwork is filed through the last name of the man of the house."

"Thank you for trying to help us," Mamá said. She put a hand on my shoulder and squeezed it to show that she knew exactly how I was feeling at that very moment.

Sargento Díaz stood up then. He waved his small hands for us to do the same. "You are welcome. And now can you please move forward? There are many more waiting. Go on through the doors. Ask that woman there. She will take you to the holding room."

The holding room was small. Luckily, there were only a few people there, including a family with two little girls. One of them had been crying recently; fresh tear tracks ran cleanly down her filthy cheeks. She was sucking on her index finger and sniffling, like the finger in her mouth was the only thing keeping her from wailing.

Mamá and I sat on the far end of the room, on a couple of folding chairs beside the family with the girls. Mamá turned to them. "Excuse me," she said, talking to the girls' mother. "Do you know where I can find some water? I need to clean my son's face and hands. He's been crying awhile."

"There's a faucet out there," the woman said, pointing to a door beside the one we had entered through. "What are you going to use to clean him? Where are your bags?"

Mamá blinked rapidly and smiled. "I don't know," she said. Then she let out a small, troubled laugh. "We don't have bags. We don't have anything. We lost everything."

The woman scrutinized us for a moment. Her eyes settled on Wicho and something passed over them, briefly, like a shadow. "I'm Reyna. I'm from Chicago. Where are you from?"

"We're from south Texas, from the valley," my mother said, offering the woman a quick handshake.

As my mother introduced us, the woman reached under her seat and pulled out a bag. She opened it and rummaged around, tugging at things until she found what she was searching for. "Here," she said. "You can use this to wipe him down for now."

"Oh, no, I couldn't." My mother looked at the beautiful blue-and-gray scarf in the woman's hand. Her eyes shimmered. "It looks expensive."

"Not worth much now, not in here, anyway," Reyna said.

"Besides, it's a good thing to help someone in need. Might be, someday you could help me."

"Thank you," Mamá said. "Que Dios se lo pague, Reyna." Then, turning to tap my knees, she said, "Come with me, Estrella. You should clean up too. You look like a plucked chicken."

"Okay," I said. Looking at her disheveled hair, I didn't have the heart to tell her she could use a comb herself. She'd find out soon enough when she looked in a mirror.

The door led us to a small yard closed off by a very tall wooden fence with an outhouse behind the main building, where we took turns taking care of our necessities. Once we were all done in there, Mamá dunked the scarf in the outdoor sink beside a well and handed it to me. "Here, you wipe your face first," she said. Then she rinsed it and used it to clean up Wicho, who complained the whole time that he was cold. Once we were all clean, Mamá stood looking around, considering the height of the fence. "I guess they don't want anyone climbing in here," she said. "Or out."

"Come on, Wicho," I called out to my brother, who had picked up a small twig and was scratching at the dirt with it. "Don't get dirty again, Papi." Then, turning to my mother, I said, "I guess he's feeling better."

"No cochis?" Wicho asked, coughing and digging harder into the dirt until the twig snapped.

He was looking for the little cochineal bugs which roamed the ground back home in Monteseco. Wicho liked watching them curl up into perfect little spheres in his palm. He never hurt them, just wanted to watch them curl and uncurl. But it was November and there were no cochinillas to be found in the dirt.

"We need to keep him bundled up. He can't get one of his fevers," Mamá said, her lips forming a small, forced smile. "I hope that cough isn't a sign of things to come."

We went back to the holding room and waited. I'd like to say it was a pleasant wait, but it wasn't. We sat there for hours without anything to eat or drink. To our relief, a priest and two nuns came by in the late afternoon and handed us soda waters and three dark pieces of flat bread. We ate the bread greedily. My mother thanked them profusely.

I couldn't voice my gratitude. I just ate and drank, more greedily than even Wicho, because it was the first morsel of food we'd had since dinner the night before, after the city council meeting.

We waited so long in the holding room that almost everyone else had been called out, and we were alone with only one man and his son. By the time the doors finally flew open again and Sargento Díaz came in and called on us, it was dark outside.

"Ah, señora," the sergeant said, holding his hands together in front of him like he was about to take communion, "I am so sorry, but I have bad news."

"Bad news?" I asked, my voice suddenly high and crackling.

"Yes, bad news," he said. "I have found the papers. Come. Come. We need to speak."

PROCESSING

At the Aduana in El Paso, things move inch
by inch. We are all detained while customs
officers sort, check, verify. Every single
thing brought in has to be inspected,
documented, pilfered through, before it

is admitted into the country. Grown men
argue, fight, wage war over tools. They wrestle
saws, chains, nails, and screws out of official
hands; the precious gems in their toolkits
cannot be given away, left behind, discarded

on the way. What will they use to sustain,
provide, build a whole new life for their
familias? Women hoist toddlers onto their backs
and rummage through linens, curtains,
and dishes older than the papers they carry

in their valises: old photographs, birth
certificates, stamped and notarized property
deeds that prove they are established citizens
in the United States. Everywhere they look,
someone is hauling a treasure in each

hand. An old man in a tattered coat
and fedora hat leans into his Silver Plated
Fritz. A young woman embraces a mannequin
head. Its eyes are blue; one of them is chipped
to the right of the iris. Its hair is red. It is not

Mexican, but the girl, with her green eyes
and brown hair, could go either way. As
the sun wanes and the day fades, everyone
shifts, sighs, sobs, closes their eyes and
prays. Everyone is speaking in Spanish,

everyone except the little girl sitting on the sidewalk, out of the way, clutching her schoolbooks. She is confused, doesn't understand why she has to throw them away. They're written in English.

CHAPTER ELEVEN

*W*E WENT BACK INTO THE MAIN room, where we had been before, and Sargento Díaz told us to sit back at his desk. "I am so very sorry this took so long," he began. "It is hard, going through so many papers, but we just had a train arrive, and everything is in disarray. As you can see, it is a long process that never ends." He pointed to the line of repatriates that was just as long as when we had arrived that morning. "They just keep coming. By trucks and in loaded cars, even on foot. So many of them. We had no idea there would be so many. We are not prepared for such a big load."

"The papers," my mother said. "You said you found something."

"Yes," Sargento Díaz said. "We found orders for repatriation in a bundle with the paperwork sent on the train from an orphanage in Missouri. I apologize for that."

"Missouri?" I asked. "But we're from Texas."

Mamá's face changed. "Orders?" she asked. "What kind of orders? From where?"

"From Monteseco?" I asked.

The clerk shook his head and waved his hand in front of us. "No. No," he said. "The court order is from Morado County, and it came with your certificado de residencia. They were right there, under the big pile of certificates for the orphan children."

"Morado County?" I asked.

Sargento Díaz nodded. "Well, as you probably already know," he began, "there is a problem with the paperwork, ¿verdad?"

"Of course there's a problem," my mother cried. "I have no idea what papers you have, but you can't repatriate someone who's never been a patriate of that country. We were born in the United States. We've never been Mexican citizens, so I have no idea what certificates of residency you're talking about. I told you before, we were kidnapped, taken from our home, and dropped off on this side of the border."

At that moment, Sargento Díaz opened a folder on his desk and turned it around so that my mother could inspect the documents within it.

Mamá snatched up the folder. As she flipped through it, her brows knitted across her forehead. Then she went back through all the papers in the file, frantically flipping between them again and again, as if she couldn't find what she was looking for.

"There's been a mistake," she finally said. "We are not Communists. We are not enemies to America."

The clerk's face changed then, and he was suddenly not so pleasant and understanding. "Really?" he asked, taking in a deep breath and releasing it forcefully while he waited for my mother to explain.

"I don't know what else to say, but we are not traitors!" Mamá said, opening the folder and flipping through the papers again. "These are trumped-up charges. They were fabricated in order to deport us." Disgusted, she closed the folder. "This is an injustice. You have to let me call my brother-in-law. He can get our lawyer to start an investigation."

The clerk reached out. His elbow rested over the papers lying flat on his desk in front of him. He motioned for my mother to hand over the papers. "Why do you lie?" he asked. His voice reverberated around the walls of the narrow office like a ping-pong ball.

My mother passed the offensive papers over to him. Her arm was a jackknife, extended straight out in front of her, the folder clutched between her fingers and thumb, waiting. Her straight back and tense shoulders said it all—she was livid.

"I am not lying," she said, straightening up, throwing her shoulders back. "I have no reason to lie."

"Well, this court order looks official," Sargento Díaz said. "And then of course, there are the certificates of residency, which I can say with all certainty are authentic."

Mamá grabbed the folder back, then sorted and perused the documents, shaking her head the entire time. "No. These are lies, all lies."

Wicho cried in my arms, saying, "I want go home," again

and again. I tried to hush him, but he fussed some more, so I put him down on the floor and told him to go look for bugs. He was quiet for a moment, and then he shook his head and climbed back up onto my lap. I breathed a sigh of relief.

Mamá pushed the papers back toward the sergeant. "Don't you understand?" she asked, leaning in toward him. "We've been set up. Someone went to a great deal of trouble to separate us from my husband and get us out of the country. That's why it's so important that you help me. I need to get back to the United States and get to the bottom of this. I need to find out what happened to my parents and my husband."

"I see what you are saying." The clerk pulled on his shirt collar, fiddled with his necktie, swiped at a drop of sweat on his sideburn, and cleared his throat. "I am sorry this is happened to you, señora. But there is a bright spot here. A good thing I tell you. See, for the purpose of getting assistance, these papers will help you. You can use them for now to get on the train. When you get to where you are going, to one of the repatriation camps in Ciudad México, you can request a meeting with the people in the American embassy there. You tell them what has happened to you, ask them to help you. They'll fix it for you there."

"Repatriation camps!" Mama's voice was high-pitched, shocked. "No. I'm not doing that. This is illegal! Accepting these forged papers and using them would be breaking the law. I won't allow you to make criminals out of us! We need to investigate this. We need to file charges against those who did this to us. This is an abomination. I refuse to get caught up in it."

"Repatriation is the only thing we process at this site. It is what we do here. Aquí, sólo eso—repatriación," the sergeant said, switching nervously between his broken English and his native tongue. He breathed out and wiped at his wide brow with a handkerchief from his shirt pocket.

Wicho was starting to whine again. Mamá took him on her lap and bounced him gently up and down. Her foot moved too, impatiently tapping her heel. "So what are you saying?"

"I'm saying, like it or not, you are repatriated," the sergeant said. "You don't have to wait here for your husband. You can go straight through to Ciudad México when the train gets here. You can go there next week."

"We can't do that!" I said.

As if he knew what was going on, Wicho started to scream again. "I hungry! I want home! I want go home!"

"You want my consejo?" Sergeant Díaz asked my mother, leaning forward and whispering as if he was trying not to be overheard by persons invisible to us. "Take these papers, señora. Take the certificates and get on the next train to the repatriation camp. They will help you settle down, find you somewhere to live, give you clothes, medicine, and food. Your baby is not well, señora. He is flushed, and I suspect he is sick. You should do what I say, señora. It is what's best for him."

THE THINGS THEY CARRIED

They carried on their way everything
they owned. There was no money,
no food, no drinking water. But tools—
they were aplenty. Honor—dignity—

was in the things they carried. On their
way, everything they owned weighed
more and more. Their livelihoods were
in the saws, the garden hoes, the buttons,

even in the tiny screws. These were not
just things they had to do without. These things
were hobbies and holidays. They were
home. Nevertheless, the people carried on the

only way they knew how—with their hopes
in wooden boxes, crates, even sewn into
the seams of their clothes. Children, babes,
toddlers, they were the heaviest things

they carried. Everything they owned
could be discarded, tossed, flung aside,
thrown—everything except the little girls,
the little boys. They were everything

they owned by law and carried on
their way. Everything they were was
gone—gone.

Chapter Twelve

*T*HE GUARD WHO ESCORTED US OUT of the customs house through a back door was young. His hat was too big for him, as was the heavy military coat, which made him look a bit like a scarecrow. A slim rifle was slung upright over his shoulder, and his thick military boots gave the impression of long, narrow feet.

Mamá took my hand, and we hesitantly walked toward him. "This way," he said in Spanish. "Follow me outside."

As we exited the customs house, the scent hit us like a tidal wave of decay. My mother pushed the lapel of her coat up to her nose. Wicho lifted his head off my shoulder and wailed, a loud, resounding cry that made the guard turn back to say, "Keep him away from the others. Most little kids here are sick. They don't always make it.

"This way," he continued, ushering us along on a narrow path behind the customs house until we came to a huge corral full of people. I couldn't believe a corral—a fenced-in area meant to keep animals from roaming—was the waiting camp. But that was where they were putting us. That was where we were supposed to stay until the next repatriation train came to take us to Mexico City.

Mamá shook her head when we entered the compound. "Wait," she called out. The guard opened the small gate to the corral. "Where are we supposed to sleep?"

"Sleep?" the guard asked. "On the ground, like everyone else."

There were no livestock in the corral, only people. I couldn't believe my eyes. Hundreds of Mexican families were standing and sitting around, eyes hollow.

Everywhere I looked, I saw mothers and fathers pulling threadbare blankets over their children's shoulders, their gloveless hands holding their own coats closed at their necks while they gripped the hands or shoulders of their little ones—children that clung to their necks, waists, and thighs. And then there were the children without any parents at all, huddling together for warmth. Perhaps the orphans Sargento Díaz mentioned.

The people here were living out of blankets and curtains in place of tents. Those who had no blankets or curtains had sewn together heavy work clothes and hung them up over ropes tied to the end of crooked makeshift poles. It was clear the people were using whatever they could get their hands on to build tents: cardboard, dried-up branches, broken crates— anything to protect themselves from the elements.

Pails, small barrels, even garbage cans provided a place to

sit. Linens lay directly on the cold ground. Babies and toddlers sucked their thumbs, wiped their noses, or scratched their heads. They lay on the ground, gripping the rolled shirts and pants they used as pillows. There must have been two thousand people huddled together in the former pasture.

The evening sky above us began to darken further, clouds obscuring the moon, and the guard looked up. "It's going to rain. You want to stay as close to the fence as possible. The best spot is over there in that corner, where the fence is highest."

"Thank you," Mamá whispered, and she put her hand on my shoulder to guide me in front of her.

We couldn't see anything. The day had worn down past suppertime. There were so many people in the corral, it was hard to imagine we could find room to stand, much less sit or sleep anywhere. "Out of the way. Out of the way," the guard kept shouting, using a wooden baton to tap people who wouldn't move to make way for us. They jumped as the stick touched them.

There were people sitting everywhere. Some lay bunched up against the fence rails, and once or twice I stepped on someone's clothes and almost tripped.

"Where do we go for food?" Mamá asked. "And water? Where can we get water? My children are tired. They need to eat. What do I feed them?"

"Someone will come by," the guard said. He pointed to the ground under our feet. "You can wait for the charity trucks there. Or there. Wherever you like, but not in front of the gate. Never in front of the gate. Repatriates are coming in day and night. There's no telling when I might need to open the gate. Understand?"

"I thirsty!" Wicho fussed in my mother's arms. He wiggled and fought her as he attempted to get out of her arms.

The guard turned around and started to walk away. He said, "Buenas noches," without looking back.

"We need to find water," Mamá whispered, peering down at Wicho.

"Down! Down!" he kept saying. He arched himself back like a squirmy caterpillar.

"There is water over there," a woman said from behind us. Her voice in the dark was a bendición, an unexpected but welcome olive branch. "Toward the back. Beside the barrels."

It took us awhile to find the water because we had to make our way through the multitude of deportees discreetly, saying, "Con permiso," and "Perdón," and always "Gracias," because we didn't want to be rude.

We had to be nice as we walked around those who would not move and stepped carefully over those who couldn't because they were either sick or sleeping.

The woman was right. There was water at the back of the corral, a trough full of clean water, sitting beside a well in the far corner. Someone had cleaned the trough recently.

"There's a cup up there, on that nail on the well," a man shouted from behind us. "But for the love of God, rinse it out when you're done. It's a communal cup."

I couldn't tell in the dark how Mamá felt about the man's

ill-mannered request, but I was deeply offended to think he believed we would pass germs to him.

"It's on the pole to your right," a young girl said, pointing behind us. I reached up and took the only cup in the corral off the nail. Then, thinking about it, I put it back.

"I'll just use my hands," I whispered.

Mamá pulled down the tin cup. She poured a bit of water onto the scarf Reyna had given her and used it to clean Wicho's hands and face. "Cold," Wicho kept saying every time the wet scarf made contact with his skin. His little lips trembled, and his tiny body shivered.

Mamá rinsed and wrung out the scarf and handed it to me to wipe my hands and face. "It's ice cold," I said, handing it back to her as soon as I was done.

"I hungry!" Wicho cried, pulling on my coat sleeve. "Trella, I hungry now."

"He's been hungry for a while." I picked him up.

"Of course he is," Mamá whispered. "He hasn't eaten anything since dinner last night, other than the one piece of bread inside."

Dinner last night. The meal seemed so long ago, I couldn't remember what we'd had. I'd been so upset over the results of the council meeting, I hadn't eaten much.

"Here." An old man sitting on the ground lifted his hand, offering us an apple. "There was a priest and two nuns here earlier, passing out food. I was saving this for later, but I can't let children go hungry. They can't go without food as long as you and I, ¿verdad?"

"No, they can't." Mamá shook her head. She took my brother's hand and guided him to take the apple.

"Thank you," Wicho said after my mother prompted him.

The old man bowed his head. Then, looking up at me, he sighed and said, "Oh, all right, you can have something too." He reached into his left pocket, took out a coarse chunk of dark bread, and offered it to me.

"No, that's okay," I said. It felt wrong, taking food away from an old man. He was rail thin, and his face was gaunt. "I can wait until the charity trucks come back. The guard said they'd come back tomorrow."

"Oh, for heaven's sake! Take the bread!" the old man groused. "I'm trying to be a good Christian. You don't want lightning to strike me down, do you?"

My mother laughed, a crisp, clear tinkle of laughter that lifted the corner of her mouth, and she took the piece of bread from the old man and handed it to me. "Thank you," she said. "That's nice of you. Wasn't that nice, Estrella?"

"Yes," I said. "Thank you."

"Thank you, Señor . . . ?" my mother prompted.

"Martínez," the old man said. "Josue Martínez, at your service. Now go on, let me sleep." The old man's eyes shone in the dark as he waved us off. Our business concluded, he settled back against the fence, pulled at the lapels of his coat, and shoved his hands in his pockets.

As we walked around, looking for a place to sit down, people asked us questions. "Where are you from?" and "Did they tell you when the next train is coming?" Some of them introduced themselves, even asked us our names. There was Sarita Infante, a very young widow with four young children; Mr. and Mrs. Gonzáles, a husband and wife from Oklahoma; and many, many more, including the large group of orphans from Missouri.

The repatriates left us alone to figure things out. They had their own families to contend with. Most of them spoke a combination of English and Spanish. Only a few of them spoke only one language or the other. But that didn't make a difference to us, because we were fluent in both.

Wicho gnawed at the small apple in his hand. He was having a problem breaking through the tough skin, so I pried it out of his hands and bit into it, breaking the skin and loosening a piece. He watched me as I pulled it out and handed it to him. His chubby fingers wrapped around it long enough to shove it into his mouth.

"Slow down. Chew," Mamá said.

I ripped a big chunk off the piece of bread, chewing it slowly and holding my lips closed with my index finger because I couldn't stop smiling. "It's the best piece of bread I've ever had," I said between bites.

"Yeah?" My mother's voice quivered, and she sounded like she was about to cry. I offered her a piece of bread but she shook her head and concentrated on making sure Wicho kept his apple clean as he ate. He had a tendency to drop things.

I was drifting off to sleep when it started to rain. The water came down hard, and we moved as close to the fence as we could get. But it didn't make a bit of difference. The rain came down straight over us, and there was nowhere to hide. Mamá took off her coat and draped it over herself and Wicho. I pulled my coat over my head and tried to keep the rain from soaking me through.

As we huddled together, my mother, Wicho, and I, other people stood shivering beside us. The orphan children's threadbare shirts and stained pants were no match for the freezing weather. I wished there was something I could do to help, but I had nothing to share with them. The only things in my schoolbag were a copy of *Little Women*, which I had been reading before we were abducted, my journal, and two pencils in dire need of sharpening.

In the middle of the night, the rain stopped. People wandered around looking for a good place to lie down. We waited as long as we could for the ground to dry, but without the benefit of the sun, the ground stayed wet most of the night.

In the early hours of the morning, Wicho helped us kick around some dirt and toss aside some rocks, and we made ourselves a little spot to sleep on the soft, damp ground. Before I knew it, I was lying down beside my mother. She stroked my cheek, pushing my hair out of my face. I heard her hum a small arrurrú for Wicho, who lay in her arms, and then I passed out.

Dear Abuela Jovita,

It is cold and damp in this corral south of the border. There is darkness and pain everywhere here. This is not the Mexico from my youth. This is not the colorful, vibrant Mexico I visited when my parents took me on a train south of the Río Grande for my birthday the year I turned ten, three years before Wicho was born.

This Mexico has sounds I've never heard before. Children wail in misery in this Mexico. Women stare into the night and make cooing sounds in the dark. They are lechuzas, watching every corner of the darkness, waiting for something to crawl so they might grasp it in their claws, kill it, and continue to wait for dawn to glow.

I am frightened, Abuelita. Here, I am not as scared of the night as I am scared of the dawn, for there is no telling what the new day will bring. Here, in this

Mexico, we are less than human. Here, we are a threat. Here, we are infected foreigners.

Pray for us, Abuelita. Tell the stars beside you to remember we are their descendants. Tell the moon to shine her magical beams upon our troubled souls. Tell the angels in heaven to find a way to send us home.

Love always,
Your granddaughter,

Estrella

Chapter Thirteen

I AWAKENED TO THE SOUNDS OF COUGHING, wailing babies, and shuffling feet. The sun had risen like it did every morning at Las Moras. But unlike the joyful sun of our hometown, this sun was dull and dim, hanging on to the horizon, afraid to shine.

All around us, people milled in circles. Filthy, raggedly dressed men, women, and children stretched and yawned. They inhaled and exhaled and stared beyond the corral fence at a foreign country, a country where we were homeless, starving, destitute. Most looked away as soon as we made eye contact with them, but some stared back. Up and down they looked, inspecting our thick coats, our fashionable shoes, our lack of luggage. I could only imagine what they were thinking.

One lady maintained eye contact, and the corners of her lips lifted just a bit when she asked, "Do you have any food?"

"What?" Mamá asked.

A small child, a boy with hollow eyes and pale cheeks, crept out from behind the woman. He clung to her leg and wiped his runny nose on the folds of her soiled skirt. "There's nothing to eat here. The priest didn't bring enough to feed everyone yesterday. Only a few people got food in the morning, and he didn't come back last night."

Like a tiny worm, guilt dug a hole and burrowed inside me, and I felt terrible for having eaten the piece of bread Señor Martínez gave me last night.

"Do you have anything you could share? I would so much appreciate it."

"No," Mamá whispered. "I'm sorry. We don't have anything."

We spent most of the day huddled together beside the fence, waiting out the rain that came and went intermittently, pouring down in sheets so dark, so dense, it made it impossible to stay dry.

I wanted desperately to go home, but whenever I thought of home, the sound of flames roaring and the memory of smoke filling my lungs jolted me back to reality.

When the guard came back with more people, Mamá tried to ask questions. "Excuse me, can you please tell me why we are being held here? Why didn't you take us to a shelter in Juárez?"

"There are too many of you," the guard said. He held the gate open while another group of repatriates shuffled inside. "The city is not equipped to take in so many people. All the shelters are full. There are waiting lists for their beds. I am sorry, señora, but this is the best we can do for now."

"But there's got to be more help out there, organizations we could call on," Mamá argued. "We're not cattle. We're human beings, for God's sake."

"People *are* helping. Donations of food and necessities from local businesses come in every day, but there are too many of you. Too many. You understand? Try to be patient. You'll be on your way as soon as the next train gets here." The guard tried closing the gate, but my mother shoved her foot between the gate and the fence.

"The train?" she asked. "But we don't want to get on a train. Why can't we stay in Juárez? At least here, our families can come looking for us."

The guard looked past my mother at me and then down at Wicho, who was holding my hand. "I know you have children to take care of, señora, but you have to go to the interior. That is where aid is rendered. That is where you will be given a homestead with monetary allotments. All of that will be sorted out when you reach Mexico City. Juárez is not equipped to take in repatriates."

"It will be okay," said Señor Martínez, the old man who had given us food the day before. "You will be taken care of, señora. Your and your husband will be given a farm to work. And startup money. You're young. You'll prosper there."

Mamá didn't believe any of it. "Wishful thinking," she whispered whenever the old man relayed something else he'd heard from one of the hopeful, the believers. "We'd need to find your father first. They won't give a woman a farm, not without her husband there to till the land," she said once, about midafternoon. Then her eyes misted and she fawned over Wicho, cleaning his face with the scarf she kept tucked in the inside pocket of her coat.

The priest and nuns didn't come that day. "They don't come every day," Sarita, the young mother of four, explained when I asked if she knew what time of day the priest usually got there. "Sometimes he comes twice a day, but sometimes he doesn't come at all. Nothing's certain. You know how the church is."

"It's Sunday," I said. "They're probably too busy for us today."

"Ah, too busy being holy for charity work," Sarita said, and she laughed a dry, humorless laugh that twisted her smile sideways.

I wanted to tell her that where I was from, the church was a merciful place, a warm, safe haven, because my uncle Tomás was the priest, and he took care of his congregation. I wanted to tell her that, but the fact was that I didn't know if it was true anymore. What if whoever did this to us had done the same to my uncle? What if they had done something worse? What if my uncle was as lost to us as my father?

The thought was too much to bear, and I forced myself to push it away.

We went to sleep starving. Wicho was inconsolable. He cried that he wanted to go home and asked for Papá over and over again. He wasn't the only one crying in the corral, though. Everywhere around us, children cried and grownups sobbed.

The following day, we milled with the others, walking in circles around that corral, aimlessly waiting for the priest to come. "We need to keep moving," my mother said. "Muscles become weak if you don't use them, and it'll keep us warm."

"What if you don't feed them?" I asked. "Isn't that worse?"

She didn't say anything. She just kept shuffling forward behind the others, looking off into the distance, thinking or daydreaming. I couldn't tell which. As for myself, I tried to distract Wicho by pulling Sarita's children into silly games like Hook the Fishy or Climb the Mountain, made-up games with ridiculous rules and even more ridiculous results.

It made Wicho wiggle, laugh, and clap when the older kids accidentally "fell off the mountain"—the corral fence—and landed on their behinds. They threw their legs up in the air, then jumped right back up, like marionettes yanked up by an invisible puppeteer.

Padre Jorge, an older priest from the Catedral de Nuestra Señora de Guadalupe, came back to the corral early Monday morning. Everybody lined up at the gate with their hands folded together in front of them. He'd lay a piece of bread in our hands, and we'd thank God and cross ourselves the same way we did at Mass when it was the Host we were receiving.

As the children stepped off to the right, one of the nuns would give us a piece of fruit out of a small sack, until all the fruit was gone, and then only the bread was passed out.

"I am so sorry, but that is all we have today," Padre Jorge said, folding the sack and putting it under his arm. The people at the back of the line groaned as they turned away. Some of the younger children cried and buried their faces in their mothers' hips, clinging to their waists. The sight of so much suffering broke my heart.

Wicho and I walked back to our place against the fence behind Mamá, holding our measly pieces of bread with both hands. The people who knew they weren't getting any fruit or bread looked upon us with envy and disgust. They ogled the apple in my little brother's hands and then looked away, ashamed.

"Por favor, señorita, can you share with my children?" Sarita called out as we walked along the fence.

I looked down at the small piece of bread in my hands and broke it in half. Mamá reached over and stopped me. She shook her head and handed her piece of bread to the young mother. "You eat yours," she said. "You need to keep up your strength."

"We'll share it," I whispered. "There's enough for both of us."

I ate my portion of the coarse, dark bread almost immediately, pulling it apart quickly and stuffing it in my mouth. I couldn't bear to have the others stare at it much longer. Guilt battled hunger, and hunger won. Because she was carrying Wicho, Mamá shoved her piece of bread in her coat pocket. When we got to our small corner of the corral, she sat Wicho down, straightened up, and stretched. Then, smiling, she pulled out the piece of bread.

Before I knew what was happening, a woman in a red dress and red mud-crusted high-heeled shoes reached over and swatted my mother's hand. The bread went flying, landing a few feet away on the ground. Mamá reached for it, but the woman pushed her away and grabbed it.

"Let me go!" the woman yelled. Mamá gripped her wrist, fighting to take back the bread.

"It's mine!" Mamá pulled on the woman's arm and they both fell back.

Wicho squealed and laughed. "Again!" he said between bites of his apple.

"No, Wicho. It's not a game," I said when he put his apple down on his lap to clap.

As Mamá struggled and took the piece of bread away from the woman, people around us started to laugh. It was mostly young people, but some of the men laughed too as they shook their heads.

I felt the urge to abandon Wicho and go help Mamá, but I was afraid of what the others might do to him. If they were laughing at the sight of Mamá and the woman in the red dress fighting over bread, there was no telling what they were capable of doing to a little one. Would they swoop in and take his apple away?

But before I could take action, Mamá stood up, bread in hand, face intense. She dusted off her skirt and straightened her disheveled hair as she brought the bread up to her lips. The woman in the red dress jumped up and tackled her to the ground. Mamá landed on her side, her arms tucked into her stomach, gripping the bread in her fist like it was made of gold.

"Eat it! Eat it!" the young people in the corral cheered when it looked like Mamá was winning the fight for the bread.

"You've stolen your last piece of bread, Amparo!" a young girl hollered.

"Hit her!" a man yelled at my mother. "Don't let her take it away from you!"

Amparo shoved Mamá to the ground on her stomach.

"Leave her be! Leave my mami be!" Wicho cried, raising his arm. He would have thrown his apple at Amparo if I hadn't stopped him.

"No, Wicho," I said. "Don't throw things."

"Don't give up!" a boy screamed when Amparo ripped the better part of the flattened, dirty piece of bread out of Mamá's hand and sat on her back.

As everyone groaned, Amparo stuffed the bread into her mouth and chewed.

"You're going straight to hell, Amparo," Señor Martínez screamed from his place against the fence, but Amparo didn't acknowledge him. She just sat there chewing, like she was at a fancy restaurant and Mamá was a chair.

"You can get off her now," I said.

Amparo stood up, dusted herself off, and walked away.

"It's a dogfight, life is," Señor Martínez said when Mamá sat up. She looked at us, and there were unshed tears in her eyes. Before all this, she never cried. "Sorry you had to find out the hard way."

Mamá got up and came to sit next to me. I took the orange the nuns had given me out of my coat pocket and offered it to her. "I didn't know what to do," I said. "I didn't want to leave Wicho alone."

"I'm sorry you had to witness that, Estrella," she whispered. "You did right to protect your brother." Then she picked Wicho up and pressed her face against his neck and kissed his cheek. He giggled and pressed his apple against her lips. Mamá pretended to take a huge bite, puffing out her cheeks and making piggy noises, and Wicho laughed. They repeated the act several times, until Wicho grew tired of it and looked over at me.

"You eat, Trella," he said, shoving the apple at me.

"No, I'm full," I said. "You eat it."

"Down," he told Mamá, and she let him go. He walked over, sat on my lap, and tried feeding me his apple. I took a tiny bite, just barely enough to taste it. It was crisp and sour and utterly delicious.

"Do you want to share my orange?" I whispered to him.

Wicho nodded. I handed him back the apple and showed him the orange.

"You should eat that yourself," Mamá said, eyeing the small, shriveled orange in my hand.

"It's big enough to share," I said. "You want some?"

"No." She opened her hand to show me she still had a small piece of bread. She looked it at like it had worms. Then she slipped it into her mouth and chewed it. "We might not get food three times a day, but at least we have running water. We can survive on these measly portions as long as we have water to drink."

I broke the pale orange into slices and handed one to Wicho. He sucked on it and made a face. "What is it?" I asked him. "Is it too sour, Papito? Does it taste bad?"

"No. Is good." He chewed on the desiccated slice of orange, closing his eyes and making more faces.

I handed Mamá an orange slice. She popped it in her mouth. "I'm going to need you to take care of your brother tomorrow," she said after she swallowed it.

"What do you mean?" I asked, holding a slice of orange. "Where are you going?" I couldn't imagine why she would leave without me. Would they even let her leave?

"I'm not sure," she said. "That's why I need you to stay here. I'm going to try to get someone to let me use their phone so I can call your uncle. And if that doesn't work, I might have to beg for money. I don't need much, just enough to pay for a telegram."

I nodded. "Okay, but why do we have to stay here? Why can't we come with you?"

Mamá took the orange slices out of my hand and split them evenly between me and Wicho, only eating one more slice herself. "I don't really know how I'm going to do it," she finally admitted. "But I don't want to expose Wicho to the elements all day, so I'd rather you stay here. I'll be back as soon as I can."

"No," I said, shaking my head. "You said so yourself on the first day—we need to stay together. I can't stay here, not without you." What if something happened?

Mamá took a deep breath and then spoke again. "Estrella, please don't be difficult. We don't know what's out there."

"So you're going to leave us all alone in here?" I asked. "With strangers? Because that's safe."

"Fine." Mamá sighed and pushed her hair away from her face. Her eyes were puffy, and the worry lines between her eyebrows were more pronounced. She took Wicho out of my arms. "Lay down now. You two need to get some sleep if you're going to run around with me tomorrow."

I dreamed of Papá that night, but it wasn't pleasant. In my dream, I stood rooted, unable to move as my father was dragged away by those fake lawmen who came for us the night of the fire. The scene played out again and again, like a defective movie reel. Papá kept turning his head back and yelling, "Stay together. I'll find you. I promise."

"It's okay, sweetheart," Mamá said, embracing me.

"No. No!" I cried into her shoulder. "It's not. It's not okay."

"Wake up," Mamá whispered into my ear. "You're having a nightmare, Estrella. It's just a bad dream."

When I opened my eyes, the light of the rising sun was a pink swirling mass that burst through the lavender and dark gray clouds high in the sky above me. The light helped bring me back to the present, but the sadness of my memories lingered. "Is it time to go?" I asked, and she nodded.

Mamá and I left the corral with a strong warning from the guards that we must return before nightfall. We walked around the plaza, looking for a pay phone, but there were none in sight. Desperate, we stopped at each business to see if anyone would let us use their telephone to place a collect international call. But many employees took one look at us with our disheveled hair and our filthy, smelly coats and told us to leave. Most business owners wouldn't even listen to us, pointing to signs that said there were no public phones in the building. Those who did at least let us speak said they couldn't afford the hours it would take to keep the line open, waiting for the operators to patch us through. Others warned us against loitering and threatened to call the police when we tried explaining ourselves.

After hours of begging for assistance and being ignored, we stood with our backs pressed against the wall of a farmacia, listless. We had no money, but a street vendor had taken pity on us and given us an ear of corn. He'd pointed at Wicho, saying, "Para el nene," before pulling up stakes and heading off to his next stop. My little brother gnawed the treat down until it was completely free of kernels, and then he just sucked on the cob until I finally took it away from him and threw it away.

My mother stopped at a jewelry store, looking at it intently. "Okay. Time to get serious." She put Wicho down on the sidewalk and pulled her wedding band off her ring finger.

"Mamá! No," I said when I realized what she was about to do. "You can't do that. What would Papá say?"

My mother thought about it and smiled. "He would say I need a new ring," she said. Then she pulled the beautiful tortoiseshell comb Abuela Serafina had given her for Christmas last year out of her bun. Her hair fell around her face and down her back in long, thick waves. She combed it through with her fingers, trying to make it look halfway decent. "I'd take off this filthy thing," she said, referring to her coat, "but I'm still wearing my dressing gown under here. It wouldn't be decent."

"I don't think you should do this," I said. "There's got to be another way."

Mamá shook her head. "We need money for a telegram, and we don't have any more time to waste." She looked at her reflection in the glass window of the furniture store on our side of the street, pinching her cheeks and pressing her lips until she looked like she had some color. "How do I look?"

"Good," I said. "You look pretty, like you always do."

"Now I want you to be quiet and let me do all the talking. Okay?"

I nodded, and we crossed the street.

For all her bravado, Mamá was not a good saleswoman. The jeweler shook his head and said he couldn't give her what the ring was worth. When she offered to take whatever he might be able to give her, he said, "These are difficult times, señora. I can barely sell what I have in the store. I can't afford to buy anything else."

"What about the comb?" she asked. "Can you just give us a few pesos for the comb? We just want enough to pay for a telegram, so I can let my brother-in-law know where we are. Please, señor. Just a few pesos."

The jeweler pushed his horn-rimmed glasses up over his balding head and sighed. "Let me see it again."

We left the jewelry store with just enough money to send a telegram to Uncle Tomás in Monteseco. The telegraph office was in a whole other section of town, so we had to walk a good while to get there. Mamá and I took turns carrying Wicho. It was faster than trying to get him to walk.

Sending the telegram didn't take more than a few seconds, and it was a bit cheaper than we'd thought. "Let's hope he gets it," Mamá said, stepping out of the telegraph office. She held the leftover coins, rubbing them between her index finger and thumb, as if the act itself would make them magically multiply. "You want a piece of bread?" she asked, looking at the panadería across the street from us. "I sure could use a piece of sweet bread."

The two coins were enough to buy us one big, hefty roll, un bolillo, as long as my forearm and twice as thick. Mamá and I sat on the steps outside the bakery and tore into that bolillo, devouring only half of it because she wanted to take some food back for Sarita's children. Wicho ate his fill of the bread and then fell asleep in Mamá's arms.

"Come on," she said when we were done feasting. "Let's get back to the corral. At least now your uncle knows where we are."

The rest of the day Mamá was distant, lost in thought, and I wondered what she was thinking. I tried to entertain Wicho, but he wasn't distracted enough by my songs or games. He would laugh between bouts of tears, but then go right back to whining, "I hungry, Trella!"

"I know," I kept saying. "Hey, you want to sing to the moon?"

"You should save your energy," Mamá finally said Tuesday night, the first day of December and our third day without real food. The few slices of orange and the small piece of bolillo were not substantial enough, and the lack of nourishment was wearing her down. She'd always been slim, but her cheeks were becoming pale and her eyes were dulling.

I couldn't be sure if the lack of food alone was causing her deterioration or if the lack of sleep was also catching up to her. She had begun sitting up long into the night, just staring into the darkness, like many other women in the corral.

"Why don't you lay down?" I asked, patting the ground beside me.

"I will," she said. "In a minute."

But the next morning, Wednesday, I found her sitting in the same exact place when dawn stirred me awake.

Thinking of Mamá's well-being as I stood leaning against the fence next to her the evening of the third day in the corral, I had the sudden urge to scream. Her voice cut through my rage like the soft vocals of a distant choir singing a long-forgotten song.

"What are you mumbling about?" she asked. She pulled me in close so she could kiss the crown of my head. "What's going on in that blessed little head of yours?"

"Nothing," I said. "I'm just hungry. I'm always hungry."

"Go get some water," Mamá advised. "Your body needs fluids as much as it needs food, more so, even, and you can fool it into thinking you're full by drinking lots of water."

Before I could answer her, Señor Martínez rested his back against the fence and leaned in so he could whisper, "Hey, guess what! I heard some of those orphan boys say there's a mercado down that street, about ten blocks away. There's a whole slew of shops, rows and rows of them, one right after the other. Those two over there, next to the well, they're going out tonight to go see if they can find anything else to eat. You should go with them, Estrella."

"You mean, break into businesses? To steal things?" Mamá asked.

Señor Martínez frowned and shook his head. "No, no. There's restaurants there, and you know what restaurants do with their leftovers, don't you?"

"Throw them away," I whispered, suddenly understanding.

"In trash cans." Mamá's eyes lit up.

I turned around and climbed the bottom rung of the fence. "Yes!" I said, attempting to look over the fence but failing miserably.

When I lowered myself again, Señor Martínez whispered, "Yes. Huge, giant trash cans filled with all kinds of food."

"And flies, and worms, and God only knows what else," Sarita said. "No, thanks. I'd rather eat dirt."

"What about your children?" Señor Martínez asked Sarita.

"There's worms in dirt too," I said. "And other things, like cattle dung and urine. You want them to eat that too?"

"Be nice. There's no need to be ugly," Mamá scolded me. "You should respect your elders."

"I know," I said. "I'm sorry. It's the hunger talking." I wrapped my arms around my midsection. I couldn't remember ever feeling this hollow.

"What about the police?" Sarita asked. "What are you going to do about them? They don't want us roaming around at night in their streets."

"I could walk ahead," I said. "I could be the lookout."

"No," Mama said. "We'd have to stay together. All of us."

"All of you? You can't take the boy," Señor Martínez said. "He'd slow you down. What if he were to cry? No. It's best to leave him here."

"I'll watch him," Sarita said. "If you promise to bring us something back. It doesn't have to be much, just something I can feed my babies."

"That was always the plan," Mamá said. "But you don't have to watch him. You've got enough on your hands with your little ones."

Sarita's shoulders softened, and she smiled at us. "Thank you," she said, and she wiped at the grateful tears that had begun to roll down her face.

I went back and forth to the trough several times until everyone in our little group had their fill of water. Then I sat down and wrote in my journal.

As I leaned back against the cold fence of the corral, I thought of another tall barrier, an old wooden fence behind our school that the district had neglected to fix. All that time, it had sat there rotting away. All that time, it never gave way.

How I wished the fence that surrounded us now would give way. I wanted to be free of that wall of planks. The people said it was the only thing keeping us safe—safe from the elements, safe from the criminal element in the city. But I hated that wall. I hated feeling imprisoned. I wanted to walk out of there and never come back.

However, Sarita was right. There were several guards posted outside the corral. We could go and come as we pleased during the day, as long as we didn't loiter and beg and make a nuisance of ourselves. But the city didn't want us roaming out at night. We'd have to be sneaky, work together, overwhelm the guards if we were going to succeed.

At this point there was a multitude of people waiting for the train in the corral. How many? I couldn't even count. Hundreds. Thousands. Could I ask them to march out of here together tonight? Except for Amparo, the people here didn't seem like the revolutionary type. Sure, there were a lot of us. There would be nothing the guards could do to stop us if we all walked out at the same time.

But most people kept to themselves, and if they weren't wandering listlessly, they were busy watching their belongings. They checked on their bags and suitcases daily, sorting and resorting, unpacking and repacking.

"Why do they go through their things so much?" I asked Señor Martínez.

"Thievery," he whispered. "There were several incidents on the train from Michigan. People are still mad about that."

"Amparo?" I asked.

Señor Martínez twisted his lips sideways and winced. "No," he admitted. "She was busy then. Taking care of her little girl."

"A baby?" Sudden understanding struck. "How did she die?"

"Dysentery," Señor Martínez whispered. "On the way in. She had to relinquish the body along the way. It angered her. Made her bitter. She cursed everyone and everything on that train."

"That's why she's so mean," I said, seeing Amparo in a new light. "Because she lost her daughter."

"I don't know about that," Señor Martínez said. "Don't know if she was like that before. Didn't know her then. Don't know her much now. Most people are decent, know how to behave, but there's a few in here I wouldn't mind getting rid of, including her. She's a predator who wouldn't pause to steal from a child. Look at her, watching those two girls over there. I swear she's got the devil in her." The girls he pointed to, Soledad's daughters, were sitting about thirty feet away. I'd talked to ten-year-old Anita briefly during our games, and she'd said her little sister's name was Perla. Perla, who couldn't have been older than six, had befriended Wicho right away, playing peek-a-boo and patty-cakes.

"She *is* watching them!" I said. "Augh! I can't bear the sight of her. If she ever looks at Wicho like that, I'll—"

"You'll do nothing," my mother interrupted me. "You'll let me take care of it, that's what you'll do."

I wanted to remind her she wasn't strong enough to fight Amparo alone, but she knew that. Amparo's arms were twice as thick as Mamá's, and the despicable woman had a big torso too. Her shoulders and back were wide and muscular, like a luchador.

I was contemplating my mother's dwindling figure, how she was looking smaller and weaker with each passing day, when a racket caught my attention.

"There she goes again!" Sarita cried out, pulling her four children around her and holding onto them like a clucking chicken. "Stop it! Leave them alone!"

Amparo kicked Perla's rump. Anita swatted at Amparo's leg, but all Amparo did was switch to kicking Anita. *Where is Soledad?* I scanned the corral and found her, getting water at the other end of the corral.

"I know you got some apples. I saw your mother hiding them. Give them to me!" Amparo yelled. She yanked Anita up by the elbow and started to rummage through her coat pockets. "Where are they? Tell me!"

At the sight of Amparo roughing up her daughters, Soledad dropped the small tin mug of water and ran to help, but it would take time to reach them. I jumped up, but Mamá pulled me back and said, "Don't. Their mother's coming. You don't need to get involved."

"You thief! Bully!" Soledad cried out, rushing toward her daughters.

"Yeah, leave them alone!" Señor Martínez yelled from behind us.

"Stop bothering them. They don't have anything," other people in the crowd yelled.

By the time Soledad reached them, Amparo had found what she was looking for. She took a knotted little apple from within the folds of Anita's coat and let her go. "Give it back," Soledad said evenly, a darkness building in her face.

But Amparo smiled and bit into the apple.

Soledad pushed her away. "You're a disgrace to mothers!

That's why she died. That's why God took her away from you. To steal from *children*—it's the worst sin."

Silence fell on the crowd as Amparo stopped dead in her tracks, turned, and looked back at Soledad. Then, before Soledad had a chance to react, Amparo leaped at Soledad and decked her.

Soledad couldn't avoid the punch. She fell to the ground on her rump, shaking her head.

"Mamá!" Anita screeched.

"Are you okay, Mamá?" Perla cried. The girls reached out to help their mother sit up beside them.

Several men stood up. One of them walked over and stood between the women. I was disgusted that it had taken anyone that long to intervene. "That's enough," the man said. "Just walk away, Amparo. No need to take it any further."

"Mind your business," Amparo said, looking straight into the man's eyes. Then she shoved the half-eaten apple into her coat pocket and walked off.

The men turned their backs on Soledad and her children and went back to huddling together against the fence.

Soledad wiped her bleeding lip and watched Amparo weave her way through the crowd. "Stay away from my children, arpía malvada!" she yelled at Amparo, her voice trembling with rage. Anita and Perla put their arms over her shoulders and held her tight. Soledad pulled them in and wept, like she was afraid she might never see them again. "I'm sorry," she whispered. "From now on we stay together, okay?"

AGAINST THE FENCE

Three gray cinder blocks, one stacked on top
of the other, push backward, hold up
broken planks so rotten they spit out nails no
matter how hard the hammer hits them.

A dog barks, sniffs, digs at their side, but they
are rooted to the ground by grass that has been
allowed to grow all summer. Mired in mud
from recent rains, the blocks lean over, fight back.

Chapter Fourteen

WHEN NIGHT CAME, THE GUARDS STOPPED walking around the corral. They rested their backs against the fence, crossed their legs, smoked cigarettes, and relaxed. We couldn't see them, but we could smell their cigarette smoke. We could hear them whistling or mumbling to themselves, until one of them called out to the others because there were civilians walking by and they didn't want to look like loafers.

I walked around the corral until I found Ángel, the oldest of the group of orphan children. If what Señor Martínez told me was true, I wanted in. My mother was all for it too. I just wanted to make sure we'd get away with it. I didn't want us getting arrested in the process.

"Will they do it?" I asked. "Will they run out of here all at once if you ask them?"

Ángel, a slender boy close to my age and almost as tall as my father, smiled. "Of course," he said. "If there's one thing they're tired of, it's being obedient. They're done following orders."

It occurred to me that his life was probably hard long before he got stuck here with us. "Was it hard, being in an orphanage?" I asked.

"Well, there's not a lot of loving-kindness there," he said. "But then again, there's not a lot of loving-kindness for us anywhere else in that country, is there?"

"No, there isn't," I said.

"Doesn't matter," Ángel said. "We take care of each other. You'll see. We'll walk out of here all at once if you think that'll make a difference. You and your mother and anyone else who wants to can join us."

"Excellent," I said. "When the tower clock strikes midnight, we'll go. All at once, one right after the other. Otherwise, it won't work. We have to overwhelm them. Push through, no matter what."

"Clock. Midnight. Got it!" Ángel went back to his side of the corral and started to spread the word first to his friends, and then to anyone else willing to listen. Before I knew it, all manner of people—men, women, and children—were walking by, pointing to the tower clock across the street from the corral, and giving me the thumbs-up.

When midnight came, Ángel hooted and his younger friends, Sergio and Rogelio, joined him in raising the signal. I moved to the gate with Mamá and Señor Martínez, followed by far more people than I expected. At least a hundred people joined us at the gate, crowding the small space. Ángel opened the gate.

Wasting no time, I lifted my arms high and said, "Go!" Together, we rushed through it, though we could only fit about four people at a time through the cow-sized gate.

The guards hastened in our direction, cigarettes and card games forgotten, all four of them. They yelled, "Get back inside! You can't be out here!"

But we didn't listen. Like bees, we swarmed out of the corral and dispersed into the streets, each with our own industrious goals. Veering off in all directions, we disappeared into Juárez.

"Hey, you there! Come back!" "We can't protect you out there!" the guards hollered at us, but there was really nothing they could do to stop us.

Wicho squealed with delight at the multitude of people running past us and scurrying behind us like hormiguitas.

Far behind us, at the gates of the corral, the four guards waved their batons and blew their whistles and screamed for us to come back, but we didn't listen. Mamá picked up Wicho and we ran, Ángel beside us with his friends close behind, crossing the dark streets and rushing from one building to another until we got to a series of one-story restaurants. We'd noticed this neighborhood when we were out looking for a phone, but hadn't had the money to eat at any of the establishments. There was an alleyway that led to the buildings' back doors, where the trash was thrown out at night.

Mamá put Wicho down and walked up to a couple of trash cans. As she took the lid off the first one, she buried her nose in the crook of her other elbow. "Oh my god," she said, her voice muffled, horrified.

I looked down into the trash can. The shadows of the moonlight hid its contents, so I pulled it onto its side to get a better look.

"No, Trella," Wicho said. "It 'mell bad."

Mamá shushed Wicho. "It's okay, baby." Then she reached into the second trash can and started moving things around. "Any luck?" she asked me.

I shook my head. "No. Just a whole lot of corn husks and empty cans. And rancid grease," I said, wiping my hands on a relatively clean piece of paper from the trash can. "Ugh. That's what stinks."

"If we don't find anything good here, we could always go farther in," Ángel said, coming over from the restaurant next door. His friends were still picking through those cans, but didn't seem to be having any more luck than we were. "We should really try to get to the mercado. There's more people that go there. More people make more trash. Makes sense, right?"

"You go ahead," my mother said. "I don't want to get too far from the corral. Wicho might get tired and start crying."

Ángel nodded. "Okay. You stay here. We'll go check out the restaurant down there by the marketplace." He paused. "Don't worry—we'll bring something back. Promise."

"Thank you," Mamá said.

No sooner had Ángel and his friends left than we got more company. I looked up from a trash can where I'd found a paper bag with a half-eaten apple, when I heard footsteps. Amparo was turning the corner.

"Having any luck?" Amparo asked. My mother didn't answer her, and I wasn't about to strike up a conversation with her either. As far as I was concerned, she could just do the world a favor and drop dead.

To her credit, Amparo respected our silence and walked off to the end of the block, where she started rummaging through a trash can at the corner restaurant. I ignored her too, but didn't turn my back on her for a second. I struggled enough with our circumstances without the anxiety that she might attack us.

During the holiday celebrations at Las Moras and in banquet halls of Monteseco, I ate lamb from beautiful floral porcelain plates, scooped out delicate, frothy strawberry sorbets and airy mousses from tall, sparkling crystal glasses with silver spoons, and sipped Mami's chocolate from dainty teacups, but I never enjoyed the anticipation of eating *any* of that as much as opening a greasy paper bag and finding not one but four red-tortilla taquitos still wrapped in butcher paper.

"God bless whoever threw them away," Mamá whispered when I clicked my tongue and showed them to her before wrapping them up and shoving them deep inside my coat pocket.

Wicho, standing behind my mother, didn't see them, which was good, because I couldn't give them to him now. Not in front of Amparo. She was likely to attack him, and then I'd have to kick her all the way to Indonesia. Besides, if we started to eat them right then and there, standing over the trash can behind the restaurant, we might miss more food in our rummaging.

None of us could afford to lose any time. Would the guards call the police on us? Probably. So we had to rummage quickly, grab everything we could carry, and scurry back with it to the people who couldn't leave the corral—good people like Señor Martínez, who was too old and fragile to walk this far.

As I put the lid back on our trash can, Amparo pushed her trash can to the ground and kicked it. I found her name ironic—she provided the opposite of protection or refuge to the women and children in the corral. She instilled hate in those who had the pleasure of having made her acquaintance.

"Nothing!" she mumbled, wiping her grimy hands on her skirt like it was an apron. "Did you find anything?"

"No," Mamá said quietly, moving on to the last trash can, a smaller bin to the right of me.

"Hey, that one's mine!" Amparo said. Her eyes were raging orbs, big and swollen in the sunken cavities of her skull, and she almost knocked me down as she shoved past me. "I saw it first."

"Seeing and owning are two different things," Mamá said. She put one hand on the lid of the trash can and put her other arm out to hold Amparo off. "Stop! There are other restaurants with other trash cans. I touched it first, so it's mine."

Amparo didn't answer Mamá. Instead, she pulled her arm back and took a swing at her. Mamá ducked, and Amparo lost her balance and fell forward. She wasn't just bigger and stronger than my mother, she was fearless.

"You tramp!" Amparo yelled as she made another run at

Mamá. Without thinking, I picked up the trash can lid and swung it, bringing it down hard on Amparo's head like a sartén. The blunt force of the lid on her head sent Amparo into a tailspin, and she grabbed at her head with both hands. Crying out in rage, she swirled around to look at me. "Why, you little—"

Whatever she was about to say got lost in the scuffle of my unchecked rage as I continued to rain blow after blow on Amparo's arms and back with the trash can lid, yelling, "Get away from her! Get your own trash can!"

"Stop! Stop! Estrellita! Por favor, stop!" Mamá grabbed my arms and pulled me in, holding me against her chest. I stood there panting, unsure of exactly what had come over me.

My arms felt heavy, burdened, like the lid I was still clutching weighed a ton. My fingers hurt, and my knuckles were pale, almost white from holding onto it.

Amparo was cowering in the shadows against the wall of the warehouse, crying. Mamá let me go and reached down to pry my fingers off the metal lid. It hit the ground with a loud *clang*. "I'm sorry," I whispered. "But I just couldn't let her hurt you again. I couldn't."

"She wouldn't have," my mother whispered. She stroked my hair, pushed it back behind my ears, and traced the line of my eyebrows across my forehead soothingly. Then she planted a quick, quiet kiss on my temple. "I can defend myself, you know."

"But you shouldn't have to," I said, swallowing my anger. Tears started rolling down my face—angry, messy tears that burned hot against my cheeks, defying the effects of the bitter winter. "Nobody should have to defend themselves, not out here, and certainly not in the corral."

Wicho, standing beside me and holding onto Mamá's skirt, started crying too. She picked him up and hugged him and rocked him. As we huddled together, I whimpered like a wounded puppy, my anger turning to shame.

"Do you hear me, Amparo?" I yelled across the alley at the woman still cowering in the shadows. "We should be fighting together, *for* each other. This is not helping!"

"I'm sorry."

Amparo's mumbled apology did nothing to assuage my resentment. "Sorry doesn't cut it!" I said. "Losing a child doesn't give you permission to hurt others!"

"That's enough, Estrella!" Mamá said.

"Estrella!" Amparo said, chuckling. She started to scoot away from us then, rubbing her shoulder against the wall as if she needed it for support. "Estrellita—you've got more than your share of darkness yourself, you know. ¡Eres carancha, Estrellita!"

"Don't talk to my daughter like that!" Mamá said, squeezing me tighter against her.

Amparo laughed again. Then she leaned her back flat against the wall, rolling her head up as if she was looking at the stars. I couldn't see her face in the shadows, but I knew she was smiling.

After a long while in which Mamá let me go, picked up the lid, and placed it back on the trash can, Amparo rolled her head sideways and said, "Can we at least share it? Go through it together, como amiguitas?"

"No," I said. "Get away from us! We could never be your amiguitas!"

"Estrella!" Mamá cried out.

"It's a big city. She can find another trash can." I put both hands on my hips and turned to Amparo again. "Why are you still here?"

Amparo didn't hesitate. She pushed herself off the wall and started walking sedately away. "Okay, you win," she said. "See you back at the corral, Estrellita."

Once Amaparo walked off, Mamá kissed Wicho and said, "Let's go. You're making me nervous."

We crossed over from one street to another, alley after alley, walking as fast as we could past all the people who had followed our lead and were lurking in the alleys, rummaging through trash cans.

"We should look for some more food," I said. "Those taquitos aren't going to go very far."

We looked through a number of trash cans, but except for a couple of potato peelings and some shriveled oranges, we didn't find anything else of consequence. When we got to an empty alley, we hid behind an abandoned car and ate our taquitos. Wicho clapped when we unwrapped them. He'd never been a big eater, but that night he ate an entire taco all by himself. When I picked him up and kissed him before heading back, he slapped my face with his greasy hands and said, "Patty-cakes, Trella! Patty-cakes!"

ESTADOS UNIDOS MEXICANOS

TELEGRAFOS NACIONALES

DE CIUDAD MÉXICO. D. F., EL 2 DICIEMBRE DE 1931

PARA CONSUL GENERAL EN CIUDAD JUÁREZ. CHIHUAHUA

VIA _____

DESTINO SARGENTO ROMERO DÍAZ,

TOCANTE LOCALIZACIÓN DEL SEÑOR JOAQUÍN DEL TORO, CIUDADANO REPATRIADO DE LA CIUDAD DE MONTESECO DE TEJAS DE LOS ESTADOS UNIDOS AMERICANOS, TEMENOS DATOS DE CONTACTO. UN HOMBRE ALTO Y DELGADO CON CABELLO RUBIO Y OJOS VERDES SE PRESENTÓ A ESTA EMBAJADA EL LUNES, DÍA 30 NOVIEMBRE USANDO ESE NOMBRE.

EL SEÑOR PARECÍA EXTRAVIADO Y NO TRAÍA DOCUMENTOS PARA VERIFICAR SU IDENTIDAD Y COMO VENÍA HERIDO, FUE REFERIDO AL SEGURO MÉDICO. EL SEÑOR NO DEJÓ NÚMERO DE HABITACIÓN, PERO PROMETIÓ REGRESAR. SIN EMBARGO, DESDE ESA FECHA, EL SEÑOR DEL TORO NO HA VUELTO A ESTAS OFICINAS.

RIGOBERTO GARCÍA COTÉS.

Chapter Fifteen

/DIDN'T KNOW THIS BEFORE, BUT THERE is nothing as debilitating or life-changing as hunger. I'm not talking about the kind of hunger that comes from turning your nose up at your vegetables and having your mother pull the plate away and send you to your room without supper. I'm not talking about the hunger you feel when you are ideando, daydreaming about exotic foods you'd like to taste because you're tired of the same old flavors and spices.

I'm not even talking about the kind of distressing hunger that comes over you when you're sitting in a crowded room all day waiting to be processed by a government not your own—a government even less interested in making you comfortable than the one that sent you there.

I'm talking about the hunger that keeps you up at night, the gnawing of intestines writhing inside you, rubbing and twisting in your abdomen like coarse, parched bedclothes that have been put through the wringer twice. I am talking about the kind of hunger that slices through your belly like a navaja or a cuchillo, slick and unexpected, leaving you breathless. The kind of hunger you never expected to feel until it is right there, in your belly, making you squirm like a worm on the dirt at night.

If Mamá felt the hunger, if she was sliced through and through by it like I was, she didn't show it, much less speak of it. I knew for a fact Wicho felt it, though. I could hear it in his weakened wails, feel it rising to the surface of his overheated skin. I could feel it in his tiny, shriveled palms when I pried them open, pulling his fingers apart like the spiraled stems of the resurrection plant when it was left out to dry and had become dormant, desiccated.

It was already Wednesday, and there was no news from Uncle Tomás. No telegrams came through for us, and he didn't show up at the corral. Mamá suspected he didn't get our telegram. "He would have come by now," she said. "We wouldn't still be sitting here if he'd gotten it."

She got up and went to fetch some water.

Ángel came over and sat beside me. "How's he doing?" he asked, nodding to Wicho.

"He's got a fever." I touched Wicho's forehead, and he pushed me away.

"I thirsty," he said.

"I know, chiquito," I said. "Mami went to get you some water. She'll be right back with it."

Ángel picked up an odd-shaped rock from the ground beside him, dusted it off with the bottom of his shirt, and handed it to Wicho. "Look," he said. "It's an elephant. Do you see its trunk here? And the tail?"

Wicho took the rock and examined it curiously. Then he tossed it across the way from us and grinned at Ángel.

Ángel laughed. "Oh, you want to play fetch, do you?" he asked.

"Don't," I said. "He'll have you bringing it back to him over and over again."

Wicho began to cry. "Hungry, Trella!" he said, and he pulled on my coat collar and buried his face in my neck.

"I know," I said. "Wait a minute. Mami's coming back with your wa-wa."

"He needs food," Ángel said.

"I know," I said. "But we didn't find anything when we went out this morning."

"It's crazy," Ángel said. "Everybody and their brother is out there now. We had to travel twice as far as last night just to get something to eat, and we had to eat it right there on the spot, before someone tried to take it away from us."

"Yes," I said, remembering my battle with Amparo. "The thing is, there's too many of us. I haven't counted, but Mami says there's at least two thousand people in the corral. The city can't support us."

"Some people are doing it in broad daylight now, walking as far as the outskirts of town," Ángel said. "They're wandering the streets, looking through every trash can they come across."

"Exactly what the city was trying to avoid," I said, looking at the guard who had brought us through the gate that very first night. "Sad thing is, I don't think the guards care anymore. I think they're pretending it's not happening."

Ángel toyed with a couple of pebbles he picked up from the ground, tossing them from one hand to the other.

I was worrying about Wicho, rubbing his hands between mine to keep them warm, when a man's voice called out my mother's name. "Señora Dulceña del Toro!" he yelled.

"What is it?" I asked Mamá, who was only a few steps away now. "What's going on?"

"I don't know." My mother put down the cup of water she'd been carrying back from the trough and looked at the gate.

The man continued to call out her name. "Doña del Toro, ¡preséntese, por favor!"

"Here!" she said as she straightened up.

"¡Venga aquí!" The man raised his arm and waved a piece of paper in the air. "¡Venga, por favor!"

I stood up, holding Wicho carefully in my arms, and followed Mamá as she wove through the crowd toward the gate, where the man was still waving. "I'm here. What is it?"

It was Sargento Díaz, and his smile said he had something good to share with my mother. "I have news," he said. "About your husband."

Mamá's voice rose. "Joaquín?"

"Papá?" I asked. "You heard from my father?"

Sargento Díaz scrunched up his face. "Yes and no," he said. "We know where he's been."

"Where?" Mamá and I both asked. We walked through the open gates of the corral to join Sargento Díaz on the sidewalk.

Sargento Díaz handed Mamá the piece of paper and shoved his hands back in his pockets. A cold wind blew our hair in our faces, and Mamá's breath left her open lips in swirls of white, puffy clouds that dissipated as she read the telegram.

"Well?" I asked.

My mother smiled, and her eyes reddened. She couldn't speak. Long rivulets of tears were falling down her face. I took the telegram out of her hands and read it quickly. My Spanish wasn't as good as I'd like when it came to writing, but I could read it well enough.

"I found him," Sargento Díaz said, puffing out his chest proudly. "I sent a telegram to my friend Rigoberto at the American embassy, and he just sent me this back. He's in Ciudad México."

"He's hurt," I said, after reading the telegram twice.

Sargento Díaz cleared his throat. "Yes," he said. "But he's been referred to a clinic. There are good places for medical attention in Mexico City. He will be all right."

"He's alive!" Mamá whispered, finally coming out of her shocked state. "That's all that matters. We need to leave. We need to get to Mexico City as soon as possible. When is that damn train going to get here?"

I'd never heard my mother cuss before. She wasn't the cussing type. But these were dire circumstances, and I could tell by the wild look in her eyes that she was coming undone.

The sergeant shoved his hands deeper in his pockets

and shifted from one foot to the other. "I don't know," he admitted.

"Well, find out!" I said. "Someone has to know! There's got to be a schedule somewhere."

"Well, the trains run in and out all the time, yes," Sargento Díaz said. "But the repatriation train, the one the government provides free of charge for you, it has not arrived. I am sorry I don't know much else, señora. But it shouldn't be long. It's been awhile since the last one."

The sergeant excused himself and walked back to the customs house. Mamá folded the telegram in half and handed it to me. She took Wicho in her arms and started walking back into the corral. "Take care of that," she said. "Put it in your journal, where it will be safe. We don't want to lose it. It's the only clue we have to your father's whereabouts."

I shoved the journal deep in the rucksack that I carried with me everywhere. I didn't trust anyone here enough to let it out of my sight.

Later that afternoon, the priest came by and handed out fruit and bread, and we smiled as we ate. The sun was brighter as it ascended into the sky. The rain clouds of the previous days had drifted away, and everyone in the corral seemed more hopeful as they looked up at the cloudless sky.

If it's true that the sun has revitalizing energies, then there couldn't have been more proof of it anywhere in the world than at that very moment in the corral. Even the children were more playful, their squeals full of energy, as they chased one another along the fence.

Then the news spread like a ray of sunshine from one end of the corral to the other, a joyful hallelujah passed down from one set of lips to another until it reached our ears:

The train had arrived.

Mamá put her hand on her chest and held her breath. She stood motionless as a statue, looking out at the horizon.

"Mamá," I whispered, tapping her shoulder. "Should we go? What about Uncle Tomás? We sent him that telegram. What if he comes looking for us?"

My mother blinked rapidly. Then she took a short, quick breath. "We have to go. Your father's in Mexico City. We have to join him," she whispered.

"We don't know that for sure," I said. "The man at the embassy wasn't sure if that was him. And he never went back."

"He's hurt, Estrella," Mamá said. "We have to go to him. He needs us, m'ija." She picked Wicho up and started to move through the elated crowd. All around us, people smiled, hugged, and kissed one another, relieved to finally see the journey continue.

"I knew the gobierno would come through for us," a man told his son. "See? I told you they'd come for us soon. Our troubles are almost over, m'ijo."

"You're going to love Mexico City," another man told his wife and children. "It's a beautiful place, a glorious place, with museums and parks and cultura, lots of cultura. Not like Detroit. Not like Detroit at all."

"I don't want to go," a girl told her brother. "I don't want to go back in the boxcar. I don't like it when they lock us in there."

"There will be food on the train," a husband and wife assured their children. "And real restrooms. It won't be like in the American train. These are our people. We'll be well fed, well taken care of from here on out."

"Where are we going?" I asked Mamá. She didn't answer. She pushed her way past people when she had to, working to make sure we boarded the train with the first wave of repatriates.

"Come on. They can't fit us all in one train. They're bound to run out of seats quickly and then we'll be stuck waiting for the next train. We have to get on this one. We can't afford to stay here one more minute." Wicho bounced in her arms and rubbed his eyes, still half asleep. "Where's your bag?" Mamá asked. "Did you put away the telegram?"

"Yes," I said, patting my schoolbag. "It's in my journal."

The repatriation officials blew their whistles and called for us to form a line and follow them. "Let's go," Mamá said.

The train was a relic. It looked like something straight out of the Mexican Revolution. At least we were allowed to sit in a coach car, with real seats and windows to look out of. But the best surprise of all came when, after about four hours of traveling, at our first stop, a group of well-dressed women came on board and handed us each a small parcel of food.

Inside the little bags were peanuts and soda crackers and a piece of fruit. I had an orange, but others had apples and grapefruits. Everybody ate their food carefully, delicately, enjoying each bite and making sure the peanut shells and orange peels didn't fall on the floor, but rather made it back into the paper sacks so that they could be disposed of properly.

For the first time in a long time, we were being treated like humans again, and we acted accordingly, smiling politely and saying "excuse me" and "thank you" as we made our way to the privy and back.

I slept a lot, lying sideways with my head on my mother's lap, comforted by the hope of finding my father waiting for us at the end of this long train ride. It took three and a half days to get to Mexico City, with frequent stops along the way, but we finally arrived one afternoon in what I can only describe as the most congested city I'd ever seen.

Everywhere we looked, there were people. When we disembarked at the station, hundreds of people milled about in our immediate vicinity alone. They sat on benches, read papers, walked about holding their children's hands, smoked cigarettes, talked. There had to be at least as many people there in that train station as lived in all of Monteseco.

In the streets, the same thing, hundreds—thousands, even—of people hurried about. Vendors hollered, policemen blew their whistles, kids zigzagged in and out of the way of pedestrians, men in white shirts and black pants held onto their hats and hurried by, and women in long skirts and rebozos followed close behind. Men in suits strolled arm in arm with women wearing more fashionable, shorter dresses and high-heeled shoes. Boys on bicycles rode by, their coats billowing out behind them. Children sold Chiclets, cigarettes, and candy at every corner our repatriation buses passed, heading to the parish that would take us in until we were situated in a more permanent location.

"I thought we were supposed to be taken to a camp?" Sarita said to a nun who was escorting us to the shelter. "We were told we'd get a plot of land."

"That's to be determined," the nun said, "when you have your meeting at the American embassy. They are the ones who tell you what your options are. Most people choose to stay here in Mexico City. But some leave to go live with relatives. Do you have family in Mexico, someone who can take you in for a while?"

"Yes," Sarita said. "I have a second cousin in Guadalajara."

"We will help you get in touch with them," the nun said. "Tomorrow. That way you can make room here for someone else, someone with nowhere to go."

Mexico City itself was intimidating. Massive buildings rose like titans out of the cement sidewalks, relegating the people to the proportion of ants, and casting dark shadows over the city.

"Industrialization," Mamá said when she saw me look up at the hulking giants. "This is where people work. This is where we might find jobs to help us pay for the papers we'll need to get back to the United States."

"We?" I asked.

Mamá shook her head. "I'm afraid so, cariño," she said. "Here, everybody works. See those children? They're all doing their share."

"But what about my homework?" I asked. "Won't I need time for that?"

"Not at first," she said. Then she looked down at Wicho and fussed with his hair, looking uncomfortable.

"What's the matter?" I leaned over to put my chin on her shoulder. "Did I say something wrong?"

"No, of course not." My mother pressed her cheek against mine. "It's just that things here are different than you're used to. You won't be able to go to school here, I don't think. Unless the government makes some kind of special provision for repatriates that I'm not aware of, school here costs money, and we won't have it."

I thought about it for a second. School back home had always been one of my favorite places to be, but I couldn't imagine going to school anywhere else, so I didn't know how to feel about that. Were all these children—in the streets right now, selling Chiclets and candy—illiterate? Then, because I didn't want Mamá to worry anymore, I said, "It doesn't matter. We won't be here that long. I can go to school when we get back home."

"Absolutely," Mamá said, and she kissed my forehead.

I sat up and watched the rest of the street scenery, with all its congestion and shadows and trash, and wondered how long it would take for my uncle to get us back to Monteseco. A few days, two weeks, a month? I refused to consider anything more than that. The idea of being in this busy city long enough to have to start going to school frightened me, so I put it out of my mind.

The parish where we were dropped off had a convent attached to it. The nuns were kind enough to give us a fresh set of clothes. They weren't new—I could tell they'd been donated by their gently used texture—but I was glad for them. It was so nice to slip into clean clothes after finally taking a bath. Both Mamá and I had been wearing our nightclothes under our coats for days, for more than a week of sleeping on the ground with only my coat and my mother to snuggle with, and we'd all stunk. Clean clothes felt luxurious after that.

After a quick snack, the nuns escorted us to the sleeping quarters—a large dining hall with thin mattresses, each bundled together with a thin pillow, which we unfastened and unrolled exactly two feet apart on either side.

The spacing was meant to give every person a bit of personal space, but Mamá pulled my small mattress toward hers and made one big bed where she, Wicho, and I could sleep together. Ángel and his brothers slept in the men's room, which was in another part of the convent. I was sad to see them go, but happy to be clean and snuggled right next to Wicho and Mamá.

The next morning, after handing out buttered bread and atole de maizena, the nuns cast a prayer upon us and sent us on our way so that we might find jobs to get us started in our new lives. "We can only keep you here for one week," they said. "We have to make room for the next train that comes through. You must find employment and a place to live soon. You must go to the American embassy sometime today and make an appointment. This is a list of places that are always looking for workers. You might want to go there first."

Mamá didn't want to go looking for work. "We have to go to the American embassy first," she said. "We have to find this man who talked to your father. Maybe he can tell us where that clinic is. He might also be able to reach out to Tomás for us. I'm not sure what they can do, but we have to start there. We can look for work tomorrow."

"What about the police?" I asked. "Can they help us look for Papá?"

She was silent for a moment, biting her lip. "I don't know how much they can do. I'm sure in a city this size, they have better things to do than find family members for repatriates," she finally said. Then she pushed my hair away from my face and traced the outline of my eyebrow with her thumb. "We can certainly ask them."

I believed Mamá had the right idea. Her priorities were clearly straight, but the clerk, Señor Rigoberto García Cotés, an elderly gray-haired man at the American embassy, didn't quite agree with her strategy. "I already told you everything I know, señora. Your husband was hurt. He had some kind of head injury. We do not know how it happened. His head hurt so much, he couldn't tell us much, so we referred him to Clínica Morales downtown," he said, when my mother showed him the telegram he had sent to Sargento Díaz.

"But you said you called them," Mamá said. "And they said he didn't go there. So where else could he have gone?"

Señor García looked at the documents Sargento Díaz had given her, the certificates of residencies for our family. "No," he said. "I am sorry, but there is nothing more I can do. I only saw him once."

"But there must be something you can do to help us find him," Mamá insisted. "Starting an investigation into this whole thing might give you some leads to his whereabouts. You do understand, don't you? This was an illegal act committed against our family. We were abducted. I am an American citizen, and so are my children. So is my husband. It's your duty to find him."

"It is not something we do." Señor García shrugged with his hands palms out. He spoke softly, like my uncle Tomás when he delivered a sermon. "I can file a report on him as a missing person and see what the police can do to help us, if they can find the time. I can tell you right now that it will likely be a long while before I hear anything back. They are inundated with work over there. They have bigger problems—crimes, burglaries, murders to solve—you understand?"

"I understand," Mamá whispered, shifting Wicho in her arms. "But we have to try."

"Yes, yes," Señor García said. "Now, I can send a telegram to this brother-in-law, this priest, Tomás del Toro, and let him know what is going on. Maybe we can make a connection, if he's heard from your husband."

"That's a lot of ifs and maybes," my mother said, twisting her lip like she did when she heard of an injustice she wanted to write about.

Señor García folded his hands on his desk. "I know, and

I apologize for that. Thank you for coming in, señora. We will try our best to do what we can to help you. Come back in two days; I should know more then. Maybe by then, your cuñado will have sent back a telegram."

Mamá shook hands with the clerk and said, "Thank you. Do you have a piece of paper so I can give you the place we can be reached?"

She wrote down the name of the convent on the paper he handed her and returned it to him. "Is there something you want me to tell your brother-in-law, specifically?" Señor García asked.

"Yes," Mamá said. "Tell him to call our lawyer, Alberto Luna, in Brownsville. He will know what to do."

The clerk wrote the lawyer's name down and wished us well as we stepped away from his desk. Then he closed the file and waved the next person over from a long line of people waiting to speak to him. I could only hope that he'd be done with this part of his duties in time to get that telegram out to my uncle before the end of the day.

ESTADOS UNIDOS MEXICANOS

TELEGRAFOS NACIONALES
DE MONTESECO. TEXAS., EL 8 DICIEMBRE DE 1931

PARA EMBAJADO Y CONSULADO DE ESTADOS UNIDOS EN
MÉXICO. CIUDAD MÉXICO
DESTINO RIGOBERTO GARCÍA COTÉS,

IT IS A RELIEF TO HEAR MY SISTER-IN-LAW AND
HER CHILDREN ARE SAFE. PLEASE ADVISE THEM THE
SITUATION HERE IS BEYOND CRITICAL. THE VILLAS
HAVE FALLEN PREY. I AM SORRY TO REPORT THEY HAVE
JOINED THE RANKS OF THE DISAPPEARED. THERE IS
MUCH GRIEF HERE. OUR STREETS ARE BARE AS MORE
AND MORE ARE VANISHED. I HAVE NOT HEARD FROM
ANYONE. NOT FROM JOAQUÍN. NOT FROM THE VILLAS. I
AM ALONE HERE WITHOUT MY FAMILY. I WILL LEAVE FOR
BROWNSVILLE IMMEDIATELY TO CALL ON ALBERTO LUNA
AND WILL KEEP YOU INFORMED AS THINGS DEVELOP.
EXTEND MY LOVE TO MY NIECE AND NEPHEW, ESTRELLA
AND LUISITO, AND DO EVERYTHING IN YOUR POWER TO
HELP THEM.

YOURS IN THE SPIRIT OF OUR LORD,
BROTHER TOMÁS DEL TORO.

Chapter Sixteen

*T*HE NEXT MORNING, AFTER RECEIVING A distressing telegram from Uncle Tomás that made Mamá cry, we walked
out feeling completely dejected. We didn't know what to do
or where to go. So we walked aimlessly until Mamá composed
herself enough to speak.

"I need to sit down," she said, shoving the handkerchief the
nuns had given her in the pocket of her freshly washed coat.
As we sat down on a bus bench, Mamá picked up an abandoned newspaper. Together, we looked through the want ads,
poring over the tiny print. Unfortunately, there was nothing
in there we could do to earn money right away. There was no
posting for an American journalist or a high school student.

It was depressing to acknowledge that at the present time
our skill sets required us to file applications, set up interviews,
go through with them, and then wait to see if we had the job.
"We don't have time for that kind of nonsense," Mamá said.
"We need money now. We need to get paid daily, in cash,

so we can put notices in every newspaper about your father. We need to hire a private investigator who knows the ins and outs of the city. We can't wait around for the police to find him. We have to do our own digging, and that takes money."

"What about Abuelo Rodrigo and Abuelita Serafina?" I asked. "Are we going to try and find them too?"

Mamá pressed the corner of her eye. "I wouldn't know where to begin," she whispered. "At least with your father, we have a lead. We know he's here somewhere. We need to concentrate on him for now."

"And rent," I said. "We'll need money for that too. The nuns said we can't stay there long. We have to find a job so we can rent a place."

Mamá frowned. "Let's hope it doesn't come to that," she said, blinking nervously. "Let's hope we can find your father before that."

There was a rumor buzzing around the convent that well-educated American women like my mother could become schoolteachers in the more affluent neighborhoods, but you needed money for that—money for the bus fare, money for nice clothes, money for school supplies and books. This was Mexico City—well-paid teachers here brought their own school supplies.

Since teaching and tutoring were out of the question as far as quick employment options were concerned, Mamá and I left Wicho in the care of Sarita, who was helping the nuns in the temporary nursery they had set up for repatriates. We walked over to the nearest plaza and got a job washing clothes for a woman named Venustiana Hernández. Up until that morning, Venustiana had four women on staff, but she said she'd fired two of them, so we could take their place at the trough.

If I had to say anything about our new boss, I would have to say Venustiana Hernández was more than mean. She was vicious. A small woman, at four feet ten inches tall—she couldn't have weighed more than ninety pounds wearing her heavy winter coat and big brown square-toed military-style boots—but she was fierce.

A metal walking cane sat on her shoulder like a dangerous alternative to a purse, so nobody messed with her. Her face said, *I am in charge.* She had eyes that bulged out—not all the way, like the eyes on a pug (that would be insulting to a breed known for having a loving disposition). No, I would say that the overzealous protrusion of this woman's eyeballs was exactly the same as the natural placement of a chihuahua's eyeballs in its tiny head.

You might even go as far as to say they shared other traits, Venustiana and a chihuahua—namely, their disposition. A chihuahua is highly neurotic and somewhat abusive, yelping and growling at every single little noise it hears. That temperament was certainly true for Venustiana Hernández.

In the early morning dawn the next day, when we first got to the washing station, we could feel her watching us.

That afternoon, I pulled a bedsheet out of the sudsy water in the washtub and started wringing it between my reddened hands. The water was hot, but I was chilled, soaked all the way down to my undergarments, and more water dripped off my elbows, rippling over the aluminum washboard and down my sides.

Next to me, Mamá leaned into her work. She scrubbed one end of a white sheet against the washboard with every muscle in her slim arm, shoulder, and back.

She looked like she wanted to scrub the life out of that bedsheet, like making it white again was the most important task in the world. The sound her scrubbing made against the aluminum washboard was rhythmic, but there was no musicality, no beauty to it. It was dull and dreary, like the sky above us.

"What's the matter?" my mother asked.

"Oh, nothing," I said. "I was just thinking about what Uncle Tomás said in his telegram. That we were the first to contact him, that he hadn't heard from Papá or Güelo Rodrigo or Güelita Serafina. It's strange, isn't it, that none of them have reached out to him yet?"

"It's not that strange," my mother said, after thinking about it for a moment. "Think about everything we've been through. I suspect their journeys haven't been any easier. It's a matter of time before they all get in touch, and then we'll be able to figure something out."

"I know," I said. "I'm just worried about Papá."

Mamá stopped scrubbing and stood up. She put her hands on her waist and stretched backward. "I know," she said.

The frown that had formed on her face when she read my uncle's telegram had not left her brow since, and I worried about her. Even with the small amount of food portioned out to her by the nuns at the convent, she didn't look much better than when we were starving in the Ciudad Juárez corral.

In fact, I thought she was paler than ever, and her frame under her secondhand dress was much leaner than she had been. It hadn't even been two weeks since our life had been upended, but she had lost a lot of weight, and she didn't seem to be putting any of it back on.

"But your father can take care of himself." Mamá sighed and rubbed her thin cheek with the back of her hand. "I'm more worried about your abuelo Rodrigo's health."

I nodded. My grandfather's heart condition had been weighing heavily on my mind. With the way we'd been pulled out of our homes, I worried that during their abduction he hadn't had time to take his medicine along, not to mention how he'd get more if he ran out.

"Wouldn't it be ironic if we were all here in the same neighborhood, and we just haven't found each other yet?" I'd been daydreaming all kinds of good-outcome scenarios in this vein all day.

"Yes," my mother said. "It's highly unlikely, but yes. It would be."

Behind me, Venustiana had left her usual spot sitting at the cement trough. Sensing her disapproval, I finished wringing out the bedsheet and put it in the rinsing tub. My shoulder and back muscles burned from the effort it took to push down, soak, and lift that bedsheet out of the water again and again until I had rinsed all the soap out of it.

"Change out that water," Venustiana ordered, because everything with her was a command.

Mamá wiped her sudsy hands on her apron as she walked over to me. "I'll do it," she said.

But Venustiana wasn't going to let me get off that easy. The boss woman raised her walking stick, creating a barrier between me and Mamá. "Let her do it," the squat woman said. "She's old enough to take care of her own business."

"In this job, just like in every job you'll ever have, you must learn to deal with all kinds of people," my mother had said yesterday, the first time I complained about Venustiana Hernández.

"You don't understand. You've never worked for anyone but Abuelo Rodrigo," I'd said. "You've never put up with someone like this. Someone mean and vicious! She's a big bully, just like that Amparo woman."

My mother had sighed. "Yes," she said. "She is mean. But she is the boss, so you're going to have to do what she says for now. Otherwise, we'll be out of a job, and then how will we get back to Monteseco?"

Now Venustiana walked back to the trough after I said I could handle the sheet by myself. I stared at her back, wishing I could just quit and get as far away from her as I possibly could. "She makes me so mad."

"Don't give into it," Mamá whispered. "Remember you are a lady—a rose in winter, beautiful and refined despite the frost surrounding you."

Mamá was always telling me how to be a lady, though I wasn't the best at listening to her advice. When I nodded, she went back to scrubbing. I closed my eyes and visualized something I had seen on the way to the courtyard this morning: a single red rose growing on a desiccated stem in the dormant garden of a beautiful home in the center of town. Had Mamá seen it too—that miracle of nature? Was that why she was saying that now?

Silent for now, I wrung out the sheet and hung it up on the overburdened clothesline. Then I leaned down, put my hands on the rinsing tub, and hauled it up. It took every muscle in my body to carry that washtub over to the edge of the street and dump out the water.

When I was done, I took the rinsing tub back, and then I used the bottom of my apron to lift the thin handle of one of the buckets of boiling water from the iron grill of the wood-burning chimenea. I put that water in the rinsing tub along with two cold buckets of water. Venustiana was right about one thing. I learned fast. I knew what I was doing, so I could take care of myself and my mother and brother. She just didn't have to be so rude.

IN SPITE OF WINTER

A lone red rose blooms on a spindly thin
twig—its frail torso and arms standing on brown
and brittle feet. Petals, like loose strands
of hair, flutter against a bitter winter breeze.

Her velvet coat is out of season, and
behind her the sky is dark and gray. A storm
thunders in the horizon, while on an extended
limb, a single leaf waves cheerfully.

CHAPTER SEVENTEEN

*T*HURSDAY MORNING, AS WE ATE OUR atole de arroz for breakfast, the nuns came to the dining hall to inform us that we would be parting ways Monday morning. If we hadn't secured jobs by Sunday, we would have no other choice but to go to the outskirts of town, to the poor neighborhoods, where people lived in shanty houses and didn't have to pay rent to anyone.

It wasn't a good situation, and the nuns didn't recommend it. So they impressed upon us the importance of finding work. If we did get jobs, however, there were several barrios nearby where we could rent a small room until we got back on our feet and could afford a small house. They would be happy to help us with that.

"Too bad the government didn't give us the land they promised," Sarita said to my mother. "I would have stayed in the States if I'd known women without husbands couldn't get any land." Some of the people we traveled with, like Sarita, had left voluntarily because they had been promised a better life in Mexico.

Mamá sighed. "I don't want land," she said. "We have land. We just need to find our way back to it."

But Sarita didn't have to worry about her immediate future. The nuns were willing to let her keep earning her keep by working in the nursery until she found other means of supporting herself, or until she got married. "Fat chance of that," Sarita had confided to Mamá. "Who's going to marry a woman with four mouths to feed? I suspect I'll be here until the last of my children is grown and gone his own way. I'll probably haunt this place when I'm dead, because I don't think I'll ever be able to leave."

"What do you think we should do?" I asked Mamá that night as we lay down on our joined mattresses with Wicho snuggled between us. "Should we rent a place here? Can we afford it if we keep working for that woman?"

Mamá tickled Wicho for a moment longer. Then she kissed him and pulled away. She put her hands flat on the pillow and rested her head on them. "I'm not particularly attached to this job," she admitted. "After today, we'll have enough money to buy something decent to wear—maybe a couple of nice white shirts and a long black skirt, something I could wear day in and day out without calling attention to myself if I took a job as a schoolmistress at one of those nice schools on a nicer side of town."

"That would pay much better than scrubbing clothes," I said. "But what about me? Could I go to school? Not at first, but later, after you made more money?"

"I hope we won't be here long enough to make it necessary to enroll you in school for the spring. But if it comes to that, then yes, absolutely. You should go to school." Mamá's eyes glistened in the dark, and I knew she was trying hard not to let her emotions get the best of her. She usually saved that for the middle of the night, when she thought I couldn't hear her. When she turned away and hid her face to sob softly into her pillow, how I wanted to reach out and touch her, but I didn't. It broke my heart to stay silent, but it would break hers to know I knew.

Mamá turned and lay on her back. She started a prayer and I followed along. When we were done, she put her hands at her sides and said, "I just wish I had enough money to hire a private investigator. I was really hoping your father would come across one of the notices I put in the newspapers."

"Me too," I said. "But we can't lose hope. He might still read one of them."

My mother sighed. "Unless he's no longer in the city," she said. "He might have already gone back up north to find a way of crossing back, thinking we were still in Texas."

"How long are we going to stay here?" I asked. "Should we try to make our way back?"

"I don't know." In the darkness, Mamá's voice sounded lost. "Go to sleep, cariño. We have to get back to the embassy in the morning. I want to send Tomás another telegram. I want to see if he's made any progress with our lawyer."

Friday morning, Wicho waved and blew us kisses as we

left the convent. We walked all the way to the embassy because taking a bus would mean using money, and we were saving every peso we could get our hands on.

"Ah, Señora del Toro, I am glad you came by," Señor García said when he saw us standing in line. "Come with me to my desk. I have another telegram for you from your brother-in-law."

Mamá's eyes lit up at the news. She rushed ahead of me and practically ripped the telegram out of Señor García's hands when he offered it to her. But as she read it, her eyes narrowed, and she pressed her lips together, her fury growing. "I can't believe this!" she said, reading the telegram again.

"What is it?" I asked. "What's wrong?"

"They won't give him copies of our birth certificates!" she cried.

"Who?" I said. "The government?"

Mamá crumpled the telegram in her hand. Then, as if thinking better of it, she unfolded the paper and smoothed it out. "The clerks at the courthouse. They told Tomás they can't give him access to our records. Not even with our lawyer there to press them."

Señor García shook his head. "They are toying with him," he said. "He is next of kin, and he has a lawyer with him. It might take longer than expected, but at some point they have to give him copies of those documents. They might have to get a court order, but I suspect it will get done. Eventually."

"You don't know our court system," I said under my breath.

"Thank you for helping us at this end, Señor García," Mamá said. "Can you please send another message to my brother-in-law? I have it right here."

"Yes. Yes, of course." Señor García took the note my mother handed him. She was asking Tomás if he knew anything about her parents, Abuelo Rodrigo and Abuelita Serafina. In the telegram she asked Tomás to please check with Abuelo's doctor in Brownsville, because she hoped that he had found a way of seeing him and keeping up with his medication.

Later that day, at the trough at work, Mamá and I worked extra fast. We were two parts of one machine, like sprockets in a timepiece—hauling water together, trying to get our loads done as soon as possible so we could go back to the embassy early enough to see if Señor García had heard from Tío Tomás.

We finished the day's work more than an hour early, which made me almost giddy with joy. "I'd be happier if I wasn't so tired," Mamá said as she took my apron and hung it on the clothesline.

"Me too." I was soaked through and through. I pushed my hair out of my face and massaged my cheeks as we walked over to the cubby station where we kept our lunch bags while we worked. My cheeks felt like cold lamb chops hanging on my face. I pressed on them, trying to warm them up.

"Oh my god, you're bleeding!" Mamá stopped and took my hands in hers. My skin was red and roughened. I'd seen the cracks at my knuckles, had even tried putting extra lotion on them at the convent, but the lotion only stung in the raw spots. They hadn't gotten any better, but they hadn't bled until that very moment.

"It's nothing," I said. "I'll put something on them when I get back to the convent. We should get going. We don't want to miss Señor García."

Mamá pulled a handkerchief out of her skirt pocket and pressed it delicately against the cracks. Her frown was unsettling enough, but she actually looked like she was about to cry. "This is too much," she said. "I never wanted this for you. You shouldn't have to bleed just to eke out a living."

"It's okay," I said. "It looks worse than it feels. It hardly hurts, really."

I wrapped the handkerchief around my knuckles and moved to the table. My mother shook her head and mumbled under her breath. Her voice was hoarse, barely disguising her distress.

"Of course it hardly hurts. Your hands are ice-cold from that freezing well water. You couldn't feel a thing no matter what was going on."

"Really, it looks worse than it is. I'll ask Sister Marianita if she has something for it tonight." Bending down to the cubby under the table, I dug out my mochila and threw it over my shoulder. Then I handed Mamá the small brown purse the nuns had given her, avoiding eye contact. She'd know I was lying.

The truth was that my hands had been hurting for days. Last night, I couldn't sleep for the pain.

"What's going on over here?" Venustiana asked as she came toward us.

"We finished," I said, smiling brightly at the sour-faced woman.

Venustiana looked at our twenty loads of laundry all nicely folded inside their baskets, waiting to be picked up by their owners, and our aluminum washtubs sitting upside down in a row on the ground. "But the day is not over," she said, pointing at the clock on the church tower. "You have time to do a few more loads."

"But we have to go," Mamá said, looking up at the clock. "We have business to take care of at the American embassy."

"You can take care of it on your own time. For now, I need you to take care of these four loads," Venustiana said, handing each of us a basket of clothes from Señora Marina's workload. Her older sister, Meme, had not come to work that day because her arthritis was acting up, so Marina had fallen behind.

Mamá put the basket back down next to Señora Marina. "I'm sorry," she said, taking the other basket from me and putting it down beside the first. "But we did *our* work, the work we were assigned for our day's pay."

"We have an appointment, and we can't miss it," I explained.

"Then you will miss it, because you're not done here." Venustiana thumped her cane in front of us.

"We can't work any more today," Mamá insisted. "Estrella's hands are bleeding, see?" She picked up my left hand and pointed to my knuckles. "The skin is cracked. We need to get to a farmacia."

Señora Marina stopped working. She straightened up and looked over at my hands. "Oh, that's bad. Put some udder cream on it when you get home," she said.

"Hey! Who asked you? Get back to work!" Venustiana tapped her cane on the ground three times. "I'm not paying for your opinions!"

"No, you're paying for our work—by the load," Mamá said. "And it looks to me like we're done with ours. So we'll see you tomorrow."

"Not if you leave, you won't." Venustiana anchored her cane in the groove between two paving bricks and folded her hands over the cane's handle. "If you leave, you don't have a job here."

"That's fine. Just give us what you owe us." Mamá raised her eyebrows and put her palm out.

Venustiana shook her head, straightened up, and reached into her pocket. Her thin lips formed a crooked, deformed little scar of a smile across her face as she pulled out a wad of money. She counted out a few pesos and handed them to my mother.

Mamá counted it. Then she counted it again. "You're short a day's pay," she said.

"No, I'm not," Venustiana said. "It's short two half-days' pay. You're both leaving without finishing out the day."

"We finished our work," I insisted.

Venustiana shrugged. "You're leaving early, so you don't

get a full day's pay. That's just the way it works!"

"It's an hour! One hour! That's not half a day's pay," I said, letting my frustration get the best of me.

"Your decision, not mine," Venustiana said.

"Fine. Keep it. Come on, Estrella." Mamá walked off, leaving me standing there, wishing there was something I could do to get our money from Venusiana. But other than wrestling her to the ground and digging it out of her coat pocket, there was nothing, so I trotted after my mother, who stalked along with her shoulders rolled back and head held high. At the end of the block, we turned the corner and walked fifteen more blocks until we got to the embassy.

"I wish I had better news," Señor García said. He took the latest telegram from Uncle Tomás and handed it to Mamá.

She held the telegram between us so we could both read it at the same time.

"No, no," I said, when I read that my uncle Tomás had exhausted every avenue and could find no sign of where the authorities had taken my grandparents. "Tío Tomás has to find them. Güelo Rodrigo is sick! How could they do this to him?"

"I know you're worried about him taking his medicine," Mamá said, "but I'm sure Abuela Serafina is taking care of him, wherever they are."

"I know she is," I whispered and tried to control my emotions. It served no purpose to cry.

Mamá folded the telegram and put it in her coat pocket.

Señor García sighed and pressed his lips together. "I'm sorry. I wish there was more I could do to help you locate your family. But as you know, these are difficult times, and there is not much more we can do from here. Just keep us posted on your current living arrangements, in case your husband or your parents get in touch with us. We can connect you to them."

"Thank you," my mother said. "I'll come back next week when we have our new address."

When we walked out of the embassy, Mamá stopped at the gate and looked ahead. "How are you doing? Are you tired?" she asked. "Should we catch a bus? I'd rather use the money to get something for your hands, but if you're too tired, we can catch a bus."

"We can't afford to be so frivolous. We should forget the farmacia and walk back to the convent. Sister Margarita will have something for my hands. I'm sure of it," I said.

"What if she doesn't?" Mamá frowned again.

We walked seventeen blocks to get back to the convent, and we were so late that dinner was already underway when we got there. The nuns had already locked up for the evening, but they weren't upset with us. They were just relieved to see us, especially after we told them why we were late.

Wicho shrieked with joy when we walked in. He abandoned his food and came rushing into Mamá's arms. He squealed when I hugged him and buried my face in his neck, snorting like I was devouring him with my kisses.

We ate our lentil soup slowly, savoring every last drop and cleaning out our bowls with the last bite of our bread. Only one bowl of lentils and one thick slice of hearty bread was allotted per person. I was so hungry I could have eaten two more bowls of soup if they'd been put in front of me.

I was right about Sister Marianita having something for my hands. After dinner, the older woman took me aside and told me I didn't have to help with the dishes in the kitchen that night. She walked Mamá and me over to the office and put a thick salve on my wounds.

"It's my own special blend," she whispered. "Just spread it over the cracks, but don't rub it in. It'll sting a little, but you'll feel better in a few days." Then she handed Mamá the small jar and said, "You can put this on her four times a day until it's all healed. You should put some on your hands too. They're not looking much better than your daughter's."

"Thank you," I said.

Mamá opened the small jar and put a tiny bit of the salve on her fingertips and worked it into the cracks on her hands.

"Don't be stingy with it," Sister Marianita said, taking the jar and putting more of the homemade ointment on Mamá's hands, spreading it gently over her knuckles. "There's more where this came from."

"Que Dios se lo pague," Mamá whispered. She tightened the lid on the small jar and handed it to me. I put it in my pocket.

That night, I couldn't go to sleep right away. My hands were burning from the salve, so I laid them on my chest and closed my eyes and talked to God for a long time. I prayed for my hands to heal quickly so that I could get another job. I didn't want to become a burden on my mother. I also asked Him to keep an eye on my uncle Tomás in Monteseco—because I was afraid that by trying to help us, he might be putting himself in danger. I prayed that he wouldn't be repatriated like the rest of us. I prayed for my father and my grandparents and every single person out there looking for their loved ones. I prayed for the nightmare of repatriation to be over.

Dear Abuela Jovita,

I pray that you can get this message from your place so far up in heaven. I pray that you can get permission to come down to earth for a moment, find my father, and whisper in his ear that he is beloved. That we are waiting to hear from him. That we want nothing more than to be reunited with him.

And if you have any influence on the angels in heaven, will you ask them kindly to protect my familia? Will you beg them to find my abuelos, my mother's parents, so that we might not lose them the way we lost you and Abuelo Anzelmo to La Santisima?

I pray that you make the angels listen to the heartbreak in my mother's sobs at night. That you can make them see how vulnerable we are in this strange land. That they whisper compassion into the ears of men so those men might give us back every ounce of stardust they took from us—the magic that was stolen from each and every one of us.

Love always,
Your granddaughter,

Estrella

CHAPTER EIGHTEEN

ONDAY MORNING, SISTER MARIANITA GAVE MAMÁ a blue polka-dotted dress and a nice coat from the charity closet.

"I'm not supposed to do this," she said. "Some would say it is unfair to offer you more clothes when there are so many others in need, but I just want you to get this job. For the sake of your children, the little one especially."

"Job?" I asked.

Sister Marianita nodded and handed Mamá a piece of paper, saying, "They are expecting you there at ten this morning. I told them you were reliable, so make sure you get there on time."

"Expecting us?" I asked, reading the address spelled out in Sister Verónica's beautiful handwriting.

"Just you," Sister Verónica said, addressing Mamá. "The lady of the house, La Señora Montoya, is looking for a tutor for her three children and a niece who lives with them. They will be going to London next summer, and she wants them to practice their English. It is a rare opportunity, one I think you are well suited for."

"Thank you, Sister," Mamá said. "I appreciate you looking out for us."

"What about me?" I asked Sister Verónica. "I need a job too."

Sister Verónica shook her head. "You would make a good nanny, but I'm afraid I don't know anyone who needs one. Perhaps you could ask your friend Ángel. They're always looking for people at the shoe factory."

"No," Mamá said. "You are not working at the factory. There is too much risk there. Besides, someone needs to stay with Wicho when we get our own place."

"He can't stay here?" I asked.

Sister Marianita blushed as she shook her head. "I'm sorry. We just don't have the staff to take care of so many children. A new train could arrive any minute. Certainly one will be here in the next few days. We need to make sure everyone here has moved along."

"Even the babies?" I pleaded.

"I'm sorry," Sister Marianita whispered.

Mamá put her hand on my shoulder. "We'll manage, Estrella." Then she picked up her purse and went off to her appointment.

After Mama left, I went to the nursery and played with Wicho. It had been awhile since he and I enjoyed a good time together. He could be a handful, but I loved him and wanted nothing more than to have him grow up feeling as loved and as safe as I'd felt all my life.

If only we could find Papá. Wicho's life would be better if we were all together, if we were, all four of us, safe and sound back at Las Moras.

Suddenly it hit me. In all those telegrams back and forth between Mamá and Uncle Tomás, nobody had ever mentioned Las Moras. Was our house still standing? Or had it been consumed by that dreadful fire?

I had to know. I had to send a telegram to my uncle and find out if we still had a home to go back to.

"Sarita," I said, putting Wicho back in the wooden crib with two other toddlers, "I've got to go somewhere. I'll be back to help you take care of him in a couple of hours."

"Trella! Trella!" Wicho cried, lifting his arms up toward me. "Up, Trella! Up!"

"Really?" Sarita said. "You're leaving him like that? Look at him. He wants to spend time with you. Take him outside. Play with him."

"But I have to go all the way to the embassy," I said. "It can't wait."

"Then you're going to have to take him with you," Sarita said. "I have my hands full with the rest of them."

I thought about it for a moment. Normally, I wouldn't even think about taking Wicho out in the middle of winter, but it was actually nice outside. *I could carry him there,* I told myself. *It wouldn't be too hard, if I took a couple of breaks to let him explore the territory along the way.* Yes, he did tend to get fussy, but I was used to that. I really needed to get the telegram to my uncle. *I'll take some snacks,* I thought, *in case he gets hungry. If he gets to be too much, I'll just take him outside and let him play for a while.*

"Okay," I said. "But I'm bundling him up."

"Good." Sarita took my brother's little coat out of the closet and handed it to me. I picked Wicho up, and she helped me put his arms through the sleeves.

"I go?" Wicho asked.

"Yes, you go," I said, and I kissed him. He scrunched up his nose and pushed my face away. I buttoned his coat all the way up to his neck. "But you can't take this off. You have to keep it on the whole time we're out. None of your shenanigans!"

Sarita laughed and handed me a pair of mittens. I put them in my pocket in case we needed them later. "He'll be fine," she said.

"He will," I said. "I'm taking some of those crackers and a can of juice, so he'll have something to snack on while we're there."

"Help yourself," Sarita said. "That's what they're there for."

The air was cool and crisp, but nothing Wicho and I couldn't handle. I walked slowly, talking to Wicho, showing him the sights as we went along, so it took me almost an hour to get all the way to the embassy.

"See?" I told Wicho when we were standing in line waiting to talk to Señor García. "That wasn't so bad, was it?"

"Bad!" Wicho yelled. "Bad!" Then he wiggled and squirmed around until I put him down. I held his hand for a while, but then he broke free and ran off. I caught up to him right before he hit the glass door leading outside.

I picked him up and walked back to the line. "You want a cracker?" I asked, putting him down on the floor in front of me and handing him a cracker out of my bag.

Wicho smiled as he bit into it. "I thirsty," he said.

I took a small can of guava juice out of my bag, opened it, and handed it to him. He drank greedily.

"You like that?" I asked.

He nodded and licked his lips. "Is good."

After another long swig of the juice, Wicho handed me back the can and wiped his mouth. I reached for a napkin and cleaned his face thoroughly.

Everything was going well until I stood up and looked around for a trash can. No sooner had I turned away than Wicho was back on his feet, making another run for the door.

I reached him just before he snuck past a woman who was entering the embassy. "No!" I said, pulling him back inside. "We have to stay in here."

"Out!" Wicho screamed when I picked him up. "Out! Out!" He twisted around in my arms. Somehow he managed to get himself turned upside down and kicked me in the face—right in my nose. The pain was excruciating. Tears welled in my eyes.

"Stop it, Wicho!" I ordered. "Stop it right now!"

That was when he started wailing. He opened his mouth and let out an ear-piercing scream that made me wish I'd never left the convent. "I'm sorry," I said. "But you can't go outside."

Wicho kept crying. His screams reverberated off the walls of the embassy.

Every person in the lobby looked at me like I was a terrible mother.

"He's not mine," I said. A woman frowned at me. "I mean— he is and he's not—he's my brother."

"Well, take him outside," a man said. He was holding a fedora in one hand and a huge envelope on the other. "We don't need that in here."

As if sensing the man's dislike of him, Wicho let out an even louder series of wails.

"Stop, Wicho," I begged. "Please stop."

"Aw," a woman said. "Take him home. He needs his mother."

A clerk with dark blond hair wearing a very nice suit stood up and yelled in perfect English, "He needs a good spanking, that's what he needs!"

He was tall and slim, like Papá. Only he wasn't my father, and he wasn't Wicho's father either. As Wicho pounded on my chest one second and wailed in my ear the next, I remembered that day in our sala at Las Moras, right before we were sent here, when I'd flipped him over and given him just that, *a good spanking.* My face flushed and my hands trembled as anger rose inside me. But it wasn't Wicho I was angry with. I was angry at the blond man. He had no business yelling at me, telling me to spank my brother.

"Give him to me," the blond man continued. "I'll take care of it!"

"No!" I screamed. "He's a little boy. He doesn't need a spanking. He needs a nap."

The blond man threw his hands up. "Then take him home!" he yelled.

I looked around the crowded room. Everywhere around me men stood silently minding their own business. Women wrapped their arms around their little ones, and children looked away and buried their faces in their parents' coats and shirts.

"I would!" I yelled loud enough for the clerk to hear over my brother's wailing. "I would take him home—if we could go home! But our government has thrown us out of our own country. They've left us out here in the cold, without food or shelter, without any means by which to live. But you wouldn't know anything about that, would you? You wouldn't know what it's like to starve and freeze and wonder if you'll ever see the rest of your family. You wouldn't know that because you've got a good job here. As long as Mexican Americans are rounded up, forced across the river, and put in corrals to freeze and starve to death, your mortgage will get paid and your children will be fed!"

"Dang right!" the man with the fedora yelled, raising a first in the air. "You tell him, chiquita!"

"Now that's quite enough!" The blond man straightened his necktie. "We will have no upheavals in this office. Young lady, I am not the enemy. I am trying to help, but I can't do my job with a baby screaming in here. I suggest you step outside with him."

While the man was obnoxious, he was right about one thing: Wicho needed the opportunity to calm down. But I didn't want to lose my place in line.

As my brother continued to cry, hiccupping and wailing intermittently, the crowd of people continued to ignore us. Men shifted their feet, raised their heads, and looked up at the ceiling while women talked to their children in hushed voices, telling them to behave.

"Where's your mother?" a woman asked. She was holding a bundled-up baby of her own. "Sometimes a baby just needs to be held by his mother."

I left the embassy without accomplishing my errand, holding Wicho firmly in my arms. He cried for half a dozen blocks. No matter what I said or did, he wouldn't stop. He only quit crying when I put him down so he could stomp around on the dead grass in an empty lot.

"I hungry," Wicho said when he stopped running around long enough to smell the aroma of food wafting from the restaurant across the street.

"Me too," I said. "Are you ready to go eat?"

He nodded and lifted his arms. "Thank God," I said, and I picked him up.

I didn't have a chance to tell Mamá what had happened or even explain what I was doing at the embassy that morning because she was too full of news and excitement. From the moment she walked through the door, Mamá wouldn't stop talking and laughing and smiling.

Thanks to the lead from Sister Marianita, Mamá had made

the leap from laundress to English tutor. "The house is on the other side of town, so I'll have to leave earlier in the morning than when we worked in the courtyard," she said. "But the pay is so much better."

"Really?" I asked.

"I'll have to take three different buses to get there, but the salary is well worth the effort. If I do a good job, there will be recommendations for similar positions." Mamá's eyes sparkled and came to life. "And then I can work two jobs."

"Two jobs!" I said, worried that she might be overextending herself. "But how would you do that? When would you be back?"

"I wouldn't be getting back as early as I did today. Today, I just met the children and conversed with them," she said between bites of the fideo the sisters had prepared for lunch. "They were very well behaved, but a little distracted. I think they were bored more than anything."

"I wish Wicho was well behaved," I said, trying to lead into the events of my day. I didn't know how Mamá would react to my taking Wicho to the embassy with me after I told her how he'd acted, but it wouldn't be right to keep it from her. "He threw a fit today."

"Really?" Mamá asked. "I suspect it's not going to be the last time. Now come on. Put the dishes away. We have to go."

"Go?" I asked. "Where?"

My mother picked up her plate. "To find a place to live, remember?"

With Wicho in tow, we headed out with a list of places to

go and people to talk to about renting a small place we could afford. We spend most of the afternoon walking from one horrific dwelling to another deep within in the bowels of Colonia Cuauhtémoc.

"Is it too much to ask to have a place be livable?" Mamá said as we walked away from an apartment building that could only be described as a slum. The apartments were nothing like I'd imagined. The rooms were stuffy and old. The walls were heavily stained and the stucco was crumbling off. You couldn't quite see to the other side through the rat holes, but it wouldn't take much more digging by the four-legged creatures for that to happen.

"Are you sure this is all we can afford?" I asked Mamá as we walked into yet another deplorable dwelling. "I smell mold."

"Well, at least this one has a real floor," she whispered so the landlord wouldn't hear us.

The landlord, Don Patricio, was a small, rail-thin man with a calm, soothing tone, and he insisted on speaking to us in what he considered *our language*. His English was passable, though he had a habit of asking and quickly answering his own questions that grated on my nerves. Even with the heavy accent and the questions and answers, we could understand him well enough, but he claimed to have a problem following our "Americanized" Spanish. We hadn't encountered this kind of criticism in the convent, so the man's comments were a bit unsettling.

"You speak funny," he said. "Your Spanish is corrupted,

like your country is corrupted, ¿verdad? Yes. I think so."

Mamá didn't care what he thought of us; she was just happy the place was modestly furnished and Don Patricio was willing to make a weekly payment arrangement with us, because she only had enough money to pay for a week's worth of rent at the time.

"I have a good job," she assured Don Patricio. "You'll get your money on time."

"See that you do," Don Patricio said. "Otherwise, ¡pa fuera! Understand?"

"Yes," Mamá said. "I know."

Mamá, Wicho, and I moved into the apartment at the far end of Colonia Cuauhtémoc that very afternoon. Sister Marianita, Sarita, and the rest of the nuns were happy to hear we were all settled in. They gave us their blessing and saw us off with a blanket, a small suitcase full of used clothes, and an even smaller bag of goodies from the pantry.

"A little something to get you started," Sister Marianita said, placing the bag in my hands. "And remember, we are here if you should need something. We hope we don't *have to* see you again, but a visit every now and then would be nice." She embraced me tightly.

"I'm so proud of you," Sarita said, hugging my mother. "You're doing it. You're making a better life for yourself and your children."

"I am," Mamá's smile was wistful. This was far from being one of my mother's greatest accomplishments, but Sarita didn't know that. She had no idea who my mother was—what she had done in her lifetime, or how she had provided for us children before this last month.

The day after we moved into the apartment, I sat around playing with Wicho and thinking about our situation. This couldn't possibly be the best thing I could do to help. There had to be more.

So I came up with a plan. Every morning after my mother woke up and went off to work, I put some fruit and chunks of bread in my bag and left the house with Wicho in tow to go look for my father.

I started by going to the biblioteca pública on Tuesday and looking through their maps of the city. While Wicho played on the floor beside me, I copied the address and directions to every clinic and hospital in the area of the embassy. I outlined every route in my journal and formulated a strategy to visit them in such a way as to economize my time and effort. I didn't want to be all over the place. Planning was imperative.

Once I had all the information I needed, I set out on my search on Wednesday. As the days wore on, I walked with Wicho into every emergency room and sala de espera and talked to every clerk who would give me the time of day. Most of them were nice and looked through their records and told me he hadn't been seen there. Some of them were rude and told me to get out, but I wouldn't give up.

On Friday morning, Wicho had had his fill of adventure and was especially cranky as we walked to the last hospital on my list for the day. He started to cough. I touched his forehead, but he didn't have a fever, so I pressed on.

"I tired, Trella," he said when I shifted him from one hip to another at the corner in front of the hospital.

"I know," I said. "One last stop, and then we'll go home. Okay?"

"No," Wicho said, and he slapped me.

"Don't do that," I said, grabbing his little hand. "It's not nice."

"Nice!" Wicho kissed me on the cheek and laid his head on my shoulder.

I opened the hospital door and stepped into the white-walled interior. The scent of bleach and something else—something less fresh, like rancid medicine or illness—hit me, and I stopped for a moment. I'd been in enough facilities that I should have been prepared for the effect the repulsive scent had on me, but I wasn't.

"Do you take after him?" the young man at the desk asked when I inquired about Papá. "Is that why you've got those tiny little freckles on your nose?"

I wasn't in the mood to be toyed with, so I got a little smart with my response. "You've got it," I said. "I look just like him. Blonde hair, green eyes, freckles, thin lips. Everything about me is like him. Except my attitude. I have my mother's attitude."

The young man laughed and looked at me closely. "I don't know," he said. "We don't get a lot of men as pretty as you in here."

I rolled my eyes. Wicho and I were *both* too tired to appreciate his flirtation.

"What are you talking about, Alejandro?" a stout older woman asked as she came in through a door behind the clerk.

The young clerk turned around and faced the woman. "She's looking for her father," he said. "She says he looks just like her."

The woman picked up a pair of glasses from the desk and put them on. "Let's see here," she said. "Hmm. What's his name, sweetheart?"

"Joaquín," I said. "Joaquín del Toro."

"Yes," the woman said. "Yes. I remember him."

Suddenly the dimly lit waiting room with its blank walls and folding chairs, dead plants, and broken-down tables became the most beautiful, most welcoming place in the world. I had found him. In this dreary, malodorous place, I had found my father!

"Let me see. I know we have an address for him," the woman said, and she turned around and left the room.

Five minutes later, Wicho toddling beside me, I stepped out of the hospital clutching a piece of stationery with an address for Papá neatly written on it. I wanted nothing more than to run down the street, jump on a bus, and go find him right away. But it was too late to go there now. Wicho was exhausted, and Mamá was probably on the first bus back to the apartment. I had to get there before she did. Besides, I wouldn't want to find Papá without her. She needed to be there for the family reunion.

For a moment before I revealed the news to Mamá, I feared she might be mad at me when I told her what I'd been up to all week. But she wasn't mad at all. In fact, she was so happy to hear the news that she put her arms around my waist, picked me up off the floor, and twirled me around the room.

"Oh my god!" she said, looking at the paper with Papá's address on it. "I can't believe this!"

"Let's go," I said, pressing my hands against her thin cheeks and pinching them with excitement. Wicho had napped a little while we waited for Mamá to come home, so he was okay for some more running around. "Let's go right now."

"Yes," she said. She turned around and surveyed our shabby apartment. "My purse," she finally said. "Where did I leave my purse?"

I put my hand on her shoulder and pressed on the strap of her purse. "You're wearing it," I whispered.

She laughed, a merry, tinkling sound that reminded me of silver bells and music, and I thought of Christmas, of how we hadn't celebrated the holiday in any way this year. But now we could, because finally finding Papá was a Christmas miracle.

It was strange how absentminded Mamá became the minute she knew we were about to be reunited with Papá. Suddenly she couldn't remember where to take the bus or even when to cross the street. I felt like I had two kids in tow as we boarded buses and walked around looking for the address on the paper.

"This is it. This is the place," Mamá said. We were

standing in front of a modest home in a quiet little neighborhood off Reforma.

There was a huge difference between the house my father was renting and the dump of an apartment we were living in.

The stucco on this house was painted red, and it didn't have any holes in it. There was a winter garden along the little path that led to the front door, and the roof was made of those fancy curved bricks they call teja roja. The house was so nice that I wondered how he'd come to live there. Was it easier for a man to make money in Mexico than it was for a woman?

"Well, come on," I said, shifting Wicho in my arms. The sun was going down, and there was a slight chill in the air, colder than the last few days. Wicho coughed, and I pressed my hand on his forehead again. It felt a little warm, but not feverish.

Mamá stared at the pretty little house in front of us. She pushed her hair out of her face and blinked hard. "I told myself I wouldn't cry," she whispered.

"It's okay," I said. The sight of her about to lose control choked me up, and I cleared my throat. "Come on. Let's not draw this out. It's getting dark out here."

The woman who answered the door was very lovely. Her white hair was up in a chignon, and she was wearing a dark red shade of lipstick on her thin lips.

"Can I help you?" the woman asked in Spanish. She put her hand on her chest, and I saw that she was wearing a small gold ring with a yellow topaz in the center of an orange enamel flower. The ring matched her mustard-colored shirt.

"We're looking for my father," I said in Spanish. "They told us at the General Hospital that he lives here. This is the address he gave them when he was treated there."

"Your father?" The woman thought for a moment.

"Joaquín del Toro," Mamá said. "We are his family. I am his wife, Dulceña del Toro, and these are Estrella and Luisito, our children."

The woman hit her forehead, like she just remembered something important. "Oh! Yes, of course! The young man we found wandering the streets."

Mamá gasped and turned to look at me. "Wandering the streets?"

"Yes." The woman opened the door and stepped out to stand on her porch with us. "I am Señora Valdez-Uriega, señora. Anyway, he was coming up the street, up there." She pointed to the right. We looked to where she pointed. "And suddenly he fell. I called inside to my husband, and we ran out there as fast as someone our age can run. And there he was, flat on his face."

"He was hurt?" I asked.

Señora Valdez-Uriega nodded. "Oh, yes, very much so."

"That's what that telegram said." I looked to Mamá. "The one we got in Ciudad Juárez."

"Where?" Mamá asked the woman. "How was he hurt?"

Señora Valdez-Uriega touched her temple. "Right here, on the side of his head," she said. "He was bleeding, but he didn't know what had happened. He kept mumbling something about a train. We took him to the hospital and they admitted him. We put a deposit on his hospital bill so they would give him the care he needed without any fuss. They don't treat vagrants well. They throw them out if they can't pay. We thought everything was fine, but when my husband and I returned the next day, he was gone."

"Gone?" I asked. "You mean they threw him out anyway?"

Señora Valdez-Uriega shook her head. "No," she said. "He told the doctor he had to go to Tamaulipas and checked himself out. But he left us a very nice note, thanking us. I still have it in the house. Would you like to see it?"

"Yes! Yes!" Mamá and I said at the same exact time.

Mamá opened the envelope and started to read Papá's note as we walked away from Señora Valdez-Uriega's house. The note didn't give us much more information as to Papá's whereabouts than what the woman had already told us. But one very important, troubling detail made Mamá come to a complete stop and stare at me.

"He doesn't know who he is—where he came from. He only remembers his name!" Mamá said. The note trembled in her hands, and I took it from her. "Your father's lost his memory, Estrella."

I read the note quickly, speeding ahead until I came to the point where he explained his diagnosis. "It all makes sense now. Why Uncle Tomás hasn't heard from him."

Mamá's face blanched, and she looked like she was about to faint. "Thank God," she whispered.

"Thank God?" I asked. "Mamá, are you feeling okay? This isn't good news."

She took the note back and looked up at the sky above us. It would be dark soon. The sun was already setting in the horizon, giving the whole city an ominous feel. "Oh, but it is," Mamá said. "He's alive, Estrella. Your father is alive and heading home to Monteseco. Don't you see? Everything's going to be okay."

Señor y Señora Valdez-Uriega,

Muchas gracias por haber venido a mi auxilio. No tengo mas manera de pagarles por la gran amibilidad que me han extendido en rescatarme y traerme a este hospital. Estoy muy agredecido. Quisiera haber podido darles gracias en persona, pero no puedo quedarme un momento mas en este lugar.

El doctor me dice que he perdido parte de mi memoria, pero que probablemente esto es temporario. No se porque, pero tengo un presentimiento que debo de partir imediatamente para Nuevo Laredo. Anoche soñe que en ese lugar encontrare respuestas a todas mis preguntas. En ese lugar se me habrira el cielo. Las nubes se van a desvaneser y podre ver claramente las raices de mi existencia.

No me despido de ustedes, porque me comprometo con esta nota a regresar algun dia y pagarles con interes el dinero que han pagado de mi parte para asegurar mi bienestar. Que dios se lo multiplique en abundancia hasta el dia que yo se los pueda pagar.

Muy agradecido,
Joaquín del Toro

CHAPTER NINETEEN

I WENT TO BED THAT NIGHT AND let the tears roll down my face as I prayed for my father to find his way safely back to Las Moras. I must have fallen asleep soon thereafter, because sometime later I woke up to the sound of my brother coughing and crying in his cot beside my mother. Mamá was already up out of her cot at the stove, bringing out a battered pot a neighbor had given us earlier that week.

"Is he sick?" I asked. Guilt made itself comfortable in my heart as I worried about all the times I'd taken Wicho out that week. "It's my fault," I admitted. "I shouldn't have taken him out so much."

Mamá turned the knob on the kerosene lamp at the foldable table in the kitchen area and brought it closer to her cot. "It's more than that," she finally said. "His tongue is developing a white coating, and his throat is red. This isn't your fault." She sat on the edge of the cot and wrung her hands.

I left my lumpy cot and went to sit next to Wicho on Mamá's cot. He whimpered and fussed when I put my hand on his forehead. "Oh my god," I said. "He's burning up."

"I've been trying to keep the fever at bay with a wet rag," Mamá said. "It seemed to help at first, but then it came back full force. And even with the aspirin, he hasn't gotten much better. Please stay with him while I go out and draw some water for a bath."

Mamá bundled up and went outside with a bucket in tow to the communal pump. When she came back in, she poured the water into the pot on the old-fashioned wooden cookstove and stoked the fire until it was roaring full force. Then she went back out four more times, bringing in more buckets of water until the aluminum washtub sitting in the corner of the kitchen was halfway full. When the water on the stove was boiling, she poured it into the washtub, then tested it to make sure it was lukewarm.

We stripped Wicho down and put him in the tub. His cheeks flushed and his eyes watery, Wicho cried, wanting to go to bed, but Mamá kept pouring water over his head and shoulders gently with a tin cup. Sitting on the floor beside him, I sang every song he loved, everything from "Que llueva" to "El barquito chiquitito," but nothing seemed to help.

When Mamá finally pulled him out of the water and gave him another dose of aspirin, he cried and spat it out. She had to crush another small, bitter pill in the cradle of a big spoon and add some sugar and water, then forced him to swallow it down. The whole ordeal took most of the night, and by the time we lay back down, it was almost three in the morning.

Mamá lit the wick on a lantern and set it next to the bed, where she sat up holding Wicho, who had thrown up several times and now had a chill. "I cold," he kept saying as he burrowed inside a blanket cradled in my mother's arms.

"He's not getting any better," Mamá whispered when I sat up in bed and watched her rock Wicho. "I wish there was an all-night clinic close by where I could take him, but I don't know of any place like that."

"Do you want me to ask the neighbors? Doña Pilar next door is very nice," I said.

Mamá touched Wicho's forehead. He fussed and pushed her hand away. "No. It'll be morning soon," she said. "We can catch the bus on the first round of the day. With any luck, they'll see him quickly at the hospital."

"What about work?" I asked. "Won't they be mad? They wouldn't fire you, would they, like Venustiana did?"

"No, I'm sure they wouldn't," Mamá said. "Señora Montoya knows I have children. She has a phone. I'll see if the hospital will let me give her a ring to let her know Wicho's sick and I won't be in today. Go on, get some sleep. I need you to be alert in the morning. We don't want to miss the bus."

Mamá and I were second in line at the hospital, right behind a woman and her sickly teenage daughter, repatriates who had just gotten to Mexico City a few days before. Their Spanish was not as good as ours, and they were staying with family nearby. The girl was coughing a lot and she had a fever, but she seemed in good spirits. Wicho, on the other hand, was no longer just fussing. He was outright crying, saying his tummy hurt.

When we were in the examining room, and Dr. Benavidez lifted Wicho's shirt, Mamá gasped. Wicho had developed a rash over his torso. "That's new," my mother said. "He didn't have that last night."

The doctor pulled Wicho's shirt off and made him sit up so he could check his back. He pressed his lips together and shook his head. "What's wrong?" I asked. "What is it?"

"Scarlet fever," Dr. Benavidez said after he checked Wicho's tongue. He took off his glasses and put them on the desk in front him. "I'm not going to lie to you, Señora del Toro. Your child is very sick. I haven't seen scarlet fever attack a child this severely in a long time. I understand you're recent immigrants?"

"Yes," Mamá said softly. "We came in a few weeks ago, by train." Mamá also explained our time in Ciudad Juárez in the corral, sleeping outside in the cold before the train came.

"What kind of constitution did he have before you traveled?" Dr. Benavidez asked. "Was he a normal, healthy delivery? How was his health in the United States?"

After my mother explained Wicho's health issues, his propensity for colds, the coughs, the medicine, the tesitos Doña Luz was always having to make for him, Dr. Benavidez decided to hospitalize him.

"Oh my god!" My mother put a hand to her chest. "How could I let this happen?"

"This isn't your fault, Señora." Dr. Benavidez put the stethoscope over his ears and listened to Wicho's chest again. "Scarlet fever preys on the weak, and your son is very fragile. He does not have the fortitude to fight this infection on his own. The poor conditions you were subjected to before you got on the train, the cold, the lack of nutrients, it's all taken a toll on him. His system is compromised. I am worried that without proper care, he will not make it."

Dr. Benavidez had Wicho placed in a special unit in the hospital. I had to sit in the waiting area alone for a while until the doctor came to get me. As we walked down the hall toward Wicho's room, he explained visiting procedures to me.

"You mean we can't see him?" I asked Dr. Benavidez as we stood in front of a room with large windows. Unlike the hospital where I first found Papá's trail, this hospital smelled clean. The scent of bleach and antiseptic was everywhere. The hallways were well lit, and the floors sparkled. I felt good about having Wicho admitted into such a facility.

"Your mother can go in, of course," Dr. Benavidez explained as we walked. "She's with him right now. But it's best if you stay out of the room. He is contagious." He then explained that, as with polio wards, Mamá had strict washing protocols she had to follow to come into Wicho's room to avoid bringing more germs inside.

My mind reeled and my eyes burned. "But I can't see him?" I asked.

"You can watch him from here," Dr. Benavidez said as we stopped outside Wicho's room. Through a window set in the room's wall, I saw Mamá at his side. Wicho was lying back while a nurse tended to him. The doctor tapped on the glass, and Mamá looked up and gave me a half-smile. "He can see you, and you can see him, but it's really best for him to be isolated right now. We can't have him come into contact with any more germs, which you could bring in without intending to. His little body is working hard to fight this disease. I know it's difficult. You are his big sister, and you want to hold him. But we have to think of him first, señorita."

Mamá left the room and came outside. She hugged me and pushed my hair back. "I'm sorry you can't go in," she whispered. Then she pulled a handkerchief out of her purse, pressed it against the corners of her eyes, and sniffled.

"Don't be upset, señora," Dr. Benavidez said. "He will get better. It'll just take time. He'll be well taken care of here."

"Yes," she said. "I know. But you have to understand. He's only two years old. We've never been apart from him, and he's never been apart from us. This will devastate him."

I tapped on the window again, and Wicho turned around. When he saw me, he let out a loud cry and yelled, "Trella! Trella!" The nurse brought him over to the little window to take a closer look at us.

Wicho was still crying for me, so I put my hand flat against the window and made ojitos at him. "It's okay, Papito," I said. "I'm here."

"Children are resilient, señora. You'll be surprised how quickly he adjusts," Dr. Benavidez assured my mother. "It will likely affect you more deeply than it will affect him. When it comes to illness, it is often the parent of a small child who suffers the most. You must trust us to do what is best for Luisito. He will be well cared for here."

Doctor Benavidez was right: Wicho's illness did affect Mamá more than it affected anyone else. He was the only thing she thought about, the only worry she allowed herself to speak of. Long gone were the days of going to the American embassy and worrying about finding my father or grandparents.

Every day after I sent Mamá off to work, I packed a lunch and headed for the embassy. I sent Uncle Tomás daily telegrams updating him on Wicho's recovery. He sent me back daily updates, telling me he still couldn't get copies of our birth certificates.

Days after we took Wicho to the hospital, Papá hadn't made it back to Las Moras, and Tomás still hadn't heard from anyone else. He was frustrated and didn't know what else to do to help us.

Every day, Mamá joined me at the hospital after work. We'd stay there, she inside the room with Wicho and me sitting on a chair in the hall by his window, until they threw us out in the evening. Then we'd go back to the apartment to eat a late supper and head straight to bed so that we might do it all over again the next day.

On the way home one night, I saw that the neighborhood had changed around us. Everywhere I looked, people had started to line up their Christmas decorations. There were Nativity sets in all sizes and shapes in window displays, on porches, even out on lawns. Poinsettias were displayed on windowsills, beside front doors, and up along porch steps.

"Look," I said, pointing at a dog sitting on a porch with a wide collar on his neck in the shape of a poinsettia. "Christmas is here."

Mamá looked around like she'd just noticed where she was. Down the street, a group of people rounded the corner. They stopped in front of the first house and started singing,

> *"En el nombre del cielo,*
> *yo os pido posada,*
> *pues no puede andar,*
> *mi esposa amada."*

"It's a posada!" I exclaimed. "Listen, Mamá. Isn't that beautiful? Sing with me!"

Mamá's face changed. Her cheeks paled, and she began to shake. Then, she started sobbing, low, soft, heartbroken sobs that tore past her trembling lips.

"No," she said. "I can't."

"What is it?" I asked. "What's wrong, Mamá?"

"I can't do this, Estrella," she cried. "I can't. I just can't."

"It's okay." I reached out for her, but she slipped out of my arms and started trotting down the street, away from the merriment, away from me.

"Wait for me," I yelled, and I started off after her. "Mamá, please wait!"

I was out of breath by the time I caught up to Mamá, five

blocks down on the other side of the street, where she stood looking up at a broken streetlamp.

"I'm sorry," she said when I put my arms around her and pushed my face against her shoulder. "I shouldn't have run away."

"It's okay," I said. "Wicho's illness is taking a toll on us both. And it doesn't help that there's no good news coming from Monteseco. Poor Uncle Tomás. He's completely dejected. I can hear it in his messages. If only Papá would make contact. It would make things more bearable."

The night was cold and damp. I could feel the darkness penetrating my clothes, moistening my skin, and filtering into my lungs. I pulled the lapels of my mother's woolen coat up and folded them over the lower part of her face.

We started walking then. "Are you hungry?" I asked. "You should eat something. How about grabbing a cup of soup at that stand? Across the street, over there, see? He's got soup."

"I'm not hungry," Mamá said, her eyes downcast.

"It couldn't be much for a cup of soup, and you should really eat something to keep up your strength for work tomorrow," I continued.

Mamá stopped and turned to me. "I'm sorry," she said. "You must be starving." Then she touched my cheek. Her hand was pale and cold.

"We should both get something," I insisted. I pressed her hand between mine, breathed warmth onto it, and rubbed it vigorously to get her blood circulating again.

"Okay," she whispered. She reached into her pocket with

her other hand and pulled out a peso. "But nothing too big for me. Just a small cup, to warm up."

I took the peso and leaned in to kiss her cheek. It was cold too. Whether she realized it or not, she needed more than that cup of soup. "I'll be right back," I said. "Wait here."

When I had procured two steaming cups of chicken soup, I turned around to look for Mamá, but she wasn't across the street anymore. I scanned the sidewalk, left and right, up and down, on both sides of the street, looking for the long forest-green hooded coat the nuns had given her, but she was nowhere to be found.

Panicked, I crossed the street as quickly as possible, searching every direction. Mamá's face was a blank stare when I finally found her sitting on a bench in the cemetery down the street. The cup of soup I gave her sat in her hand untouched. No matter how much I begged her to eat it, she couldn't bring herself to put the spoon in her mouth.

"At least drink the broth," I urged, taking the spoon out of her hand and helping her lift the lid off the soup. "You need to eat. You don't look well, Mamá. Think of Wicho. Stay strong for him."

My mother sipped at her soup to appease me, but she didn't eat the measly pieces of chicken and vegetables at the bottom of the cup, saying, "You can eat that if you like. I'm done with it."

"The nourishment is in the broth," I said, repeating something Doña Luz used to say when I was being difficult and wouldn't finish my caldito at home.

"You should eat it anyway." My mother pushed her cup toward me on the bench. "Shouldn't go to waste."

I took the cup and tossed back the caldo dregs. There wasn't much there, so it wasn't hard to chew and swallow. I put the cups together, one inside the other, and waited for Mamá to gather herself so we could go to the corner to catch the next bus. But Mamá didn't move. She sat on that bench in the middle of that dark cemetery and looked out at the shadows of tombstones all around us.

"Mamá?" I asked after a while. "What are we doing here?"

My mother didn't look at me—she just focused on the graves. "I don't want any of us to die here," she finally said.

"We're not going to die." I swallowed hard at the idea of losing her.

She turned to me then, but her glazed eyes didn't quite look at me. "I could never go back if one of you was buried here."

"Then maybe we should get out of the cold," I said.

Mamá winced at my words. "I'm sorry," she said. Then she scooted in, sidling up to me on the bench until our bodies were touching. Putting her left arm around my shoulder and taking my hand in hers, she said, "I'm being terribly selfish right now, aren't I?"

I gave her a peck on the cheek. She was so cold. "Please don't cry," I begged, taking my handkerchief out of my pocket and wiping at her eyes. "Nobody's going to die. Wicho's all right. You saw him. He's fine."

"We have to go home, Estrella," she whimpered. "We have to get on a train and find a way to get back across the border.

We'll swim if we have to, but I'm not staying in Mexico any longer than I absolutely have to."

I nodded and pressed my handkerchief into her hand. "Yes." I kissed her forehead. "We should do that."

"As soon as possible," she said, putting her hands on my cheeks, anchoring me with her dark, wild eyes. "As soon as he's out. As soon as they give Wicho back to us, we're buying train tickets and heading north."

During the rest of the time Wicho spent recovering in the hospital, Mamá barely ate. I cooked whatever I could find in the kitchen, served her supper, and sat beside her at the table, encouraging her to eat as if she were my child and not the other way around. For her part, Mamá would move her food around on the plate with her fork and look out the window absently. When I begged her to go to the American embassy to see if either Papá or her parents had resurfaced, she would nod in agreement but forget all about it by the following afternoon.

On Thursday, December thirty-first, Wicho was officially out of the hospital. My mother, holding Wicho in her arms and grinning from ear to ear, looked like a skeleton. She was gaunt and pale, but with my brother's arms wrapped tightly around her neck, the brightness returned to her eyes.

"Thank you for our belated Christmas present!" she told Dr. Benavidez as she pressed Wicho's face to hers and planted loud, affectionate kisses on each of his cheeks. "He looks like an angel."

"Glad to be of service," Dr. Benavidez said. "Now, if you

would sign here. He's all yours. After you pay the bill, that is."

"You wouldn't keep him, would you?" I asked. "If we couldn't pay the bill?"

Dr. Benavidez took off his glasses and tapped his beard with them. "Hmm," he said. "I don't know. He does eat a lot. And he's got some kick! He's going to be a champion fútbol player. The nurses can attest to that."

"I know," I said, thinking of all the times he'd kicked me since he'd started walking.

"Where do we pay the bill?" Mamá asked.

At the direction of the doctor, we walked to the front of the hospital, past the front desk and took the hallway to the left, all the way down, until we reached the cashier's window. The window was outlined with papier-mâché decorations in the shape of angels, and there was a sad little poinsettia sitting in a tin cup on the desk.

As the cashier, a pretty young girl with too much rouge on her cheeks, said how much we owed the hospital, I thought I would faint.

"Can we afford that?" I asked my mother quietly, so as not to embarrass her.

My mother cleared her throat. "No," she said under her breath. "But what choice do we have?"

"You can pay half of it now," the cashier said. "If you don't have it all today."

Mamá let out a sigh of relief and said, "God bless you, child. I thought I was going to have to give you my firstborn in exchange."

The young cashier laughed, a loud, chuckling sound that made her whole body shake. "It's Christmas," she said. "You shouldn't have to give all your money away at Christmas. Just pay something toward the bill. Whatever you can afford. It's not like the hospital is going to shut down because one baby got sick."

"Merry Christmas," Mamá said as she handed over a small wad of money. "And thank you again."

On the way home, Mamá laughed at everything Wicho said on the bus. She couldn't take her eyes off him as he pointed at the buildings all decked out for the holidays. He was fascinated by the sights and sounds of Christmas in another country. He'd never seen so many Christmas artifacts as when we walked through the mercado to buy him a toy.

He touched everything he saw and could have stayed there and played all day, but Mamá finally convinced him to pick between a donkey and a rooster for his Christmas present. He picked the donkey and carried it with him onto the bus back to the apartment.

"He got fat," Mamá said as she bounced Wicho on her knee.

I touched Wicho's pink cheeks and stroked his dark hair. He pushed my hand away, snarled, and then grinned at me. "He looks the same to me," I said. "Same wickedness and everything."

"I missed my little cherub," my mother said, pinching Wicho's little hands. "¡Qué chulo, muñeco!"

"No, Trella! No!" Wicho squealed when I tried coaxing him out of Mamá's arms to sit on my lap. "Leave me 'lone!"

"But I love you, chiquito!" I said.

He squirmed and hid his face in Mamá's neck until he was sure I wasn't going to try to pry him away from her again.

NEW YEAR'S RESOLUTIONS

Just three this year, because that's all I can handle right now.

1. Take better care of my family, especially Wicho!
2. Find a way to get us back home right away! Beg! Steal! Borrow! Whatever it takes!
3. Be a better sister and daughter.

CHAPTER TWENTY

*I*F WE DON'T PAY THE RENT next week, will we have enough money to get two train tickets?" I asked Mamá from my cot across our apartment that night.

Outside, a series of firecrackers exploded and lit up the sky, sending sporadic rays of light through the bare window. They languished over her pillow, above her head, and cast dark shadows over her small face. "Yes," she said. "Señora Montoya gave me a Christmas bonus. And I didn't give them everything I had at the hospital."

"We should do it, then," I said. "We should go take a train and follow Papá to Nuevo Laredo. I bet if we ask enough people, we can get a lead on him."

"We can leave first thing in the morning," she said. "That way, he can't say we owe him anything."

A grin quivered to life within me. It crawled up to my lips and fluttered there for a moment. "What about Wicho?" I asked. "Will he need a ticket?"

Mamá shifted on her lumpy cot. It squeaked and squealed like a tiny violin. "No," she said. "He's a baby. He can sit on my lap."

"Or mine," I said. "He'll want to move around."

Mamá giggled. I could see the shadow of her smile curling itself upward. "He always does," she whispered, then yawned. "Go back to sleep. We'll need to get up bright and early to pack our things."

I thought about the things we owned. The things we'd carried here from the convent. The things we'd accumulated since: a suitcase full of worn used clothes, a rusty washing board, a tin washtub with a matching bucket, a set of chipped cups and plates, an old frayed towel, and three wooden spoons. Except for my clothes and schoolbag, I didn't want any of it.

"You're right," Mamá said the next morning when I refused to pack anything except our clothes and toiletries. "We need to travel light. This stuff can only get in the way. We need to move quickly."

The train was cold. We were packed tightly into our seats beside an old woman named Gloria. She smelled like old roses and rancid oranges, but the scent didn't bother me. I'd smelled so much worse in the last couple months.

Even though she was in good spirits, Mamá's cheeks were gaunt and pale. But her eyes shone brightly when she cast them on Wicho, who was looking healthy and happy since his release. He was taking the vitamins that Dr. Benavidez had prescribed. He was also eating well, because my mother made sure he ate his fill, even if it meant she took smaller portions of whatever we were having.

"Try to get some sleep," Mamá said, taking the cores of the apples we'd just eaten for breakfast and putting them inside the paper sack for disposal. "You'll want to sleep as much as you can now, because once we are off this train in Nuevo Laredo, we'll have to start looking for your father."

"I was thinking the same thing," I said. "He's not likely to know where to go or what to do, so he'll have visited many places and asked a lot of questions."

Mamá nodded. "He probably talked to half a million people by now. You know how gregarious he is." She pushed Wicho's wispy dark hair out of his face and kissed his forehead. "I'd like to visit a church at some point. La Parroquia de Nuestra Señora de Guadalupe is about half an hour from the international bridge."

"To give thanks and to ask Him to make Wicho all better," I said.

Mamá thought for a moment. "Yes. And to ask them if they can call your uncle Tomás to come pick us up after we cross over. We'll need protection from the people who made us disappear in the first place."

We had talked about it extensively the night before while we'd waited for the sun to rise: If we couldn't find Papá, if he'd already crossed over into Texas, we were going to brave the Río Grande. We'd have to scope out a good place to cross and then wait till night to actually do it. My uncle would have to be there to pick us up so we wouldn't get caught. It wasn't the best plan in the world. But we were willing to do it if all attempts to find Papá failed.

As I pondered all the *what-ifs* in our plan of action, a strange thought struck me, and I couldn't help but give it voice. "What if Uncle Tomás isn't around anymore? What if he was repatriated too?"

"Then we'll find someone else," Mamá said confidently. "We'll call on the Damas de Dios or Nina or Donna. We'll call whomever we have to call to stay there. I won't let them deport us again without a fight. What they did to us is unconstitutional. Your father and I won't be caught with the same net again."

My poor father. I could only imagine the terror he must feel, the overwhelming despair he must have been enduring, not knowing where he belonged. I hoped that whatever else was going on with him, he was healing and recovering his memory. I needed him to get better, not just for myself but for my little brother, so I closed my eyes and sent out a little prayer on his behalf. "I know you won't, either of you," I said.

"We will find our way home, Estrella," Mamá said as she closed her eyes and leaned her head back.

"We will," I whispered. "We'll find our way back to each other. I can feel it. Papá's been looking for us, Mamá. We're getting closer and closer to each other with every passing mile. We'll be reunited soon. You'll see."

As we traveled out of town, the scenery changed, and I started to see more and more familiar sights, the kind of things I would find when I got back to Monteseco: a pasture full of cows, a rooster weathervane sitting atop an old barn, and barbed wire—miles and miles of barbed-wire fencing.

That's when I remembered my favorite tree on our property at Las Moras, a massive oak, ancient and benevolent. Its golden center was pierced through by the barbed-wire fencing it had encapsulated, devoured—taken into its heart.

ALONG THE BARBED-WIRE FENCE

Along the barbed-wire fence, an oak has
matured. Its golden heart pierced by the barbed
wires of the barricade it has engulfed. Four lines
of barbaric fencing, swallowed up, imprisoned

within fifty rings of stout, slow-breathing
bark. The anchoring posts push and tug
with the passing seasons, but the oak is stoic,
unmoved—its heavy trunk incorrigible.

CHAPTER TWENTY-ONE

*I*T TOOK TWO AND A HALF days on a train and more than three hours on a bus for us to reach the frontera, but almost three full days after leaving Mexico City, we were standing in the plazita in front of the parish in Nuevo Laredo, the closest border town to Monteseco we could reach on our limited resources.

Before we went looking for Papá, we visited the sanctuario and filled every saint's ear with our prayers. We lit a great many candles and touched the Lord's glass coffin in the back of the church, begging him for his misericordia and protection on this, the most important step in our journey. We tried phoning Uncle Tómas, but no one answered at the parish.

When we left the church, Mamá went straight to the newspaper and put in a notice, a plea for assistance in finding our beloved father and husband, who was sick and needed medical attention. Then she bought two elotes on sticks, and we sat on a bench at the plazita, huddled together for warmth. We watched the people as we devoured our ears of corn, in case my father should be wandering around right under our noses.

"It's highly unlikely that we should chance upon him out here, out of the blue like that," Mamá said. "But stranger things have happened."

"I was thinking," I said. "If he had any kind of money, Papá would have bought food from a street vendor like we just did. He wouldn't have gone to a restaurant. He would have eaten what's out here. These people are out here day in and day out. We should ask if they've seen him."

Mamá chewed and swallowed the food in her mouth. Then she shook her head. "That would only work if we had a picture," she said. "Descriptions don't work very well. People see what they want to see. They remember strange things that color their perceptions. There's too much at stake to run from person to person. We need a better strategy. We need something tangible. If only we'd gotten ahold of your uncle. He could have come down here with one of those pictures he keeps at the parish."

"That's it!" I said. "We should get someone to draw a picture of him. There are artists who do that. They sit out here with their little drawing pads and ask if you want your picture drawn. Remember? We did that once, a long time ago, when I turned twelve and we came down here for the feria."

Mamá put her ear of corn down on the paper on her lap and shifted in her seat, looking down the street. "That's a possibility," she said. "We should ask around. See if there is such a person out here on a Sunday afternoon."

"Let's go!" I said. "I'll go this way and ask every vendor and store clerk down the street until I get to the avenida. Then I'll turn right and right again at the end of that block and make my way back around. You go that way and turn left down there, and we'll meet behind the plaza when we're done."

"No," Mamá said. "Whatever we do, we do it together. I can't afford to lose you too."

"Nothing's going to happen to me," I said. "And we can get this done quicker if we separate. We can cover twice as much ground if we do that."

"Don't ask me to do that, cariño," Mamá said. "Don't ask me not to worry, not to stop you from making mistakes. I'm your mother, Estrella."

I stood up and put my arms around her and kissed her on the cheek. "Ay, Mamá," I said. "You'll never stop being my mother. But you have to stop acting like I'm a little girl. In case you haven't noticed, I've grown up quite a bit the last few weeks. I found out where Papá went, didn't I?"

My mother sighed and pushed the hair out of my face, pressing it behind my ear. "Yes," she said. "You're growing up, but that started long before we got here. You've got your abuelita Jovita's spirit. Nothing is too hard or too hopeless for you. It's a great way to be in the world. Who am I to take that away from you?"

"Really?" I asked. "You think I'm like her?"

"In every way that matters." Mamá pulled on a strand of my hair as if the thought frustrated her. "Go on," she finally conceded. "Get going. I'll meet you behind the church in about an hour. Don't make me worry."

I took off down the street, asking every vendor I found if they knew of a person who could draw a picture of Papá just from my description. Most people laughed and just shook their heads. Some of them made jokes.

"Sí, pero nomás hago figuras de palitos," one man said. It wasn't funny to me to have him offer to draw me a stick figure of my father.

When I was hot and tired and about to give up, a disabled man sitting on a bench outside a small store front stopped me. "Was he tall?" he asked. "This man that looks like you."

The disabled man was missing his legs, so his plaid pants were folded under his thighs. But he looked comfortable and clean, so I knew right away he wasn't a beggar. He was just sitting outside, being neighborly.

"Yes," I said. "Yes, he is considered tall. He's five-eleven."

"That's tall," the man said. "What is his name?"

I told him, and he nodded.

"There is a tall man that works over there." He used his thumb to point behind him.

I looked back there, for some sort of business where my father might be of service, but all I saw were houses. Poverty-stricken, wretched little houses in need of repair. Then, farther down the road, I saw a cantina with a faded drawing of a giant beer bottle on the wall between the front door and a small barred window. I could tell by the lack of lights that it was closed for the day. There were no vehicles in the driveway either.

"I don't think my father would work there," I said hesitantly. "That's not quite his kind of place. Maybe when he was young, I don't know. But I've read his journals, so I don't think so."

The man, who'd introduced himself as Don Reynaldo, shrugged. "Well, he looks like you around the eyes and mouth. Kind of serious. Frowns a lot. Has strong opinions about things, and he's not afraid to speak his mind."

That sounded like Papá. "Does he talk with his hands all the time?" I asked.

Don Reynaldo grinned and nodded. "Never puts them down. Just full of energy and charisma. Charmed his way into a job the first day he got into town. Keeps the place clean—and safe. Nobody fools around in there anymore."

"You think he's there right now?"

Don Reynaldo shook his head. "No," he said. "Not yet. But later tonight, after seven. When the church people go home and turn in for the night. That's when Paula opens up for the others, the beer followers, the blind believers. That's when your father shows up to help. That's when she needs him."

I thanked him and ran for Mamá.

"A cantina!" Mamá looked like she was about to faint when I found her and told her. Her face blanched, and her eyes narrowed. Then she pressed her hand against the side of her lip and chewed on the inside of her cheek as she thought about it for a second. "No. Absolutely not," she finally said. "You can't come with me. You'll have to stay here. You can wait inside the church with Wicho where it's safe, while I go investigate."

"But that's not fair," I said. "I'm the one that got the lead on him. I want to be there when he sees you. I want him to see us together—you, me, and Wicho."

Mamá shifted Wicho in her arms and started to walk toward the parish. "We don't even know if it's really him," she said. "And a cantina is no place for a girl like you."

"But it's okay for *you* to go in there?" I asked, frustrated and angry that she couldn't trust me. "What are you afraid of? It's not like I'm going to suddenly start taking shots of tequila. Please, Mamá. Don't make this more difficult than it has to be."

Mamá took my hand and squeezed it hard. Then she brought it up to her lips and kissed it. "Come on," she said. "We'll light a candle and say a prayer. Because if that is him working over there, he's going to need some divine intervention."

After a while, we left the church to look for a place we might sleep for the night. There was a little hotel with decent rates a few blocks away, but Mamá wasn't ready to commit to anything.

"We'll only spend that kind of money if we absolutely have to," Mamá said as we made our way back to the parish. "If that's not your father in there, we'll come back and stay here. I'm sure by tomorrow we can get ahold of your uncle, and then we'll have other options."

When the time came, I took Wicho from her and cradled him high up on my shoulder, and we headed down the street. The cantina was dark and dank and smelled like urine and vomit. The rankness hit me like a sack of rotten potatoes, turning my stomach and making me want to run back out the minute I stepped through the threshold.

Heads turned as we stepped into the room. There were only half a dozen patrons in the cantina, but they all looked us up and down before they went back to their drinks.

A waitress put out the cigarette she'd been smoking on a small dish at the bar, uncurled her legs from under her stool, and stood up. Then she picked up a wet rag and came over to us. She leaned over and started wiping the top of a nearby table in slow, gentle circles. "Are you lost?" she asked in Spanish.

Mamá didn't answer her. She didn't have to, because at that very moment my father walked through a back door. His hair was longer, and he had a scraggly beard, but it was him. His attention was on wiping his boots on a siderail at the end of the bar, so he didn't see us standing there, holding our breath.

"Papá!" Wicho squealed, and my father froze.

"Papá!" I cried out, and I ran to him. He turned around then, his eyes shining, his lips moving, mumbling something incoherent under his breath.

I flew at him, wrapped my arms around his waist, and pressed my face against his chest as tears of joy and relief poured out of me. When I looked up at him, Papá's lips were trembling. They pulled back, like they were trying to figure out how to speak. Then the word he'd been trying to say came out: "Estrella?"

"Yes! Yes!" I cried. "That's me! That's my name, Papá! Do you remember me? Do you know who I am?"

"I do." Papá's face crumpled as if he couldn't hold his emotions back any longer. "I do remember you! And your brother too. I remember my Wicho!"

"Thank God we found you, Papá!" I said as he caressed my cheek with his fingertips. "We've been so worried."

He looked at my mother then, standing there, staring at him from across the room like she was made out of stone—a living, breathing statue. "Dulceña," Papá whispered. "Mi amor."

Mamá started shaking then. As my father released me and walked toward her, she rubbed away her tears with the back of her hand and swiped at her nose. "Joaquín!" she cried out as Papá hugged her and my brother to his chest.

He kissed her then, a long, full-blown kiss on the lips that made everyone in the bar cheer. The spectators whistled and hooted and clapped—a deafening sound that thundered around us as I walked over to join my parents.

We stood holding one another for a while before my father finally pulled back and said, "Come on, let's get out of here."

Papá took Wicho in his arms and took my mother's elbow. He steered us out the back door and escorted us out into the alley.

"Where are we going?" I asked as we exited the cantina.

"To my place," Papá said. "Josefa lets me stay up there as partial payment for my services." He pointed to a stairwell running sideways up to the second floor of the cantina.

"Services?" I asked. "What exactly are you doing here, Papá? This doesn't seem like a proper job for you."

"I stock up the bar, clean up the place, take out the trash—literally and figuratively, if you know what I mean," he said, motioning for us to go upstairs.

"No," I said. "I don't know what you mean."

Mamá patted my arm. "Never mind, Estrella. Let's get inside so we can talk in private."

I went up first, with Mamá following right behind me.

My father's little room was no bigger than the apartment we'd rented in Mexico City, but it was certainly nicer. There was a small kitchen area with a potbellied cast-iron stove in the center of it. To the left of the stove, there was a small kitchen table and two sturdy-looking wooden chairs. He didn't have any sofas, but he had a nice bed big enough for two people. Over the bed was a big quilt with a star pattern. It wasn't a fancy bed, but it certainly better than the lumpy, narrow cots we'd slept on.

As it turned out, Papá had a compelling story to tell. After his abduction, the men drove him all the way down to Matamoros, and he'd been put on a train immediately.

"I have a vague memory of it. They must have beaten me senseless in order to throw me on that train," he said. "Because I don't remember any of it. I'm pretty sure I lost consciousness and was out for a few days. Because when I woke up in Mexico City, I couldn't remember anything."

"You were out that long?" I asked, horrified. "The whole time you were on the train? Didn't anybody try to help you?"

"I was all alone in a boxcar," he said. "There wasn't a soul in there with me."

"Your parents were with you." Mamá put her hand on my father's arm. "They must have been, for you to come through it almost unscathed."

My father smiled and caressed my mother's hand. "Except for the memory loss," he said. "I knew my name, but there was a lot I couldn't remember. I didn't get my full memory back until I saw you just now. The doctors said it would come back eventually, when I least expected it, and it did. I heard m'ijo call out to me, and boom. There it was. All of it—like I'd never forgotten it."

Over dinner, which Papá prepared on his tiny wooden stove in his room, Mamá and I shared our plan to brave the river and have my uncle Tomás come pick us up in his car on the other side.

"He can do that. He won't have a problem with that," Papá said, nodding as he chewed and swallowed his fried potatoes. "We'll have to go out there tomorrow morning. Find a good place to cross—a shallow place. We can't afford to get Wicho wet. Not with everything he's been through."

I put down my fork because I remembered something. "What about that place I read about in your journal, Papá?" I asked. "You know, where you crossed down here with the horses you stole from the Rangers? You remember that? How you brought them to Mexico and gave them to the soldaderas?"

Mamá giggled, and Wicho laughed—a strange little sound

that sounded a bit artificial because he had no idea what we were talking about.

My father grinned. A bite of potatoes formed a funny-looking lump in his cheek. He squeezed my arm as he chewed, then took a swig of his coffee. "I do," he said. "I do remember that place. It's upstream from the ferry at Los Ebanos."

"That's an idea," Mamá said, pushing her empty plate away. "Do you think you can take us there tomorrow? To see if it's still safe?"

"Morrow!" Wicho squealed. "Morrow! Morrow!"

"Yes, tomorrow!" Papá took Wicho and lifted him up in the air, high over his head. "We'll go there tomorrow. Just a small family of four, taking a moment to enjoy the scenery on a short drive out through the countryside. Perfectly acceptable, I think."

My father lifted Wicho up in the air several more times, making airplane noises with his lips every time. Wicho squealed and laughed and made airplane noises too.

"Yes," I said. "Perfectly normal. But where are we going to get a car?"

"You let me worry about that," Papá said. "Now it's off to bed for both of you. I'll clean up the kitchen. We can sort the rest of the details in the morning."

Before lying down, I recited the small oración I'd composed to the Archangel Miguel when I'd visited his statue in the parish earlier that day. The Archangel Miguel was the Brave Conqueror, the fearless protector of children, and I felt the need to reach out to him before we set out the next day.

After praying, I lay in bed working through every scenario I could possibly think of long after my parents fell asleep. I listened to the blissful sound of their breathing and thanked my lucky stars that we had finally found each other. But I worried that our battles had barely started.

Papá could get us across the river, but what if the lawmen of Monteseco were keeping an eye on Uncle Tomás? What if they followed him, called the border patrol, and had us all picked up, including my uncle for attempting to assist us during our "illegal" crossing, even though we were American citizens?

There were so many things that could go wrong, and I'd thought of dozens of them already. *Go to sleep,* I told myself. *Close your eyes and count your blessings, or at least count sheep!* Although that had never worked for me. I had never been able to visualize sheep that needed to be counted. I doubted anyone could.

I must have fallen asleep at some point, because when I opened my eyes again, a thin ray of sunlight was flickering through the rough-sewn curtain of Papá's room. The wavering light danced in front of me, and I closed my eyes again.

Then a thought entered my mind, and I could actually see it unfolding, a solution to our dilemma—a way to ensure we wouldn't get arrested after we crossed. It was brilliant, and I couldn't wait to share it with my parents.

I threw back the blankets and looked down at the sleeping forms of my mother and father, curled up on the floor like two cochinillas while Wicho lay sprawled out beside me on the bed.

"Wake up, Papá," I said, shaking my father's shoulder. "We need to get you all cleaned up!"

"Huh?" Papá lifted his head and squinted at me through one open eye. "What needs cleaning up?"

I giggled. His thick blond hair was all matted and plastered against his skull on the left side of his head. "You," I said. "Now come on. Get up!"

I pulled on his arm, and he groaned. "No," he whined. For a moment he sounded just like Wicho.

"Come on," I said. "I have an idea."

My parents got up. Wicho needed to pee, so I took him out to the privy. As I stood looking out at the world around me, I realized that beyond the apprehension and the nerves, I felt hopeful. I had prayed so much that at some point I had transcended into confidence.

The sun was shining brightly, warming my cheeks, but the cold January wind numbed my lungs and face, reminding me of how cold the waters of the Río Grande would be when we finally got in it. Nevertheless, we couldn't let that deter us. If we found the right place, we could walk all the way across. We could bear those cold waters if we didn't have to swim.

"So I'm going to need a suit," Papá said after I told him the plan I'd concocted while they slept. He was sitting still in his chair in the center of the room, back straight, head thrown back, with a towel wrapped around his shoulders and neck while I shaved off his scraggly beard. He really had no business trying to grow a beard. It was patchy and rough and just didn't look right on him.

I moved the razor delicately over his chin and across his cheek. "Yes," I said. I whisked the razor around in the basin beside me on the small square kitchen table. "You need to be more than clean-shaven and bathed. You need to be well dressed. You need to sell it, Papá. If they believe you're Anglo, they'll let you just walk on through. You know. You've seen how they act with each other."

I tapped Papá's shoulder to let him know I was done. He pulled the towel off his shoulders and wiped his face with it. "I guess I could borrow a suit from Señor Ramírez down the street. He works at the bank, so he wears good clothes every day. He's a nice enough man. He'll let me borrow something."

Mamá, who was keeping Wicho busy on the bed while I helped Papá clean up, smiled and said, "It's not like you wouldn't be returning it. You could send it right back in the mail for him."

"There you go," I said, wiping the razor down and putting it back in its wooden box. "Now remember, it's important that you show up in that suit in Monteseco too. It's not just for crossing the border. You have to make sure they think you've managed to get the law on your side. To present yourself at the courthouse in a suit, asking to have copies of your family's birth certificates, would make it easier for you. The clerk's a young guy. He won't think to call the sheriff's department before you're out of there with the documents in hand."

Mamá nodded and chimed in. "He probably won't say anything until after you leave."

"But it'll be too late," Papá speculated. "I'll be on my way down to the river to fetch you by the time the sheriff's office hears about my reappearance."

He threw the water out into the street and wiped the basin clean before hanging the wet towel over a nail in the corner of the room. I put the shaving kit high up on a shelf over his bed where I'd seen him reach for it.

Mamá left Wicho playing with his toy donkey on the bed and came to stand in front of my father. She took his chin between her fingertips and inspected his freshly shaved cheeks. "There's the face I love." She stood up on her tippy toes and kissed his chin.

Papá pulled Mamá into an embrace. I flushed and looked down at the floor—I knew they were still deeply in love, but their lingering kiss wasn't something I saw very often. At home, where they had the room to wander off, they were more discreet with their affections. It didn't surprise me that they should want to kiss all the time now. They must have thought they'd never see each other again. I know I'd had my doubts along the way.

"Okay, you guys," I said. "That's enough. There are children in the room."

"You wouldn't be here if it weren't for such kisses," Papá teased.

Mamá's thin cheeks flushed bright red almost instantly. "Joaquín!" she cried. "You can't say such things!" She slapped

Papá's shoulder and pretended to push him away.

Papá threw his head back and laughed. Then he turned and winked at me. "She likes me. You know she likes me."

"Stop it," I said. "We have business to take care of. Now, where does this Señor Ramírez live?"

A PRAYER FOR PROTECTION

Bravest of all angels in heaven,
beloved Archangel Miguel, stay
with us as we brave the treacherous
waters of the Río Grande. Lead the
way with your mighty sword as we
face our greatest adversary. Steer
us clear of the precarious precipice.
Walk before us, light our path, and
protect my beloved family from
those who would clip our wings.

Chapter Twenty-Two

Señor Ramírez was very interesting. He claimed to have a love for the dramatic and spoke with an animated, cheerful tone of voice. His eyes sparkled with mischief when my father told him exactly why he needed to borrow a suit. And he clapped after I told him the story of how my father had stolen the Rangers' horses and crossed the river to deliver them to the soldaderas. He was so taken with our plan to get back to Monteseco that he did more than lend my father a suit. He wanted to help in every way possible.

"I haven't had this much excitement in my life since my family and I went to live in Montana. What a fiasco that was. You'd think they'd never seen a Mexican," he said when Papá asked him if he was sure he wanted to get that involved. But Señor Ramírez insisted that he be allowed to help us. The first thing he did was drive us out to the river to scope out the crossing point in his Ford sedan.

"I haven't been out here in a while," Papá said, looking out the window from the passenger seat. "At least a few years. But it's just a bit farther down the road, south of here, where the campesinos' wives wash their clothes on this side of the border."

"How far south?" I asked as Señor Ramírez crept along, driving on the road ever so slowly, a vuelta de rueda.

"Are there any landmarks we can look for?" Mamá reached into her pocket and handed Wicho his toy donkey.

"Not really," Papá said. "We'll know we've gone too far if we see the ferry that crosses over at Los Ebanos. There's a thick cluster of trees on this side of the river, and among them there's a huge tree that looks like a witch. The campesinos call it Llorona. A narrow dirt path to the right of it takes you all the way down to the river."

"There!" I said. "Is that it?"

"Yes," Papá said. "That's it. Turn left, Señor Ramírez. We're here."

As we drove through the village, people stared at us. Men touched the brims of their hats and nodded. Women stood at their doors, sat on their porches, or watched us from windows, and children stopped running around, lifted their heads, and gawked while they shaded their eyes from the sun.

"¿Van pa'l río?" a boy asked, running alongside the vehicle.

"Yes," I said in Spanish. "We want to look at it."

"They're going to the river!" the boy called out in Spanish to a group of women sitting on a porch. Then he stopped running and waved good-bye to us. I waved back. Wicho stood up and looked out the back window. I took his little hand and made him wave at the boy. He pulled his hand away, sat down, and went back to playing with his toy donkey.

Not long after that, we stopped the car and had to walk the rest of the way down a steep barranco. We could smell the water before we saw it. As we stepped carefully down an incline where the narrow dirt road became nothing more than a well-worn footpath, we heard the water gurgle and gush as the river moved south toward the Gulf of Mexico.

"Will you look at that," Señor Ramírez said as we broke through the brush and came upon the riverbank.

Mamá stepped forward to admire the view. "El Río Bravo," she said. "They don't call it the Fierce River for nothing."

"I don't think we're in the right place. It looks pretty deep," I said, thinking of my little brother and his delicate condition.

"Looks can be deceiving," Papá said. "Let's go check it out."

We walked along the riverbank, looking up and down the long stretch of land for signs of the women who were supposed to be washing their clothes there. "Ah, here you go," Papá said from a few feet ahead of me. He leaned down and picked up a sliver of soap. "See these?" He pointed at several other gray slivers of soap. "This is it. This is where they wash."

Mamá came up from behind me. She was holding Wicho's hand as he walked beside her, making his way slowly toward us by stepping on the bigger rocks on the edge of the water.

"We have to make sure," she said. "We can't just assume it's the right place."

"I can do that," Papá said, reaching down and unlacing

his boots. He tossed them off to the side onto a bed of light-colored pebbles. He took his socks off and shoved them inside his boots. "Be right back." He ran into the water fully clothed, hollering as he went. "Oh my god!" he screamed back at us. "It's freezing!"

"What did you expect?" Mamá yelled. "It's January, for God's sake!"

Whooping and hollering like a pup, Papá continued moving toward the other side. I suspected he was putting on a show for me and my brother, because he kept turning around and grinning at us.

The cold waters of the Río Grande never came up past his knees, but his pants soaked up the water, and before long he was wet all the way up to his waist. On the other side, he finally stood still. He put his hands over his eyes to shade them from the bright noon sun and surveyed the waters first to his left and then to his right. Then he turned around, waved, and gave us the thumbs-up.

When Papá came out of the water, Mamá was waiting for him with a fresh towel. He wrung out the legs of his pants, one at a time, while he was still wearing them. Then he toweled off his feet and put his socks and boots back on.

"Wish we had more time to spend out here," Papá said, standing up and looking out at the river. "It's the perfect place for a family outing."

"Not in January, it's not," Mamá said. She made Wicho stand up and dug the pebbles out of his fist because he didn't want to relinquish them. "Come on, Joaquín. Let's go. It's too cold for Wicho out here. We don't want him to get a cold. He's still pretty weak from the scarlet fever. And I don't know what happened to his vitamins. I had them in my purse, but then we got on the train and I lost track of them."

"Someone took his vitamins?" I asked.

Mamá frowned. "I must have misplaced them," she said. "I can't imagine anyone wanting to steal a child's vitamins."

"Some people will take the hide right off your back if you turn away from them," Señor Ramírez said as we started back to the car. "Can't trust anyone these days, and not just because they're bad. Your country's economic crisis is hitting us hard too. We depend on those American dollars on this side of the border."

We got back to Papá's room over the cantina and ate a quick almuerzo of salchichas con huevos. The sausage was spicy, and the eggs were soft and melted in my mouth. When we were done, Papá put on his borrowed suit and said, "I'll see you on the other side at midnight. Don't be late." Then he hugged and kissed us all and walked out the door.

At the window, I watched him jump into Señor Ramírez's car—Señor Ramírez had a visa and could wait on the other side of the international bridge for him. Once they joined up, Señor Ramírez would drive Papá to Monteseco and drop him off at my uncle's parish.

We waited around the apartment all afternoon, only venturing out to go to the privy because Mamá said we should save all our strength for the river crossing.

When she lay down and took a nap with Wicho, I tried

writing in my journal. But there was too much going on in my head, so I slipped out and went for a walk. I meandered over to the church, lit a candle, and prayed that my father had made it safely across. I wandered around the cold, empty church, visiting one santito after another, touching their feet after pressing kisses onto my fingertips, and praying.

At the altar of Nuestra Señora de Guadalupe, I found a vase full of white roses. *More winter roses,* I told myself. It wasn't so much odd as rare to see roses blooming in the winter here.

The roses were sitting in a modest crystal vase with enough water to keep them fresh for a while. I touched their petals and remembered a similar arrangement Mamá had put together at the last minute because a storm was coming and she wanted to save them from the freezing rains. That was my mother's nature, always trying to protect those who were unable to protect themselves.

After leaving the church, I walked down to the panadería and bought two fluffy conchas for me and Mamá and a marranito, a piggy-shaped gingerbread cookie, for Wicho, with the peso my father had given me when I shaved off his beard. He'd pressed the large coin into the palm of my hand and said, "Thank you, señorita. Your steady hand is much appreciated." I'd giggled and pocketed the coin because I'd been dreaming of buying a piece of sweet bread ever since I'd spotted the panadería the day before.

When I went back to the apartment, Mamá was awake and sitting at the table with Señor Ramírez. "Did he make it?" I asked. "Did he get across without any trouble?"

"Like a fish swimming downstream," he said. "He just swam right through customs. Just like you predicted, Estrella. No questions asked. Of course, it helped that he's wearing my best suit."

"Oh, thank you! Thank you!" I dropped the bread on the table and hugged Señor Ramírez. He smiled, a pursed little smile that made his eyes crinkle at the corners.

"No need to thank me yet," he said. "There's still the matter of getting the rest of you across. I'll be back tonight to drive you down to the river. Eat your pan dulce and get some rest. We'll see you at ten."

After Señor Ramírez dropped us off at the river, Mamá, Wicho, and I made our way down to the river's edge and took a moment to hold hands and pray together before we entered the water. I went first. Mamá followed with Wicho cleaved onto her right hip, folded safely within the crook of her arm.

There was a waning crescent moon overhead, so I couldn't see much. But I knew we were in the right place because Papá had marked the exact place we should enter the water with a stick buried into the sandy riverbed.

The river water was quick to flow into my shoes, soaking my socks and numbing my toes. "Chilly," Mamá said. She kept her eyes on the water at her feet. We shivered along, one treacherous step at a time. It didn't take long for my limbs to shake and my lips to start quivering.

"It's so cold," I said, my lips trembling as I tried to talk.

"Don't think about it," Mamá said. She pointed ahead.

"We're almost there. See? We just have to get to that willow tree. That's not too far."

We walked forward slowly, taking our time, until we were close enough to the willow to reach out and hold onto the branches to steady ourselves.

"We made it," I said.

My mother wrapped her arm around me and kissed my temple. "Yes," she said. "Yes, we did."

Then, as if the sun had suddenly burst through the horizon, the whole bank of the river was awash with light. Every muscle in my body tensed, and I looked up as three vehicles shone their lights on us. "You there!" a voice called out. "Come on out here. Come on—out of the water! Don't make me come after you!"

"What's your name?" a patrolman asked Mamá when he helped her out of the water.

"You don't have to answer that," I told Mamá.

Mamá turned around and nodded at me. "I know," she said.

"Have it your way," the officer helping me out of the water said. He put cuffs on me without asking any more questions. Then he tugged and tested them and used them to pull me away from the river's edge.

"Are you Dulceña del Toro?" the first officer asked Mamá.

"What?" Mamá looked shocked.

"Is this your daughter Estrella?"

I looked over at my mother who looked as shocked as I was. "Come on. We have your husband in the car."

We walked beside the two border patrolmen and saw that

they did indeed have my father in the back seat of one of their cars.

"I'm sorry," Papá said when Wicho, Mama, and I sat next to him in the backseat of the patrol car. "They're everywhere. I couldn't have avoided them."

"Don't apologize, mi amor," Mamá said. "You tried your best."

"That's not all," my father whispered. His voice was more than low, it was solemn.

"What is it?" I asked.

"Las Moras," he said, taking a deep breath and expelling it slowly. "It's gone."

Mamá gasped. "What do you mean, gone?" she asked. "The house burned to the ground, didn't it? I figured as much. Don't worry, Joaquín. We can rebuild it. And even if we can't—even if we're not allowed to stay, Tomás can rebuild it."

"He sold it," Papá interrupted Mamá. "The city owns it now. They knew Tomás needed the money to get us back, so they offered him a 'fair price,' and he took it. You must understand, he had to do it. He was desperate."

"I understand," Mamá whispered.

After a long silence between us, I asked, "Did you ever get copies of our birth certificates?"

Papá nodded. "They're in my pocket," he said. "But the patrolman wouldn't even look at them."

The driver of the patrol car started the engine. The officer in the passenger seat turned around and swung his arm over the seat. "You can show them to the captain up at the customs house," he said. "We just pick you up. They do all the sorting out up there. You understand?"

"Yes," Papá said. "You've said that. Three times. But I got it the first time."

FROM THE GARDEN

With leaves severed off their fragile
shoulders, their leaflets stripped from
their tender limbs, naked roses wilt.
Their creamy complexions blush

shamefully on white tablecloth. Later, up
to their ears in water, they tremble inside
crystal vases. Pale and perplexed, they
shiver—safe from an impending frost.

CHAPTER TWENTY-THREE

W E SAT TREMBLING IN A BLANK, barren room up at the customs office, Mamá, Wicho, and I. The officers had given us towels to dry off and blankets to wrap around our shoulders. But there was no comfort in knowing that we were about to be sent back to a country that was not ours. All my energy, all my courage, had dissipated. But I couldn't cry. My eyes were dry of tears, and I was numb inside.

Papá had been called in and out of the room to speak to customs officials about our immigration status. He told them everything we'd told him, from the fire to splitting us up to the corral in Ciudad Juárez and the train to our reunion, but he wasn't sure it was doing any good. It wasn't until early morning, when my uncle Tomás and our lawyer, Señor Alberto Luna, showed up, that things started to change.

"I got us a hearing in the morning with Judge O'Riley. I've known him for years. He's a fair man," Señor Luna said, tapping a brown folder on the table in front of him with his index finger. He needed to clip his fingernails. They were too long, and they made a scratching sound every time he emphasized the contents of his folder. "He's not going to deny the validity of these birth certificates. You and your children are US citizens, and as such you have rights. What happened to you was illegal. These trumped-up charges don't hold water. They were fabricated to get you thrown out of the country as quickly as possible, and they did it under cover of night without even a court hearing. But you have a right to a fair trial—a trial where you *and* your lawyer are present. I'm going to insist he reinstate your citizenship."

We weren't criminals, my family and I, but they still put us in a cell at the jailhouse for the rest of the night.

"At least they kept us together," Mamá said. She sat down next to me on my cot and set Wicho down on her lap.

Wicho started shaking and making funny noises in the back of his throat. Mamá touched his forehead and tried to get him to settle down.

"What's going on?" Papá asked. He left the window where he'd been looking out at the sliver of moon in the sky to come stand by my mother. "Something wrong with him?"

"I don't know," Mamá said. "He's drooling a lot."

Papá picked up Wicho and held him in his arms. "Hey, little guy?" He pushed my brother's dark hair back and looked into his eyes. "Talk to me, son."

Wicho started crying then. With his mouth full of saliva, he sounded like he might choke if he kept it up.

"It's okay, Wicho," I said, standing in front of them and

rubbing Wicho's back in circles, the way Mamá did when she wanted to soothe him to sleep. "We're okay. Don't cry, chiquito. Want me to sing you a lullaby?"

I started singing "Los tres cochinitos" for him, and slowly, Wicho stopped shaking so much. He stopped crying, and his breathing became more regular. "Again," he said when I stopped.

I offered him my arms, and he went into them. He curled up on my shoulder, and I sang him the song again as I paced the length of our cell. Papá sat down on the cot next to Mamá and wrapped her in his arms.

As I laid him down on the cot on the other side of the room, Wicho looked up at me and said, "I love you, Trella."

"I love you too, piojito," I whispered, and kissed him on the forehead. Then I sat down next to him gingerly, so as not to disturb him. I continued singing until he was completely asleep.

Mamá mouthed the words, "Thank you," from across the room when I signaled that Wicho was out for the night.

Papá lay back and crossed his feet in front of him. "I'm just going to rest my eyes for a moment," he said. But he was snoring within minutes, a light little whistle that made me close my lips tightly to suppress a giggle.

The next day, Alberto Luna presented our case in a front of a courtroom full of people. I didn't know why so many people were there watching the day's trials, but I didn't care. I was just glad we were finally being heard.

Judge O'Riley was a very old man with a very long, straight

nose, at the end of which sat a set of small, round spectacles. He had to lift his glasses often to read, before putting them back on to look out at us huddled together como golondrinas on the bench in front of him.

Alberto Luna had a lot to say to Judge O'Riley as he introduced the facts of the case. He had even more to say when he told of our trials and tribulations after our abduction—because that was what he called it, an abduction. He told the judge of our time in the Ciudad Juárez corral, sleeping with no blankets or shelter in the winter weather. He detailed Wicho's contraction of scarlet fever and the time we spent in the hospital, worrying about his survival. He told of Papá's beating and his time in the train, injured and alone. Mr. Luna left no detail out, and then he summed up how every single thing he mentioned should not have happened to US citizens.

"Now, I know that it is common that children as old as Estrella and even as young as little Luisito here be left behind with a trustworthy family member when their parents are 'repatriated,'" Alberto Luna argued. "But we urge you not to break up this family. We ask that you to take a careful look at all the evidence. There was never a real trial—or any trial at all. And since there were never any grounds for the repatriation of the del Toro family to begin with, I ask you to uphold Joaquín and Dulceña del Toro's US citizenship so that they might remain here with their children, where they most certainly belong."

Judge O'Riley pursed his lips for a moment and shuffled the papers in front of him. He cleared his throat several times, and then he said, "While I see that the children are US citizens, I have to consider the validity of the charges against their parents of violating the Immigration Act of 1924 before I make a decision. I am going to take a recess to look over the case more closely, make some telephone calls, decide what to do. But before I go into chambers, I have to ask Brother Tomás del Toro here if he is indeed willing to take the children in if I rule against the parents? Can you, sir, make sure your niece and nephew are well taken care of? That you take them to visit their parents regularly and stay connected to them?"

Why would the judge even consider separating us?! I was about to stand up and tell him that I did not want to stay in the United States without my parents when Wicho started to shake again.

I tried whispering to him, saying, "Calm down, baby. It'll be okay," but Wicho's whole body tensed up. He threw his head back and started making those guttural little noises again. His little neck was taut, rigid, and his eyes had rolled to the back of his head as his body shook more and more violently with every passing second.

Papá grabbed him. He pulled Wicho's eyelids open and cursed under his breath. "A doctor!" he yelled out into the courtroom. "Is there a doctor nearby?"

"Wicho! Papito! It's okay! It's okay!" I kept saying. I felt completely helpless as I watched Papá hold Wicho against his chest. But no matter how much I called out to him, Wicho's tiny body shook uncontrollably.

"I'm a physician," a young man said, tapping my shoulder.

I moved out of his way and backed up so that he could get in and tend to my brother. "Hold him still for a moment."

As the young doctor examined my brother, Wicho made pained grunting noises that told me he was trying to fight this thing that had ahold of him, but he couldn't do it. Not all by himself.

"Please, doctor," Mamá cried from behind me, "what's wrong with him?"

The young physician set Wicho down on the bench on his side and held him steady with his hands on his arm. "He's having an epileptic attack. How often does this happen?"

Papá looked to my mother for the answer. "Just once before," Mamá said.

"Very late last night," I said.

Then, to everyone's relief, Wicho stopped shaking, and his body began to relax. The tiny muscles of his neck softened and smoothed out. He opened his eyes and looked straight at me. Then he took a deep, staggered breath and cried out as he exhaled. "Trella!" he called in a scared little voice.

"It's okay. I'm right here, chiquito," I whispered, taking his little hand and massaging his palm with my thumb. "How do you feel? You want some water?"

Wicho shook his head. "I tired," he whispered, closing his eyes.

"He'll want to sleep now," the physician said. "I suspect the ordeals of your travels have taken a toll on him."

Wicho opened his eyes and lifted his arms. "Trella," he called out. I looked to the physician for permission to hold him.

"Is he going to be all right?" Judge O'Riley finally asked, and we all turned around to look at him. He'd left his bench and was standing a few feet away from us.

The doctor turned around and looked at the judge. "Yes," he said. "This is the result the bout of scarlet fever, complicated by malnourishment and stress." Then, turning to my parents, he said, "He needs to be treated immediately."

Judge O'Riley patted his belly. He pressed his lips together and nodded. Then he said, "Very well. We'll take a recess then. Father Tomás, can you take the child to the doctor's office? I'll try to move things along quickly here, but I don't think the child should have to wait for me to rule before he receives the care he needs."

My uncle jumped up and swooped Wicho into his arms. "I'll take care of him. I promise," he told my parents as he followed the doctor out the door at the back of the courtroom.

The judge turned away, but before he walked off, I stood up and called out to him. "Judge O'Riley, can I say something?"

The judge raised his eyebrow and looked around the courtroom. "Make it quick, young lady. I've got a docket full of cases that need my attention."

"I just want to say that this wouldn't have happened to my brother if we hadn't been abducted and deported to Mexico," I said. "My brother has always had a weak constitution, but having to starve in a corral in the middle of winter, being exposed to the elements and the waste of people living in filth, well, that just made it worse. It's a miracle he survived the ordeal. He almost died of scarlet fever in Mexico City because he was exposed to all manner of disease in that corral. Sending us back to Mexico, where we would continue to struggle to survive, would be dangerous for my little brother, but separating our family would be worse for him. It would devastate him. I beg you, let us stay here together. Please—give us back our lives."

Judge O'Riley's eyes brightened a little, and he sighed. "I can see you love your family very much."

"I do," I said. "They're all I've got."

The judge nodded. "Thank you, young lady. I will take your impassioned words under advisement. You folks sit tight. We won't be long. Mr. Luna, I'd like to see you in my chambers for a moment."

I clung to Mamá's arm the entire twenty-eight minutes it took Judge O'Riley and our lawyer to come out of chambers. When court reconvened, the judge took his seat and addressed everyone. "I have been a judge in this great country of ours for more than forty years, and in that time I have had to make some pretty hard decisions—decisions that I wasn't always proud to make, decisions which still keep me awake at night because they were based on laws that weren't always fair and just to the people involved. But as an old man about to retire, one with one foot out the door and the other one in the grave, I can honestly say I've had about as much nonsense as I can stand. And I'm just not willing to add this verdict to my long list of regrets—I refuse to rule in favor of a mandate that, because of its very nature, hurts children by leaving them either homeless or orphaned. So it is the order of this court that the charges of improper entry against Joaquín and Dulceña del Toro be dropped and that their citizenship in this country be acknowledged. That they be released immediately so that they may take care of their children with the freedom and liberty afforded all citizens of this country."

The gavel hadn't even hit the judge's bench before people in the courtroom began to whistle and cheer. Papá and Mamá hugged each other. Albert Luna grinned. Papá wiped at his eyes. "I never doubted it for a minute," he said, hugging me to his chest. "Dios mío, but I'm crying."

"Crybaby," I said to him, and we all laughed, a sad little laugh that said we knew that despite our victory, it was still a sad day for the hundreds of thousands of people who were still destitute and unwanted in a foreign country that didn't trust their American ways.

My family had lost more than our home and our land. We had lost my grandparents. That would have to be the next step for us after making sure Wicho received proper medical care—finding and bringing Abuelo Rodrigo and Abuelita Serafina back to Texas. We'd also have to find out what happened to Doña Luz and her family, make sure they were okay. But that would take time and money, both of which were in short supply. How long would my grandparents be able to survive, if they had received the same treatment we had?

As for myself, I could only feel grateful that my parents, Wicho, and I had survived. The house, the land—that could be regained or replaced. We had each other. We were together again, and that's what mattered most in the world.

TOO LATE

Too late the prickly pear decides to
grow tough skin and thorns outside.
For in its youth, when sun was high
and water low, its tender heart was soft,

exposed. Now, the sun's hot licks
and water's wicked whip have
made it hard, and crude, and thick.
And trapped within it years of abuse.

Dear Abuela Jovita,

Today is Día de los Tres Reyes Magos—Three Kings' Day! The most fortunate day of the year. This morning we passed by our lost property for the last time as we drove out of town. I took up my pen and wrote a poem about the cactus that's been blooming and thriving at the gates of Las Moras since before I was born.

I thought of you when I wrote it—not because you were anything like that prickly pear, but because it is a miracle that you weren't. It is a miracle that despite all the things that went wrong in your world, you stayed loving and kind not just to your family but to your people. I hope I never grow thorns or become so tough, so hardened by life, that I lose touch with my true self—my identity as a mexicana, a loving, courageous woman!

Thank you for staying with me throughout this long journey. And thank you for watching over us and listening to the rantings and ravings in this journal. I want you to know I couldn't have survived our ordeal without you. Your love for our family carried me through. You are my inspiration in life. You are mi fortuna!

Love always,
Your granddaughter,

Estrella

AUTHOR'S NOTE

WHILE I WAS RESEARCHING THE INJUSTICES inflicted upon mexicanos and Mexican Americans in the summer of 1915, a period known as La Matanza, for my first historical novel, *Shame the Stars*, I stumbled upon the topic of repatriation (a gentle euphemism for "deportation"). I am referring specifically to the deportation of mexicanos in the 1930s.

Although the subject matter was unrelated to La Matanza and I should have moved on to other sources, I couldn't stop myself. I sat at my desk and read in awe about the deportation of over one million Mexicanos—six hundred thousand of them American citizens—and I knew immediately that I had a sequel on my hands. I knew that this was the struggle that would befall the next generation of the del Toro family in Monteseco, Texas.

The topic of deportation of undocumented immigrants in America is nothing new. Those of us who live on the border between Mexico and the United States have heard about the issues surrounding immigration and deportation all our lives. But this remains a highly controversial subject, one mired in the social and political issues that surround it.

The raids, roundups, and removal of mexicanos conducted by Immigration and Customs Enforcement (ICE) agents in recent years have divided many people in this troubled region—so much so that I, like many teachers in Texas, have had classrooms with several empty desks, because parents were afraid to send their children to school. Raids, roundups, and unconstitutional deportations: None of this is new. What is also not new, but what I find completely unacceptable, is the fact that most Americans still do not know that we've done this many times before.

The US government has a history of systemic deportation of "Mexicans" in our country. In the 1950s, the Eisenhower administration brought about "Operation Wetback," and the George W. Bush administration in the 2000s began yet another wave of deportation that has flowed through time, targeting, rounding up, and sending mexicanos back to Mexico well into the present day.

It is important to me as a Mexican American author to write about repatriation, because the majority of American students sitting in classrooms today are unaware that most of the mexicanos who were repatriated in the 1930s were in fact US citizens, born and raised in this country. Many of these deported US citizens did not even speak Spanish. They weren't allowed to speak their native tongue in American schools. To do so meant a lashing. However, the government did not care that these "Mexicans" were US citizens who considered themselves American.

How did these Mexican US citizens fare in Mexico, a country they did not know—did not recognize as their own? They were lost. They were forgotten. They were destitute. The living conditions in Mexico were horrendous. There are accounts of people being harassed, persecuted, herded like cattle, and made to sleep on the ground among thousands of other repatriates while waiting for a train to take them into the interior of Mexico. Some who had reached their destination, an empty patch of land afforded them by the Mexican government, slept huddled under a tree with their children before they were able to build a shelter for their families.

Starvation, deprivation, disillusionment—these were the things that awaited more than a million mexicanos in Mexico in the 1930s. What was most frustrating to them was the knowledge that they had been forced to leave homes outfitted with all the amenities they had worked so hard to obtain to go live like animals in open fields or rat-infested ghettos in "the land of their forefathers."

Although I did a lot of research on the subject of repatriation during the 1930s, I had to find ways of incorporating those facts, and that's where the art of fictionalizing historical events came into play. I took inspiration from the books and articles I read as well as first-person interviews on YouTube. The small mention of two thousand repatriates huddled together in the winter of 1931 in a corral behind the customs house in Ciudad Juárez in Francisco E. Balderrama's 2006 book, *Decade of Betrayal: Mexican Repatriation in the 1930s*, outraged me, and I knew that the incident needed to become a scene in my novel. But I had no details of that occurrence, so I had to put myself in that position, envision the environment, create the scenes, give voice to the characters as best I could. I had to recreate it if I was going to bring the injustice of it all to light.

Throughout the creative process, I asked myself some hard questions. *What is important here? Why do I need to depict this or that incident?* And at the heart of it all was my need to tell the truth intertwined with my frustration at the inhumane treatment of mexicanos and the demoralization of an entire group of people—mi gente. The YouTube video, "Deportation of Mexican Americans During the 1930s," uploaded by the California-Mexico Studies Center, in which a woman explains how she and her family were ordered to walk on trays of disinfectant before entering Mexico (so that they would not infect the cattle) appalled me, and I knew I had to find a way of weaving that deplorable act into my novel too.

I think the circumstances surrounding the repatriation of mexicanos in the 1930s need to be shared with readers, especially young readers in schools, because they do not know about this part of our American heritage. Like La Matanza, the repatriation of mexicanos in the 1930s is not in our American social studies books.

My hope is that teachers will look upon this companion to *Shame the Stars* as a means to open up more conversations into topics that are important and relevant in our society.

Deportation, then and now, must be discussed in schools. Students need to inform themselves as to the issues that affect their peers, their neighbors, and their homeland. To remain ignorant of the inequalities of the past is to learn nothing from our mistakes and to perpetuate the cycle of injustices. I hope this book opens up minds and hearts. I hope this book helps us fight prejudice and social inequality. I hope this book helps us heal and become whole.

FOR FURTHER READING

Books:

Francisco E. Balderrama and Raymond Rodríguez. *Decade of Betrayal: Mexican Repatriation in the 1930s.* Revised ed. Albuquerque: University of New Mexico Press, 2006.

Vicki L. Ruiz. *From Out of the Shadows: Mexican Women in Twentieth-Century America.* Oxford: Oxford University Press, 2008.

Fernando Saúl Alanís Enciso. *They Should Stay There: The Story of Mexican Migration and Repatriation During the Great Depression* (Latin America in Translation/en Traducción). Chapel Hill: The University of North Carolina Press, 2017.

Online:

Francisco Balderrama, "America's Forgotten History of Mexican-American 'Repatriation,'" interview by Terry Gross, *Fresh Air*, NPR, September 10, 2015: npr.org/2015/09/10/439114563/americas-forgotten-history-of-mexican-american-repatriation

Robert R. McKay, "Mexican Americans and Repatriation," *Handbook of Texas Online.* Texas State Historical Association: tshaonline.org/handbook/online/articles/pqmyk

Araceli Cruz, "Mexican Repatriation During the Great Depression, Explained," *Teen Vogue*, August 30, 2017: teenvogue.com/story/mexican-repatriation-during-the-great-depression-explained

Videos on YouTube:
Democracy Now!. "Decade of Betrayal: How the U.S. Expelled Over a Half Million U.S. Citizens to Mexico in 1930s," February 28, 2017: youtube.com/watch?v=g9V7QDgW9mo

"Deportation of Mexican Americans During the 1930s," interviews uploaded by the California-Mexico Studies Center (CaliforniaMexicoCtr): youtube.com/watch?v=UE9DbivsjkE

GLOSSARY

abuelo / abuela (ah-BWEH-lah/ah-BWEH-lo): grandfather / grandmother

abuelito / abuelita (ah-bweh-LEE-to/ah-bweh-LEE-tah): a more endearing form of grandfather and grandmother

aduana (ah-DWAH-nah): customs / Mexican border crossing station

amiguitas (ah-me-GHEE-tahs): young female friends

anacahuitas (ah-nah-cah-oo-WEE-tahs): Texas wild olive, an ornamental tree

¡Ándale! (AHN-dah-leh): Go!

aquí (ah-KEE): here

atole de arroz (ah-TO-leh deh ah-RROS): sweetened rice porridge

atole de maizena (ah-TO-leh deh maee-ZEH-nah): sweetened cornstarch porridge

arrurrú (ah-rroo-RROO): lullaby

a vuelta de rueda (ah VOOEHL-tah deh ROOEH-dah): slowly, like the gentle turning of a wagon wheel

bendición (behn-dee-SEEON): blessing

bestias (BEHS-tee-ahs): beasts

biblioteca pública (BEE-bleeo-teh-cah POO-blee-kah): public library

bienvenidos (bee-EHN-veh-nee-dos): welcome

bizcochos (bees-KO-chos): biscuits, sweet treats, cookies

bolillo (bo-LEE-yo): bread roll; sometimes large, sometimes small, and shaped like a wide French baguette

buenas noches (BOOEH-nahs NO-chehs): good night

buitres (BOOEE-trehs): vultures, scavenger birds

caldo / caldito (KAHL-do / kahl-DEE-to): broth soup, usually including vegetables and chicken or beef; caldito is a small portion

campamocha (kahm-pah-MO-chah): praying mantis

carancha (kah-RAHN-chah): owl; in Brazil, a scavenger bird; in this context it is used in its slang form, meaning "fierce" or "a real fighter"

cariño (kah-REE-gno): beloved

Catedral de Nuestra Señora de Guadalupe (kah-teh-DRAHL deh noo-ehs-TRAH seh-NYO-rah deh gwah-dah-LOO-peh): the Cathedral of Our Lady of Guadalupe

cenizos (seh-NEE-zos): a medium-sized ornamental shrub with delicate silvery to gray-green leaves and a profusion of purple blooms

certificado de residencia (sehr-tee-fee-KAH-do deh reh-see-DEHN-see-ah): a document that asserts that a person can and does reside in a particular territory in Mexico (several other Latin American countries also use them)

champurrado (chahm-poo-RRAH-do): a traditional chocolate drink thickened with ground maize flour and spiced with cinnamon, cloves, and star anise

chanclas (CHAHN-klahs): any of a variety of sandals from flip-flops to wedges to slingbacks

chimenea (CHEE-meh-neh-ah): chimney

chiquito (chee-KEE-to): little one, baby

chivas (CHEE-vahs): goats

cochinillas (ko-chee-NEE-yahs): cochineal bugs; in South Texas they are often called roly-polys

colonia (ko-LO-nee-ah): neighborhood

comadres (ko-MAH-drehs): female friends, neighbors, or godmothers to another's child

comal (KO-mahl): a smooth, flat iron skillet or griddle typically used to cook tortillas on the stovetop

como (KO-mo): like

cómo (KO-mo): how

¿Cómo te llamas? (KO-mo the yah-mahs): What's your name?

compadres (kom-PAH-drehs): male friends, neighbors, or godfathers to another's child

conchas (KON-chahs): a sweet pastry that looks like a seashell

con permiso (kon pehr-MEE-so): Excuse me

consejo (kon-SEH-ho): advice

corazón (ko-rah-ZON): dearest, sweetheart

corrido (ko-RREE-do): a narrative folk song, usually to commemorate a hero or victory

cuchillo (koo-CHEE-yo): butcher knife

cuerda (KOOEHR-dah): rope

cuñado (koo-NYAH-do): brother-in-law

Damas de Dios (DAH-mahs deh dee-OS): Ladies of God

desaparecidos (deh-sah-pah-reh-SEE-dos): the disappeared; missing persons

Día de los Tres Reyes Magos (DEE-ah deh los trehs rey-yehs MAH-gos): Three Kings' Day, January 6, a day to celebrate the Nativity story of the three kings, or Three Wise Men (Melchior, Gaspar, and Balthazar)

¡Dime! (DEE-meh): Tell me!

Dios mío (deeos MEE-o): My god

Don / Doña (DON/DO-nya): Mr. / Mrs.

donas (DO-nahs): doughnuts

el más picudo siempre sale adelante (ehl mahs pee-COO-do see-EHM-preh sah-leh ah-deh-LAHN-teh): slang derogatory phrase, roughly translated to "the most conniving one always gets ahead"

elotes (eh-LO-tehs): ears of corn

espinas (ehs-PEE-nahs): thorns

esposos (ehs-PO-sos): husbands

está bien (ehs-TAH bee-ehn): very well; that's good

farmacia (fahr-MAH-see-ah): pharmacy

fideo (fee-DEH-o): thin noodle

frontera (fron-TEH-rah): border (in this context, it is referring to the US/Mexico border)

galletitas (gah-yeh-TEE-tahs): small cookies

gobierno (go-bee-EHR-no): government

güelo / güela (GWEH-lo/GWEH-lah): grandfather/grandmother

güelito / güelita (gweh-LEE-to/gweh-LEE-tah): a more endearing form of grandfather and grandmother

golondrinas (go-lon-DREE-nahs): swallows, a species of small, singing birds

grupitos (groo-PEE-tos): little groups

hija mía (EE-hah MEE-ah): my daughter

hormiguitas (or-mee-GHEE-tahs): tiny ants

ideando (ee-deh-AHN-do): having fanciful thought, daydreaming

jacalitos (hah-kah-LEE-tos): hovels, poor dwellings, huts, shacks

jacaranda (hah-kah-RAHN-dah): a fast-growing ornamental tree with a profusion of small purple blossoms

jarro (HAH-rro): pitcher

La Mano Pachona (Lah MAH-no pah-CHO-nah): the hairy hand (or claw); a common antagonist in Mexican folktales, the disembodied hand is often used to scare little ones who won't go to sleep

La Parroquia de Nuestra Señora de Guadalupe (lah pah-RRO-kee-ah deh NOOEHS-trah seh-NYO-rah deh GWAH-dah-loo-peh): the Parish of Our Lady of Guadalupe

lechuza (leh-CHOO-zah): owl; in folktales this is often a witch who turns into an owl and takes flight at night

librería (lee-breh-REE-ah): bookstore or bookshop

Llorona (yo-RO-nah): the Weeping Woman; in folktales Llorona is said to have drowned her children and thereafter was cursed to wander the earth, roaming along river banks looking for them, crying out, "Oh, my children! Where are my children?" Children are often told that she will take them away if they don't behave.

luchador (loo-chah-DOR): wrestler

marranito (mah-rrah-NEE-to): a sweet bread made with molasses and shaped like a piggy

Matanza (mah-TAHN-zah): the slaughter; in this context, a reference to the summer of 1915 when Texas lawmen waged war on the "rebellious" mexicanos living in South Texas, specifically the valley along the US/Mexico border, for the purposes of eradicating them and taking control of their properties for the newly arrived Anglos

mercado (mehr-KAH-do): market square, where goods and produce were sold by local vendors, usually located in the center of town

merienda (meh-ree-EHN-dah): a snack in the middle of the afternoon, between lunch and dinner.

mi amor (mee ah-MOR): my love

m'ija (MEE-hah): contraction of "mi hija," which translates to "my daughter"

m'ijo (MEE-ho): contraction of "mi hijo," which translates to "my son"

misericordia (mee-seh-ree-KOR-dee-ah): mercy

mojados (mo-HAH-dos): derogatory term for an undocumented person, which implies they swam across the Río Grande to cross the US/Mexico border

monte (MON-teh): forest or the woods

muy (MOO-eh): much

navaja (nah-VAH-hah): knife or blade

niño (NEE-nyo): little boy

¡No habra otra matanza! (no ah-BRAH O-trah mah-TAHN-sah): There will not be another slaughter!

¡No te dejes—correle! (no teh DEH-hehs—KO-rreh-leh): Don't give in—run!

¡Otra vez! (O-trah vehs): Again!

oración (o-rah-see-ON): prayer

pa fuera (pah FOOEH-rah): out

panadería (pah-nah-deh-REE-ah): bakery

pan dulce (pahn DOOL-she): Mexican sweet bread

Papito (pah-PEE-to): little one (boy)

¡Para alla! ¡Muevanse! (pah-rah ah-YAH moo-EH-vahn-seh): That way! Move!

Para el nene (pah-rah ehl NEH-neh): for the baby boy

¡Parecen avispas desquiciadas! (pah-REH-sehn ah-VEES-pahs dehs-kee-see-AH-dahs): They look like demented wasps!

perdon (pehr-DON): pardon me

piojito (pee-o-HEE-to): baby louse; in context it is meant as an endearment

plazita (plah-SEE-tah): a small city square, a place for socializing in town

¡Por aqui! (por ah-KEE): through here

presentese (preh-SEHN-teh-seh): identify yourself

primitas (pree-MEE-tahs): little female cousins

¡Que chulo, muñeco! (keh CHOO-lo moo-NYEH-ko): What a beautiful baby boy!

Que Dios se lo pague (keh dee-OS seh lo PAH-geh): May the Lord repay you

¿Que pasa? (keh PAH-so): What happened?

ranchitos (rahn-CHEE-tos): small ranches

rebozo (reh-BO-so): shawl

relanpagos (reh-LAHN-pah-gos): lightning bolts

repatriación (reh-pah-trah-SEE-on): repatriation/deportation

resfriado (rehs-free-AH-do): a cold

rinches (REEN-chehs): slang term for Texas Rangers

sala (SAH-lah): living room

sala de espera (SAH-lah deh ehs-PEH-rah): waiting room

salchichas con huevos (sahl-CHEE-chas kon woo-EH-vo):
sausage and eggs

sanctuario (sahnk-too-AH-ree-o): sanctuary

Santa Muerte / La Santisima (SAHN-tah moo-EHR-teh/lah sahn-
TEE-see-mah): the Holy Spirit of Death /The Saintly One

santito (sahn-TEE-to): little saint

sargento (sahr-GEHN-to): sergeant

sartén (sahr-TEHN): pan

semitas (seh-MEE-tahs): mild sweet bread made with star anise

señora (seh-NYO-rah): madam, lady

señorita (seh-nyo-REE-tah): young lady

Sigan adelante (SEE-gahn ah-deh-LAHN-teh): go on

Sí, pero nomas hago figuras de palitos (see, PEH-ro no-MAHS ha-go
fee-GOO-rahs deh pah-LEE-to): Yes, but I only draw stick figures

soldaderas (sol-dah-DEH-rahs): female revolutionaries/soldiers

solo eso (so-lo EH-so): just that

Somos humanos (so-mos oo-MAH-nos): We're human

sopitas (so-PEE-tahs): small cups of soup

susto (SOOS-to): fright

tamal (tah-MAHL): a dish of seasoned meat wrapped in a cornmeal
dough and steamed inside a corn husk; the husk is removed
before eating

tesitos (teh-SEE-tos): small cups of teas

tío (TEE-o): uncle

tlacuachito (tlah-koo-ah-CHEE-to): baby possum; in context, a term
of endearment

trocas (TRO-kahs): trucks

vacas (VAH-kahs): cattle

¡Vamonos! ¡Adelante! (VAH-mo-nos AH-deh-lahn-teh): Come on! Let's go!

¿Van pa'l río? (vahn pahl REE-o): Going to the river?

¡Venga aquí! (VEHN-gah ah-KEE): Come here!

verdad (vehr-DAHD): yes, true

UNITED STATES OF MEXICO

NATIONAL TELEGRAMS

FROM MEXICO CITY, D.F., DECEMBER 2, 1931

TO THE GENERAL CONSULATE IN CIUDAD JUÁREZ,
CHICHUAHUA
FOR SERGEANT ROMERO DÍAZ

REGARDING THE SEARCH FOR MR. JOAQUÍN DEL TORO,
REPATRIATED CITIZEN FROM THE CITY OF MONTESECO,
TEXAS, US, WE HAVE EVIDENCE OF CONTACT. A TALL,
THIN MAN WITH BLOND HAIR AND GREEN EYES PRESENTED
HIMSELF AT THIS EMBASSY ON MONDAY, NOVEMBER 30,
USING THAT NAME.

THE MAN APPEARED TO BE LOST AND HAD NO DOCUMENTS
TO VERIFY HIS IDENTITY AND, BECAUSE HE WAS
HURT, HE WAS REFERRED TO A CLINIC. THE MAN DID
NOT LEAVE AN ADDRESS, BUT PROMISED TO RETURN.
HOWEVER, SINCE THAT DATE, MR. DEL TORO HAS NOT
RETURNED TO THESE OFFICES.

RIGOBERTO GARCÍA COTÉS

Mr. and Mrs. Valdez-Uriega,

Thank you very much for coming to my aid. I do not have any other means of paying you for the great kindness which you have extended to me in rescuing and bringing me to this hospital. I am very grateful. I wish I had been able to thank you in person, but I am unable to stay one more moment in this place.

The doctor tells me I have lost part of my memory, but that this is probably temporary. I do not know why, but I have a feeling that I am supposed to depart immediately for Nuevo Laredo. Last night, I dreamed that in that place I will find answers to all of my questions, that in that place the sky will open itself up to me. The clouds will disappear and I will see clearly the roots of my existence.

This is not a goodbye, because with this note, I promise to return and to repay with interest the money you put down to ensure my health. May the Lord multiply your efforts in abundance until the day comes when I can pay you back.

Very gratefully,
Joaquín del Toro

ACKNOWLEDGMENTS

FIRST AND FOREMOST, I NEED TO thank my family: my husband Jim, who keeps me sane by taking care of all the little things and some of the big things, like driving me to author visits and speaking engagements so I can rest along the way. I have to thank my son and his beautiful wife, James and Carelyn, who gave me the greatest gift of all, a gorgeous granddaughter named Juliana, the shiniest, newest, most precious estrella in my universe. Thank you also goes to my son Steven, who is the best tech support in the whole wide world. I'd like to also thank my baby boy Jason, whose smile brightens my days no matter how much it rains.

I'd also like to extend my gratitude to my kid-lit family, my Texas-ink brothers and sisters: David Bowles, Diana Lopez, Carmen Tafolla, Lupe Ruiz-Flores, Carolyn Flores, Cynthia Leitich Smith, Beth Fehlbaum, and the rest of the Texas authors and illustrators who are out there looking out for one another, giving each other advice, a smile, and a warm hello every time we meet at conferences, festivals, and book signings. You all make this a great place to be and a great path to follow.

I must absolutely thank my beta reader, Maria Elena Ovalle, for offering to look at this through a librarian/ historian's lens. Bless you and thank you for your eagle eyes. You honor, validate, and greatly improve my work.

Last, but not least, I'd like to thank my publisher and editor, the smart, talented, and versatile Stacy Whitman, who believes in me so much. I can't hold the enormity of my gratitude to you in my heart all at once for fear that it might burst. You make a difference, Stacy. You build dreams. You give us hope. Thank you for starting Tu Books. Thank you for believing in us!